HITCHED

KIM SESSION

ISBN: 061551328X

ISBN 13: 9780615513287

In loving memory of
Shaniya Davis

ACKNOWLEDGMENT

Thank you to: Diana Bloomfield, The Bolins, Sondra Blake, Dr. Roger Hall, Pete Collins, editor Mindy Reed, Writers' League of Texas, Reverend Melissa Anderson, Chapel Dulcinea, Spike Gillespie, the country of Slovakia, all the great couples I have married over the years, and last but certainly not least, Tom White and Ella Iris.

INTRODUCTION

It was bitter cold. The moon was the only source of light, but it only shone in quick flashes. Dead branches, like the knobby fingers of a giant witch, reached overhead as if in worship, obscuring the sparse illumination. The sharp edge of the K-100's barrel pressed hard into Ivy's back, threatening her to fall forward, but if she lost her grip she would career down the uneven mounds of ice, snow and debris under her feet. She questioned what in the world she did in life to have God place her here? Here being the dense Carpathian forest just outside of Bratislava on Christmas morning. Her assailant pushed the pistol harder, then harder again into her. Ivy could not understand a single word of the Slovak words spitted out to her. *Probably cussing*, Ivy surmised which wasn't fair as she wanted to cuss too, but wasn't willing to take any chances of paying unfairly for any more sins. After all, she was a wedding minister back in her small Texas town just outside of Austin and under normal circumstances wasn't allowed to do such things. But this circumstance was far from normal. "Holy crap," she muttered to herself as her right ankle twisted inward causing a sharp shooting pang to bolt up past her knee. She was directed by the gun to spin around.

It was as if a stick of dynamite exploded. The trigger was pulled again and again. At first she stared in disbelief and then she went flying backward like a comet before landing in the soft snow hard on her back. The pain was unbearable, a renegade jack hammer going crazy inside her chest. And then every feeling, every last memory and every lingering haunting question faded to black.

CHAPTER ONE

Misty Falls, Texas is the type of place that if you Google it, it will suggest a magical small town where you will want to raise your children (even if you don't have any). If you visit in person you won't be let down and will want to patent and can the smell of the air and call it something like "Enchanted Forest Waterfall."

The town consists of a population of 1,826, and the wooded scenery alternates between white picket fences and opulent ranches with unmarked red dirt roads cooled off by loblolly pines. Its two main thoroughfares are shaded by emerald leafed pecan, pine and oak trees. These same roads are quite curvy and rise and fall in gentle swells as you ride over gurgling creeks that interrupt from time to time. And conveniently, the town is only thirty minutes away from Austin, the state's capitol.

There are actually two Misty Falls; one is tall and the fall is full and wide, the water spilling over a plate of limestone landing fifty feet later in a jade green swimming hole. The pool is in a canyon like setting, with ferns and other lush vegetation growing up the cliffs that surround it in a semi circle. It's the perfect place to impress out of town guests with a cold Texas style BBQ picnic, but it's crowded as hell on the weekends. The other fall is twelve miles away, less impressive and doesn't attract any tourists, only locals who don't want to be bothered. The townies like to think that their home should be world renowned for the falls but would bitch to high heaven if that actually came to pass. What they don't realize is that it is really famous for a beautiful open air creekside Spanish style chapel off the beaten track, tucked up in the hills, perched on the highest hill top, that hundreds of couples from all over the world get married at each year.

Chapel Desiderio's weddings are mostly performed by Ivy Weiss for the traditionalists and another wedding minister who simply goes by the name of Punch for the liberals and/or atheists. Punch didn't fit the typical successful preacher stereotype and that gave Ivy hope when she started out. After all, as Ivy realized one day when they went swimming at Misty Falls number one, Punch's legs and arms were wrapped in tattoos varying from the typical skulls and flames to the more absurd including a pair of eyes on her shoulder blades, and something unrecognizable around her belly button (Ivy was too polite to ask). Punch also dived in head-first, tumbling into the water in a flurry of sommer saults from the top of the cliff as Ivy floated on a raft in the water below, praying for her new friend's safety. Punch was also a published author with a book called "Bitch." And to top things off, Ivy later found out that Punch was gay. Not that Ivy was conventional, but she wasn't married and never had been, which before meeting Punch had made her even more insecure in her chosen profession.

Ivy took a seat at the patio just outside the chapel's gift shop and waited for her next couple to arrive. To date, she had performed four hundred and seventeen weddings, one hundred and twenty-three vow renewals and thirty-seven commitment ceremonies at Chapel Desiderio alone. As she waited, she mused over a couple of things: the chapel's name for one; it meant Chapel of Desire in Italian, which she was finding ever more appropriate, but the relation to the amount of people she was marrying and the fact that she remained single unnerved her. The second thing she thought about was the fact that no one seemed to be paying attention to the statistics that their commitment would most likely crumble like sand through their fingers, that heartbreak was right around the corner as marriage was the number one cause of all divorces. But Ivy never allowed herself to dwell on such things. That would mean she was giving it power. *Love was the most powerful thing in the world*, she thought, redirecting her ever wandering mind. *If you held tight to that belief perhaps you might even slow down the divorce rate.* And right then she stopped thinking about it. Tonight would be wedding number four hundred and eighteen.

It was a Wednesday evening, which was an unusual time to get married, but the chapel's calendar had become so full on the weekends that many engaged couples, who waited until the last minute to book, found themselves suddenly resorting to weekday weddings just to get it in before their engagement dragged on another year or two.

Chapel Desiderio had a gift shop in the fashion of an old stucco cottage painted a warm golden yellow. It had a red tile roof. Curving flowered vines snaked their way up connecting the two. Tall skinny dark green shutters adorned every window along with flower boxes that hung below them. If someone blindfolded you on your way, you might think you landed in Tuscany. The gift shop sold bottles of its own brand of wine and champagne, cards of congratulations, cake cutters and bubbles among other paraphernalia that would only suit newlyweds. A bronze plaque hung above the front door that read, "Thanks for choosing Chapel Desiderio. Now it's time to Decide Rio." The gift shop was situated next to the ever expanding parking lot and a had a tiny patio to relax on just outside of it. Its ornate wrought iron treillage was like a veil offering protection from the blazing sun. Ceiling fans spun lazily and occasionally the air would swoosh a hot blast that sent a section of Ivy's hair jumping to the other side of her face. She smoothed her hair out with her palms and reached down into her bag for an elastic to pull it together in a low pony tail. If the wind was bad down here that meant her hair would be landing in chunks in her eyes and mouth while she was conducting the ceremony. The weather-worn wood floors of the patio were covered with terracotta potted plants with bright orange, red, yellow and purple flowers, all with enormous petals. Ivy had picked one set of several tables and chairs that filled the remaining space. She knew this one wouldn't collapse as long as the couple didn't weigh over 180 pounds a person. After all, she had never met them before, so *it was a Weiss decision.* She laughed at her favorite pun. Ivy reached back down again to her bag on the floor and pulled out a plastic bottle of her homemade iced tea. The ice cubes were all melted but one. It was about to dissolve any second. She pulled it out and sucked on it before it liquefied. She wiped the sweat off her brow with the cool sweaty bottle. She went through the drill in her mind. Once she had them seated, she would collect their marriage license and payment before leading them up the trail to the chapel, almost a half mile away to perform the life altering deed, the couple usually huffing and puffing along the way. Ivy had learned that if the couples were Texans like the next couple she was waiting for, they not only liked everything big, they often were big. She contributed it to an overall lack of concern with nutrition and an idolization of alcohol (favorite meals usually consist of Frito Pie, Chicken fried cheeseburgers, fried beer and any gooey Tex Mex concoction washed down with enormous pitchers of tequila saturated margaritas). It was a far cry from her California days where everyone ate salad for breakfast, lunch and dinner.

As she waited for the love birds, voluptuous wind chimes clumsily swayed and bumped overhead politely singing a peaceful melody. The patio was surrounded by a park like setting with tall, thin, dark blades of grass. Shady trees ornamented with hanging moss-potted flower baskets, stone benches, water fountains, and bronze sculptures of whimsical characters filled the grounds. One sculpture, typical of these represented, was of a young child reading a book. The child rested on a log with one shoe missing while a little singing bird merrily perched itself on his hat. At his feet, a dog with a smile and uplifted tail grinned at no one in particular with the other shoe in it's mouth. None of it had anything to do with weddings, but oddly enough no one seemed to notice or care.

Loud squealing and laughter arose from the trail. Ivy turned around to see what was going on. Then, a couple in their late twenties sporting huge glass-like rocks on their left hands that glinted in the sunlight, came frolicking down. They were encouraged by a photographer's oohing and aahing. The photographer was someone Ivy had never worked with before. She assumed it was Freeze Spindleton, the former rock journalist from New York, who Punch had raved about lately. The description fit: creepy skinny and odd looking. Ivy had tried to warn her that he wouldn't know the ins and outs of weddings and she'd be setting herself up for pissed off brides once the honeymoon was over if she referred him. Obviously her advice had fallen on deaf ears. Punch strode ahead of the them with a smug look on her face. Ivy did a once over at the twosome; she was always curious to see the difference in the couples who chose Punch over her. Just then, the bridegroom complete in top hat, leaned over to his new wife while taking a bow and stuck out the longest silver-studded tongue Ivy had ever seen and pointed and twirled it around the inside of her ear before licking her face with it. They both stopped dead in their tracks and grabbed each other's buttocks, squishing them and spanking them. Maybe Freeze Spindleton was the right choice. Ivy had to turn and look away before she was tempted to scream something trite like, "Get a room!"

"Hey Ivy, you just starting?" Punch stood next to her attempting to cool off under the fans.

"Oh, hi Punch. Yeah. My couple should be here any minute though." Ivy looked down at her watch it was seven o'clock, the time the ceremony was supposed to start. It wasn't unusual for couple's to be late to Chapel Desiderio. It wasn't an easy place to find off a bizarre trail of several country roads without any signs of life before reaching it. "They're from Texarkana so maybe they're having a hard time finding it." Ivy looked up and winked at Punch trying desperately to avoid seeing what her new newlyweds were up to now.

Punch made a mental note that it was time to tell Ivy to cut the peculiar wink she had picked up, perhaps when she was a teenager to impress the boys. She had been doing it forever, but it always looked like the first time as it caused the whole side of Ivy's left face to curl up with it. But Punch didn't want to embarrass Ivy or have her think she was picking on her. And in a way, it suited her.

Through the corner of Ivy's eye, she couldn't miss the groom getting down on the grass on his knees, whisking his hat off his mop of long brown hair that hung in ringlets and setting it down on the grass beside him. His hands reached up, bunching up the bride's taffeta gown, exposing her panties and tan pierced tummy. He then bit the upper edge of her underwear, pulling it down with his teeth. He proceeded to bury his face into her stomach pulling the dress back down over his head and wagging it like a puppy dog underneath.

"Looks like you did a good job," Ivy said, her eyes gesturing towards the couple and pinching the fleshy roll around her belly.

"Yeah," Punch looked over at the couple as if their behavior was an every day occurrence on the chapel's public grounds. "Wrote a bitchin' ceremony for them Ive. You gotta check it out." Punch proceeded to open her journal to show Ivy the hormone inducing literature when her seven o'clock pulled up. "Never mind," Punch said and slapped her black leather book back shut. "Same bat time, same bat channel tomorrow?"

Ivy told her yes as she got up and walked over to greet her couple. She was relieved that she didn't have to wait much longer in the sun and that she had tomorrow to look forward to with Punch. The couple was older, in their late sixties and both widows. Ivy could tell at first they were scared thinking Punch was their minister. They sat in their car taking in the scenery before slowly lifting themselves out of the seats of their dusty white Cadillac, which was parked lopsidedly in the handicapped zone. Ivy walked over and greeted them, much to their relief. She directed them to her favorite table to go over last minute details hurriedly before they could see only god knows what the newlyweds were up to now.

She took out her checklist for the wedding and confirmed that the wedding was still an elopement, and that among other things, no one would be giving Hazel away. When they told her they were expecting Louis's nephew and his wife to arrive as guests, she asked if anyone objected to the wedding. She assumed no one did in this case but it was also an attempt to stall as the previous couple weren't quite out of sight yet. Couples didn't tend to like this question.

It wasn't nearly as much fun as hearing that the ring bearer would be the couple's dog, rabbit, or pet monkey. It was not her favorite question either, and once upon a time she didn't bother with it until an ex husband showed up with a deer rifle to a wedding she performed a few months prior. Luckily Justin, the young community college student who worked part-time at the chapel's gift shop, (and who Ivy harbored a secret cougar-esque crush on), had been picking up litter off the trails. Before the wedding began, Ivy watched him when no one was looking. His shoulder-length brunette hair blew in the breeze and she pictured him a tight pair of swimming trunks. She fantasized about photographing him and sending the proofs to Abercrombie and Fitch, setting up his fortune in the modeling business. Him forever thankful to her and paying her back in kind. He was someone who looked like he ate granola for breakfast, lunch and dinner but he had a sexy healthy earthy appeal with his wide open smile, the bright whites of his eyes and his flawless skin. As he was picking up trash near the bridal dressing room he noticed the magnum toting ex husband sprinting up the trail towards the wedding that was now probably somewhere near the exchange of vows. He sprang to life and ran up the trail behind the man, trying to catch up as he yelled warnings to the wedding party. Just a few feet in front of the ceremony, he jumped in front of the armed man, grabbed

the barrel of the gun and pointed it up in the sunny sky as the man
shot several rounds. With a tight fist, Justin punched the man on
the inside of his arm as he held it in a Jiu-jitsu elbow hold. The best
man and the two groomsmen made sure the man stayed pinned to
the ground who was in height and weight much larger than Justin.
Justin confiscated the rifle and pointed it at the man on the ground
as he struggled with the groomsmen. Ivy and the couple stood
horrified in shock. But then Ivy found herself even more attracted
to Justin and it took everything she could to not fawn all over him
and stay professional after the fiasco. The maid of honor had called
911. Remarkably she was able to get a signal in the isolation of
the hills and the phone call went through. The police arrived and
arrested the man within a matter of ten minutes.

Hazel and her husband-to-be cast glances at each other on that
question, then each slowly responded, "No." But Ivy took it more
to mean they questioned what their deceased exes were thinking,
if they were thinking. She then collected her fee and their license
and then they made their way up the trail to the chapel. She saw
the other newlyweds descend into the black abyss of a limo waiting
for them in the parking lot. With the speed that Hazel and Louis
walked even with the help of canes, the nephew and wife would
need them to have a good head start, she thought. The trail was
dimly lit with strings of white lights strung from tree to tree that
Hazel and Louis seemed to remark on every one as they trudged
along. The sun had almost set by the time they reached the chapel
and the gas lamps that hung on the lofty walls began flickering.
Even with the slow start, everything went without a hitch.

On Thursday mornings Ivy and Punch went out for coffee and tried to unwind and catch up before the busy weekends. Then they would go bookstore hunting in nearby Austin.

"Oh my, do you know him?" Ivy whispered in Punch's ear as they emerged from the rows and rows of fiction books written by authors with last names beginning in D, E and F.

"Who? Oh, yeah. Hey Jeffers!" Punch yelled and waved in large gestures to the man sitting at the table signing books for a couple of troublesome looking teenage boys. A couple of the patrons lifted their gazes from the books they were reading to shoot her dirty looks. "What? It's not a library," she retorted to them in self defense. Her black high top sneakers were tied with shoelaces with ends that traced the ground. She wore no socks and her long bare legs strode three feet ahead of Ivy's ruffled dress hem.

He looked up at Ivy and Punch and flashed a grin, the likes of which Ivy had never seen before. He had a day's worth of blond stubble, sun kissed skin and squinty blue eyes.

Ivy felt a flood of warm electric blood surging between her legs. She thought it the equivalent of a hard on when it happened and thanked God that these types of thoughts and feelings could only be between oneself if you chose thanks to the Lord's gift of free will. She felt her breath draw in and then become shallow and quick.

The man looked up from the book he was signing, "Hey Punch! What's shakin'?"

Ivy just stared at the young, trim "Jeff Bridges" type before her. "Jeez Jeff, what do you think?"

His name really was Jeff. Ivy smiled inside at the coincidence.

"Buying another copy of the best damn book in the store." Punch flipped over the book she was holding, the pale inside of her arm revealing crosses engulfed in torrid orange and yellow flames. The title of the book read "Bitch" and featured a large photograph of a woman's ruby red nails-a perfectly polished and manicured hand giving the bird against a glossy black background. She smiled at him proudly once he had the time to read the subtitle which read "A Journey to Self Actualized Radical Feminism." The two teenage boys looked at each other, smirked, and walked off.

Jeff smiled and shook his head. When he looked back up again he asked if Punch was going to introduce him to her friend or not.

"Oh, yeah. Excuse me. My mama never did teach me any manners. This is Ivy. Great person, sucky writer. She shadows me to suck the literary juices out."

Ivy felt the heat rising from her groin to her cheeks. It was true. She couldn't write worth a damn but did he have to know that? Now what was he going to think of her when part of her job required so much writing? He was going to think she was a real fraud, that was what he was going to think! Ivy took a quick mental inventory of her pros and cons and hoped Jeff only saw and sensed the good ones: sort of attractive, too pale but feminine, definitely pretty brunette hair; her entire life everybody had told her she had pretty hair if nothing else. True, she was short, unfortunately only five foot four, which probably looked more like four feet standing next to Punch who was six feet and one inch tall. She sucked in her stomach, just a little water retention in the the tummy that could by the way, be easily fixed again. But she was a hard worker, a great cook with a sophisticated palette, and now it's been confirmed: a terrible writer. She hoped Punch wouldn't tell him what she did for a living.

"Don't see no problem in that as long as one ain't counting on it to fill up the bank account," Jeff retorted in Ivy's defense and winked at her reassuringly.

To Ivy's surprise Punch didn't answer. She was busy calculating the inventory left on Jeff's table.

Ivy wondered if she was dreaming. She loved his wink. It was just like hers. Smooth and full of character. But why didn't she dress better? Did she remember to shave her armpits this morning? She hoped she had kept her arms close to her body when she shook hands with him. He probably thought she and Punch were lezbos. She scanned the enormous poster propped up next to him. "Points of Passion" it said in a large Gothic print of jagged metallic gray with a navy blue shadowy background and the outline of a man's dead body on the ground with multiple bright red seeping stab wounds. "By Jeff Hunter" it said at the bottom. The name sounded familiar.

"New book?" Ivy asked him as she pointed to the poster.

"Naaw, this one's eleven years old."

Punch jabbed Ivy in the rib cage with her elbow. "Yeah, eleven years old, but still, it was a best seller," she said. "But who cares right Jeff? No one cares what you did ten years ago let alone eeee-leven!" she howled.

Ivy looked up at Punch wondering where the sudden bite of sarcasm came from. The elbow jab also hurt and she had to rub out the soreness. Punch turned away when she caught her friend's eye. It was pointless to try to teach Punch any etiquette.

Jeff turned to Ivy. "They are making a movie of it locally so the bookstore and publisher thought it might be a good time to re-issue it."

Ivy thought it impressive, even if it was a thing of the past. She had met many other writers accompanying Punch on these bookstore runs but none ever had a best seller. The others were merely regional or local writers with some notoriety and the last one she went out with was actually a famous bird book writer, if there was such a thing. Ivy reminded herself for confidence sake, that Kirk, the bird watcher/writer had liked her almost to the point of obsessiveness (all of her friends and family told her she was being crazy-he was just in love and, in a healthy way) and at least he did not mind her inability to write well even though her job description required it.

Kirk was only one of many she met at these bookstore forays whose help she tried to solicit in both the literary and romance department. And she usually succeeded, at least in the romance part. Just then she thought she heard God telling her she was a bad girl, but she promptly justified it to Him and anyone who could hear her thoughts for that matter. After all, she couldn't possibly meet anyone through work as they were always marrying someone else, already married, or on a date. There was no point in hanging around receptions hoping for that one single guest to take notice of her as her profession tended to make people in the atmosphere uneasy once the alcohol was flowing. She was sensitive to the "when is the minister going to leave" glances that were shot towards her. They thought she was a Bible thumper and although she was far from any right wing tendencies it wasn't her place to inform people otherWeiss she laughed to herself. So, she challenged, to anyone or anything that might be paying attention, who was better for her than a professional writer? Ivy further rationalized it to being attracted to what completed you. It was true of many of the couples she married: the funny ones married the poker faces and the lookers married the nerds, the old married the young or more specifically the young and poor married the old and rich, the type A personalities married lazy people, and the ones who could eat no fat liked the ones that eat could no lean so between the two of them they could lick the platter clean. Ivy pictured a fat man and skinny woman licking a plate clean and promptly put the image out of her mind.

Ivy smiled at Jeff as he stared deep into her eyes. Ivy wondered how many various shades of pink to scarlet she was turning and realized she must have matched her ruffled dusty pink blouse about four shades ago. Thank god she at least wore something pretty. But that was nothing new as she always did. She wondered sometimes if she was always compensating for not being beautiful. The blouse and skirt were Chloe. Hand me downs from her mother. She felt like she wanted to crawl into a cave and hide -not alone- with him, and that they should be naked. She looked upward and prayed God wasn't seeing through her and couldn't help the little snorting chortle sound that came out of her mouth and nose simultaneously.

Then the dreaded question happened.

"What do you do for work Ivy?"

"Oh, um, I work as a wedding officiant." She chose the word officiant instead of minister to better appeal to certain types, and he was one of them. It was clear the word officiant was going to score more points with a guy like Jeff. She knew it still sounded pretty "churchy" but a lot of people found it interesting, for some reason or another, which Ivy was grateful for even if most found it peculiar. Her job was interesting to her, but she couldn't imagine how it would sound interesting to anyone else. After all, how many people get to perform a vow renewal for a transvestite couple? She had done that last Saturday without warning, and was utterly confused as to who was the bride and who was the groom. Then there was the bride two weeks ago who tore up her marriage license in a hissy fit in front of all her guests and wedding party and then burned it to smithereens with her Bic lighter because the groom was ten minutes late. But since Jeff already knew Punch, who was in the same profession, any mystique was probably lost. *It's probably lost its punch*, she thought and was amused at her unintended pun. She made a mental note to keep the snort under wraps this time as it didn't go with the way she looked or the way she wanted to be and often wondered why she was cursed with such a character defect.

"That right?"

Punch subtly tugged on the back of Ivy's blouse.

Ivy turned to look at her but couldn't understand what she was doing.

"Ivy, we need to go, I've got a meeting across town in 30 minutes," Punch said.

"Oh, I'm sorry, I don't remember you telling me about it. Nice meeting you Jeff."

"How 'bout dinner sometime?" Jeff asked Ivy. "Can I get your phone number?"

The grip on the back of Ivy's blouse was becoming stronger and her blouse was pulling tight around her chest. Ivy looked down. The top button of her blouse had come undone and was now hanging by a limp thread. What the hell was Punch doing? She decided not to pay attention to it. Punch had her eccentric ways that didn't always sit well with Ivy. Ivy grabbed the last card out of the light blue silk lining of her purse, which had become stuck in the fabric. *Another embarrassing moment*, she thought as she tried to pull it out in time before Punch's grip won out. She got the last card out and gave it to Jeff as she was dragged out of the store. But first she tripped. Luckily she didn't fall. She caught herself in time but her low heels had become entangled in her dress hem thanks to Punch's tenacious pull on her in the opposite direction.

The silver Buick was parked immediately outside the glass doors of Barnes and Noble. Drops of rain in various circles and oval shapes of differing sizes decorated it as if it was wrapped in sheer bubble wrap or had caught some rare blistering disease. As Ivy slid into the wide cushy passenger seat she made one last glance inside through the shadowy glass doors at Jeff who was still staring and smiling at her. *You just never knew when love was going to find you*, she thought. She pulled the bottom of her dress up from the wet street into the car and shut the door feeling suddenly cozy in the cocoon of Punch's vehicle.

Punch put the keys into the ignition and backed out of the parking space without thought. Her tires skidded and squealed on the wet pavement nearly running over an elderly man steering his wheel chair bound wife across the street behind them.

"Punch! Look out!" Ivy screamed obviously loud enough for the old man to lower his hand before it could give any sign of a recognizable gesture.

Punch slammed on the breaks and was silent as she readjusted her rear view mirrors and straightened the car up and then backed out of the space one more time.

Oh boy, here we go, thought Ivy. It had been a while since Punch had been like this. The worst part about it was you never knew when it was going to strike. "Okay, what's going on?"

"Don't worry about it," she said as she cranked the air conditioning knob as far as it would go to the right to blizzorama. Even though it was raining outside the temperature had to be at least 100 degrees.

"I am worried about you. Too late. Tell me what's wrong Punch," Ivy said as she flipped the vents in the other direction. It was a bad enough hair day with all the rain and humidity, who in the hell needed any kind of wind screwing up things even worse?

Punch remained silent and stared straight ahead as she drove.

Ivy dug in her purse for her pot of Clinique lip balm. Frizzy hair was one thing, but peeling lips with it were atrocious. "Punch, now come on. We've had this conversation before." She vigorously rubbed the waxy ointment back and forth with her index finger and then wiped the excess off with a Kleenex. "I am straight and I always will be."

"Oh Ivy forget it. You think I'm still hung up on that?" She turned to look at Ivy who was now staring straight ahead out the window, afraid to not be on lookout. "That's not where I'm coming from. Stay straight. I don't give a rat's ass. I gave up on you a long time ago."

"Punch! He just asked me on a date. It's not like I am marrying him." She forcefully threw the lip balm back in her purse for emphasis.

Punch just shook her head. They drove the next twenty minutes in silence. Punch pulled the car up in front of Ivy's house; a brick and mortar cottage draped with vines and heavily decorated with potted plants going up the four steps to the front door. Ivy politely got out of the car, said goodbye and wished her luck with her "meeting" before slamming the door. She still held out hope that Punch would fill in her in, but Punch continued to stare straight ahead and put the car in reverse and then backed out of the driveway as Ivy watched making sure she didn't hit any of the potted avocado trees she had lining the driveway.

Ivy collected the pamphlets and letters decorated with wet polka dots that were jutting out of her mailbox, accidentally dropping them all on the damp porch floor before she could manage the doors. She swept them back up and then opened the screen door, holding it open with her foot as she let herself in the front door and immediately started preparing for the weekend. The mail would have to wait and she set it on her coffee table in the, "I'll get around to it hopefully before the lights, water and electricity get shut off and I wished I took care of it earlier" pile.

The laptop was fired up, more Starbuck's French Roast was brewing, the aroma sweeping the air. She lit a candle and put in a cassette of Vivaldi's Four Seasons. Setting the mood was important before beginning any task. And she especially needed the calming atmosphere after being jolted by Punch's erratic behavior. Her calendar was in place to compare to the charts she had made for the following days. She had to make sure all the musicians were in order with their various cues of starting and stopping of the odd assortment of songs they were set out to perform- everything from "Going to California" by Led Zeppelin to "Cannon in D" by Pachelbel. She saw that Carlos Lucas, a classically trained Spanish guitarist from San Antonio who could do it all authentically, was scheduled to play at one of the weddings, which put her mind slightly to rest. He was a pro unlike most of the musicians that people hired. That was one thing about the music scene in Austin so nearby, it was actually a curse because people loved to have their "friends" play at their wedding or hire a band they saw during one of their last intoxicated weekends on Sixth Street. Musicians who didn't understand wedding protocol had an uncanny way of fucking things up, for example, by playing the bridal march for the Maid of Honor. Ivy covered her mouth in embarrassment even though she hadn't said the word out loud.

All rituals were clearly mapped out and would be appropriately and aesthetically set up. She marked in her calendar how early she would need to get to each wedding to make sure things went smoothly. Guests would be clear on the reception's locations and maps would be printed out if they took place at another location. All the marriage licenses she had collected from the week before, as well as this weekends, were to be mailed off on her weekly

Tuesday visit to the post office, which she clearly notated on her calendar by marking the number of them so none would go unrecorded. There was nothing more embarrassing than getting a call from one of the clerks at one of the many courthouses in Texas about an over the edge bride that never received her official license. And there was nothing more time consuming than driving all over the state or city trying to fix one. The courthouses liked to pride themselves that anything could be fixed. But it was always at the officiant's expense. And then she had to make sure the wording of the ceremonies she was scheduled to perform over the weekend had no errors; no one liked to be called the wrong name especially on their wedding day as she learned during one of her first jobs. There was a lot to do in a short amount of time. Punch always chided her, telling her she took on too much. But Ivy felt she owed it to her couples who had put so much faith in her. Besides, she also got embarrassed easily and would do anything to spare herself from that emotion by overcompensating in other areas in case she did screw up somewhere else. If she had learned anything positive from her parents it was about having a strong work ethic.

She hadn't been home thirty minutes when Jeff called asking her out for the weekend. She apologized, explaining that she had five weddings, three rehearsals and four receptions she was attending in the next three days and wouldn't feel comfortable going out on a date with all that happening around her. As badly as she wanted to go, Ivy knew she wouldn't possibly have the ability to compartmentalize and forget about who's wedding was coming up next, whether they had unity candles or the sand ceremony, what the name of the best man was, or if she was confusing that persons name with the father of the brides name or the musicians or the caterers. Two of her weddings were at bigger venues in

Austin, which only made her more uptight. It meant that she would have to work in tandem with snippety "OMG" sorority types that liked to be in the wedding coordinating business these days as the local community college and the major university in Austin recently started offering a degree in the wedding business much to her dismay. Whenever she was taken away from Chapel Desiderio, she felt as if she was being unfaithful. The chapel had become her home away from home. But Jeff was persistent and talked her into seeing him that night. It was times like these that she was most grateful that she didn't have any pets or babies. Getting ready for a date could take up a lot of time without all the other distractions begging for attention. Never mind work. It was ten minutes until six o'clock now and she was due at the restaurant at seven not leaving her a lot of time with the driving. Ivy's driving was like her writing.

CHAPTER TWO

Jeff had asked her to meet at the restaurant and she thought that a good idea for the first date. She was impressed with the classiness of his suggestion. Besides, there was no sense in someone driving all the way out to Misty Falls or knowing where she lived so soon. A little mystery was always good, she reminded herself according to all the dating books she had read. Someday she too would get married. Unfortunately even with as many men as she had dated, none had ever popped the question. Maybe it was because she became impatient within three to four months of dating, believing it would never happen, then would talk herself out of liking the person; justifying to herself and them the reasons (if they cared to hear the reasons, which most were so shocked at the sudden breakup that they chose not to have their balls busted further), and would move on to celibacy or the next runner-up to save face. She had left all of them. At the same time she concerned herself with her unmarried status, knowing that the pattern had to change if she was ever to become a Mrs. . But she couldn't help herself. It was like setting herself up for something to worry about, and worrying had a certain comfort to it. She liked thinking about things and worrying about them. It gave her a sense of purpose to pursue perfection. Like cooking. Something to look forward to. Something to get absolutely down pat right. But suddenly she was wondering if she had that correct-maybe they had all really left her and just to be nice made it seem like she had left them. She hoped this time things would be different whatever the case.

She felt different about it already. Or maybe she felt hornier than she had in a long time. She wasn't sure if she was confusing the issues but vowed silently to herself and to everyone else who had lectured her on her hastiness to leave relationships, that she would not give up so easily from now on. No matter what. It had been almost a year and a half since she had been with anyone including just a simple first date. She wasn't getting any younger.

She bathed in her favorite rose and jasmine bubble bath by a new designer named Frederik Caron and dusted the fine powder that matched the scent on her damp body after she stepped out of the free standing tub. Once in her robe, she propped herself up on her bathroom counter to get close to her medicine cabinet's vanity mirror, the only way that she could see herself up close with her height, and swirled her foundation sponge in its creamy circle of peachy tan goo, swept it over her face, re-lined her lips in burnt rose and her eyes in pewter, and pinched the outer corners of her eyelashes upward between her thumb and index fingers. It was still raining but the air remained hot and humid. She found a light beige Bill Blass silk dress to wear. While putting it on she

thanked God her mom was a former model and as a perk she and
her sister Iris got only designer hand me downs. Sure, some had
missing buttons and others had small stains and she had to have
every single one altered, but who cared? She pinned her hair up
in a loose chignon and to finalize the look put on a pair of gold
earrings. She looked the best she had in a long time. The humidity
and fresh makeup suited her skin and hair giving her a soft glow.
Before dressing she had researched her naked body in the mirror;
it wasn't bad, but it wasn't great. Ten pounds could make a lot
of difference especially with her height, which was something
she inherited from her father. Her father. Her mind drifted to a
vision of him lying on the hospital stretcher in the living room.
Family and hospice surrounding him. Tufts of his Just for Men
dyed black hair gently swayed as the enormous bay windows were
open letting in the Pacific breeze. The sight was almost peaceful
except for the intravenous tubes stretched to bursting capacity. A
few times a day he would wake up in small fits, a result of his brain
aneurysm that eventually did him in. At one point he punched one
of the doctor's in the face who was hovering above him and at
another point he refused to wear any clothes, which finally showed
Ivy what her mom had seen in the man. For someone who was so
short, so small framed, and such a tyrant, he was incredibly well
endowed. She shrugged the thought off. It wasn't nice to think of
your father like this. She tried to recall what she had been thinking
of before her mind went to the gutter as it often did. Oh yes, she
was thinking about her weight. She knew ten pounds could make
a lot of difference because it wasn't that long ago she had seen
the ten pounds off of her. But she loved to eat and made a habit
of it when no one was looking-especially pan fried olives, which
she realized she had prepared and eaten almost every night before
going to bed for the last eight years straight. She had found a way

to incorporate it in her diet at all times. She made a point to not
make the olives tonight before bed. She was sure she could do it.
She felt good and things were going to change for the better from
this moment forward. A new and even better life awaited her. Her
friends and family would be so proud of the change.

At precisely six thirty Ivy got in her creamy yellow 2004 VW
bug and drove to meet her date. Oscar Pully's was located on the
west edge of downtown Austin tucked in a remote alleyway. She
circled around for a parking spot, which made her more than a
little late. This caused her considerable anxiety. Ivy was always early
or on time. Punctuality was her middle name. Tardiness, when she
was the cause, had sent her to the emergency room at St. David's
Hospital for panic attacks on three separate occasions, which had
made her even more tardy creating a never ending cycle. She broke
her rule and paid for a valet rather than park on Sixth Street, which
got a later crowd. There was no hostess at the the cherry wood
podium when she walked in. As she stood waiting to be seated she
scanned the scene revealing a restaurant filled with trendy tattooed
and pierced types and lined with red leather booths. She wondered if
Punch had ever frequented the joint. The pungent odor of marijuana
blew past her as three musicians squeezed past awkwardly carrying
their instrument cases which looked like suitcases that had been put
in the washer and dryer. The drummer really was carrying an old
suitcase and sat it upright behind his kit. He perched himself atop
it and started screwing a high hat on its stand. His foot thumped
on its pedal and made the two pieces of brass open and close like a
sea clam. She reached her right hand into the bowels of her clutch
purse and fished for her lipstick. As her hand caught the familiar
slick feel and oblong shape of the tube she noticed that above the
seating hung flickering gas lamps and black velvet paintings of
topless voluptuous and perky breasted blonds. The atmosphere was

not what Ivy had imagined and without knowing, her hand lost grip of the lipstick. She saw Jeff seated at a booth at the far end of the restaurant talking to a waitress. The waitress turned around and looked at Ivy approaching and turned on her heel. That was nice thought Ivy. He was waiting for her before he ordered anything. As she made her way to him, she saw through her peripheral vision the sizes, colors and shapes of various nipples staring at her, poking fun. Jeff stood up and there, at the top of his head, were the biggest boobs of them all.

Once Ivy arrived at the booth he gave her a quick tight hug. Ivy wished secretly one didn't have to go to such formalities as conversation and eating after the loving embrace. She felt she was ready to jump in the sack with him already. They sat back down and Ivy, in between setting her purse down and unwrapping the thin napkin from around her silverware, knocked over her skinny glass of ice water. It landed straight in her lap. She looked down. The water made her dress see through revealing the decidedly unglamorous but comfy grandma panties she wore underneath. She had chosen them just to be safe in case something like the hug that just happened made her lose control. It was another trick she learned in her dating books about how to be self contained on the first few dates. But nowhere in the books did it warn of potential hazards of wearing something sheer over them. *Lord,* she thought. She just wasn't cut out for dating. She had no cool whatsoever. Little did she know Jeff was thinking the same thing, but found it refreshing.

The waitress returned and dropped off a bottle of Corona with a lime wedge stuck in its mouth.

"So, you look absolutely stunning," Jeff said as he grabbed the lime out of the bottle's neck and pointed the beer at her. His eyes rolled up from her chest to her eyes just as she caught them.

Ivy pretended not to notice and told herself no man could possibly help doing such a thing in such an environment. Besides, no one had ever used the word "stunning" to describe her-ever. Maybe attractive, maybe petite (as in short only), maybe pretty, but stunning? No, she knew that had never happened. She felt the warm gush between her legs again and crossed them which bumped the table upward and the second water refill was about to go down before Jeff caught it.

"So, you and Punch work together?"

"Yes, you could say that. We work at the same chapel basically performing weddings. She does mostly the atheists which are a lot these days and I do the rest- everything from Buddhists to Christians and whatever else is in between; marrying the couples, writing ceremonies, delivering the legal documents to the courthouses, whatever the couples want. Sometimes they want you to help pick the color theme and the flavor of cake. There's a lot more than chocolate and vanilla these days boy let me tell you! The hem length of the bridesmaids dresses, the men sometimes need help with the little things like how to pin on the boutonnière so they don't fall off ...." Ivy looked up at Jeff. He was trying to catch a waitress's attention. The waitress had just noticed him and was making her way over. Ivy told herself to shut up and reminded herself she was a better listener besides which, Ivy had learned a long time ago; authors love to talk about themselves. Her cell phone went off. Embarrassed, she excused herself for the faux pas. She reached down in her purse which was sitting next to her on the booth to turn it off but couldn't help seeing the name displayed in the small window. It was someone from the chapel. Holy shit! She did have a wedding tonight. It was the first time she had ever screwed up. She needed to excuse herself to go to the bathroom and put in a desperate call to Punch to cover her ass. But how was she to do that with her now see through dress? She didn't have a choice. Perhaps if she walked fast no one would notice.

When she returned, Jeff was shifting in his seat rolling his hips from side to side. He was looking around the restaurant with a bored look on his face and seemed almost let down when she returned. She was sure she was misreading it. He was probably just nervous. When he saw her, he smiled and looked down at her waist. His expression changed when he saw the grandma panties showing through underneath. He had to laugh and so did she as she held back the tears that were about to gush out.

The place was hot and she imagined his blue jeans were probably plastered onto his butt and the booth in various sticky and deliciously sweaty patches. She made a mental note to change her train of thought and lighten her too serious mood. She broke her second rule and ordered a glass of wine.

Jeff noticed Ivy's abrupt halt in the conversation around the time the cell phone went off and that she was visibly self conscious. "Oh well, I uh," he laughed at himself for the lame way he hadn't been attentive and not being sure where she left off. "Sorry about that. Let me start all over. Well, see, I'm basically just a washed up, has been writer. Had the success with the book you saw earlier, *Points of Passion*. Ever hear of it?"

Ivy shook her head no and told him not before today as she wiggled back into a comfortable position in the booth. She hadn't been able to reach Punch but hopefully she would check her voice mail soon and get to the chapel and marry the couple for her. *Please Punch please.* And where was her wine? Her nerves were getting the best of her but at the same time she had no intention of breaking the date and marrying the couple. That would be rude. Jeff had a one of a kind pull on her and Ivy hoped that this power he had meant something. Perhaps finally she had found someone she was going to stay with through the trials and triumphs that were sure to follow. As she sat down she pictured him as the adoring playful father type and knew without a doubt that a child they would create together would be not only beautiful but smart and creative. She told herself to get a grip on her thoughts. What she was doing according to herself-help books was "projecting" and it was dangerous. It meant you were making someone into who you wanted them to be instead of letting them reveal themselves over time to you. She realized the hazards of doing such a thing, but boy oh boy it sure was fun and how far off could she be anyway? *No, things would be different.* She felt it. Knew it in her heart of hearts because she was a changed woman and was going to stick things out this time.

Jeff continued his story about his book while Ivy listened intently while eying the progress of the shrinking wet spot on her dress. "Well, basically it's a thriller about a serial killer who stabs his victims all at the same points in their bodies. I did a great job with it, if you don't mind my saying so." He looked at her with the crinkly blue eyes and boyish grin and then continued. "So anyway, that's about it. Been trying to coast off of it while getting some other stuff off the ground, which hasn't happened, yet. But that's what we writers do right, Ivy, write?"

A new waitress who had just been tying her apron around her tiny waist came carrying Ivy's wine and precariously set the glass down on the table along with Jeff's third bottle of Corona and then strolled past without eye contact or conversation. Jeff's eyes rolled up and down her tall narrow framed body dressed in light blue jeans as she walked away. Ivy pretended not to notice. After all, Ivy swooned as the cheap sweet Merlot soaked into her virgin bloodstream, no one had ever seriously called her a writer. Three glasses of wine later her dress had completely dried and she danced for the first time in public with Jeff to the vintage shuffles the band played. They went back to Ivy's home after their shared meal of sliders and curly fries. They made furious love against all of Ivy's good intentions and Jeff never left the house until....

CHAPTER THREE

Five Years Later

The bailiff in a controlled and powerful voice ordered everyone to rise as the judge made his entrance. He was middle-aged with a thin limp of black greasy hair that swooped from the right side of his head to just above his left eyebrow and rested on the upper rim of his plastic framed glasses. It had an edgy effect, making Ivy want to walk over and flick it out of the way. The color of his face shifted from ghostly white to beet red. *Great. An alcoholic*, thought Ivy as she tried to recount the multitude of character flaws of people with such an addiction: serious financial, work and relationship problems, intricate alibi systems and worst of all, impaired thinking. *Great.* His stomach was out of proportion to the rest of his body and his chest pushed hard into his shiny black robe propositioning bursting seams at any moment.

Ivy replayed the words of the subpoena in her mind as the judge read the day's calendar. After five years of being with Jeff, he apparently didn't know her correct name, and more importantly neither did he know his daughter's. The snort chortle started to make it's way out of her mouth and nose as she recalled the part of his petition demanding she change Olive's last name to his. Little did he know that like a dumb ass she had given Olive his last name. She thought about Olive's name and how it came about. It was one of the few things that Jeff had shared a love of with her. Her little exotic dish. And before he left her, when she thought he might at least give her a pat on the tummy and a big hug and kiss about the surprising news, she decided to name their child, if it was to be a girl, Olive, short for Olivia. As an added blessing, the name's abbreviated version stayed in the tradition of her family as well. All girls were named after plants or flowers. Her great great grandmother's name was Lily Rose, her grandmother's name was Violet, her mother's name was Fern or Ferny depending on whether people met her in her post modeling days or during them. Her sister's name was Iris, her name was Ivy, her daughter would be called Olive. Ivy's mother didn't care for the choice and would forever bring it up arguing that it did not flow with the rest of the names in the family. Ivy would then tell her mom she named her after the olive branch as a hint for her to back off. She got a grip on her thoughts as the sinking realization that she was now sitting in a courtroom being sued by Olive's father sunk in.

"Hunter versus Weiss" the judge ordered.

Ivy turned her head to the right to look up at LuAnne Dalton, her attorney, for direction. LuAnne shook her head "no" as in "stay where you are." And Ivy did, mulling over the sounds of their last names together. Yes, Jeff was a Hunter of some sort and she had proven to herself that she was far from being Weiss by hooking up with him. *I am not Ivy Weiss, Ivy stupid*, she thought. The name was the wrong one for her; she wasn't wise and she wasn't Jewish either like it sounded, which often caused confusion with newly engaged couples who weren't sure if it was even legal for a Jew to marry them and what the ramifications would be if she did. More than once Ivy explained that even if she was Jewish, the marriage would still be recognized in the State of Texas. And just like like former secretary of defense Caspar Weinberger and musician, Bruce Springsteen, she too had only been born into a Jewish sounding surname.

Ivy and LuAnne had met less than two weeks ago on a Saturday, the day after Ivy came home to the enormous bright yellow Post It sticking to her front door, which loudly announced that she was in big trouble. LuAnne wanted to meet her right away.

LuAnne Dalton's office resided in a high rise off of Rio Grande in an old money section of historic Austin that consisted of huge oak trees that shaded sophisticated mansions and charming eclectic bungalows of every European and Southern style. Ivy was sure the high rise pissed off the old timers, but LuAnne was a force to be reckoned with and as much as they hated her, Texans were also proud at the same time.

LuAnne was a giant. With big wet eyes. The type of eyes Ivy thought the Beatles were singing about in "Come Together" about the guy with the joo joo eyeballs until she found out later that it meant bad karma looking eyes. She had dishwater blond hair in a Dorothy Hamill haircut grown out a couple of inches. She wore a baggy bright gum ball orange colored cotton blazer and matching pants.

"Ivy?"

"Yes." Ivy put down the copy of *Architectural Digest* she was pretending to be calm enough to read.

"Hairyew? I'm LuAnne. Come on back."

Ivy followed behind, watching LuAnne's wide pant cuffs get caught up in one another as she took each step down the dreadfully dark hallway. The office was quiet except for the sound of LuAnne's humongous clogs thumping the carpet before slapping the bottom of her feet and the swishing of her pants. The cleaning crew must have been there earlier as the entire suite hung with the thick aroma of the new lavender scented Pinesol. She flung open a door to an office and it crashed with a loud bang into the wall. Ivy tried to see if it left any dents but LuAnne quickly directed her to sit down in a bright blue upholstered chair. The morning light did a little dance through the shutters on LuAnne's hair as she lowered herself behind an enormous mahogany desk topped with lots of family photos stuck in the crevices of strewn papers and files. She said, "What's going on with you and this prick you got yourself tangled up with? He a damn Yankee?" She placed her elbows on her desk and rested her head in her hands, knocking over several files without seeming to care.

When Ivy sensed there was no longer any point in waiting for LuAnne to pick the items up, she informed LuAnne of Jeff's history.

"No, he's not a Yankee." She hoped that was the right answer. It was hard to tell if LuAnne was joking or not when she asked the question.

LuAnne nodded to indicate she was paying attention.

"Um. He's from West Texas. Alpine to be specific." No reaction from LuAnne so she continued. "He was the only child of an oil driller. Guess his mom just stayed at home and kept over the house and his education for the most part. Both parents passed away right after Jeff had the hit success with *Points of Passion*. From what he told me, they believed they were leaving him with everything, including their home, as he was their only child. But in reality, they left nothing to him but the tremendous debt they were in."

LuAnne leaned in closer, curious to hear how the story was going to unfold.

"So, Jeff had to use a lot of the money, most of the money he made on the book to get the bill collectors to let Mr. And Mrs. Hunter rest in peace. He sold their home and made nothing from it. Apparently his parents thought they were leaving it to him free and clear according to their will. It's pretty sad because he was the only child and they really thought they were doing something for him."

Ivy waited for LuAnne to give some kind of reaction of empathy but none was available.

"So anyway, all of this that I am telling you was according to Jeff. How much of it is the truth I really don't know. Could be some of it or none of it, but I doubt all of it. I say that because several years ago I was at a wedding reception of a couple I just married. There was an elderly couple there who I sat next to during dinner. I found out they were from Alpine and about the age of Jeff's parents. Turns out they were quite close. When I mentioned that Jeff was my boyfriend, they not so subtly broke away from me and began making the rounds of talking to other people. I didn't catch on right away. Then they met up with another couple and they tried to latch onto them for awhile. I finally realized they were trying to avoid me. And when I left, they were talking to the bride and groom who had confused and frightened looks on their faces as I congratulated them and handed them their gift before leaving."

LuAnne reached down and picked up her files only to knock other items off her desk. She said, "When we get to court don't ever look at him, it will rattle your nerves. Say a nursery rhyme in your head or stare at the clock the whole time he speaks. Don't listen to his lies, it will make you angry and that's what we don't want showing up. Silence is power. Emotionless silence. If you don't know the answer to something or it takes you time to think, don't be afraid to take your time. Don't have any contact with him. If you screw up, don't worry; I am here to fix it. My questions are intended to bring things to the judge's attention. It doesn't matter how he answers. My questions will paint a picture of him. He's going to feel like a one-legged man in a butt-kicking contest." She slammed her mug down on that one causing coffee to splash all over her documents.

Ivy took a few moments not knowing what to say or do next. "Well, what do you think the likely outcome of this will be?"

"I know you're probably no different than all the other folks in the world who think it's the lawyers that make or break a case. That's partly true, but it ultimately comes down to the judge. And dad gumit, this judge we are going before makes some very strange rulings. I went before him not that long ago and it was bullshit. Not a soul could believe the outcome; even the bailiff who works down the street at 7-11 on the weekends was surprised. Shoot the breeze with her when I'm fixin' to get me a slurpee and she told me so. The judge is ugly as a mud fence, too, by the way."

LuAnne was not matching the vision of the high powered attorney she had been made out to be but, *too late now,* thought Ivy. "LuAnne, the biggest thing that scares me is the fact that he wants primary custody. And now you're saying this judge…"

"Now, that won't happen." She was quiet for a minute and then continued. "Ivy, it's a fucking control game. The guy's pissed. He wants the power you used to give him back. Simple as that." She paused giving Ivy some time to register what she was saying. "Look at you, you're a nice girl. A wedding minister for Christ's sake. And you're cute as a possum. You come from a wealthy family so you're rich, at least compared to him, you have his only child, the guy's a total failure. He has nothing and this is really all about him wanting your money is my guess?"

Ivy shrugged at the pathetic truth of the last statement. She had far more than Jeff, but wasn't rich by any stretch of the imagination. Just thinking about the part of the petition that asked her to pay him child support made her turn clammy. "Why? I just don't get this. Why now? Why like this? I tried to let him be a dad. He never wanted anything to do with it. Left me when he found out I was pregnant." She pictured the night she told him. She had brought back two double decker cheeseburgers and two brownie explosions from Dairy Queen on her way home from work. The cravings had set in early. As she was piling her cheeseburger in between the buns with cottage cheese from the refrigerator, he walked through the front door and she joyfully broke the news. He looked at her and her food with disgust and left the house without saying a word. A couple of weeks later she had returned to work and when she came home, he and all of his belongings were gone. " I literally came home one day and he had completely gone away. No note, no nothing. After that I never asked anything from him. I never brought up the word court-ever. I thought I was giving him what he wanted and raising our baby on my own. I just don't understand any of it."

"How old is the child?"

"Olive's 7 months old now."

"The men freak in these situations Ivy. Sometimes delayed reaction," she rolled her right hand in the air as if saying this was a perfect example. She continued, "I don't know why. Just a difference in the sexes. The asshole in them comes out at times like these and you got yourself a real asshole to begin with. Isn't he a writer?"

"Yeah."

"What does he write?"

"He wrote a novel called *Points of Passion*. It came out a while ago now but it did well. I know what you're getting at LuAnne, but he doesn't have any money. I don't know what he did with it all. He hid things from me. Probably didn't even try but I just never caught on. Everyone told me it was cocaine. I don't know. Of course I was the last to ever hear anything about it. No one could believe that I didn't know, but honestly, I didn't."

LuAnne stared at her for a moment trying to get a better reading on the young woman in front of her. The last remark gave her a sudden naïve quality that could work well for her in court. The more she appeared the victim the better. "Well like I said, we'll try to limit the visitation to the extreme and we'll try to prevent you from paying child support to him. I can guarantee you one thing for sure - the fucking prick won't be getting sole custody."

LuAnne watched Ivy. Ivy was staring down at the carpet in a trance. "Unfortunately you picked a loser Ivy. Now you have to suffer the consequences. Forever, most likely. He might go away again. But in the meantime he is here. We'll do what we can. Just know that your life is going to be hell for a while little darlin', in case you haven't figured that out."

Ivy got up from her chair and took her wallet out of her purse to pay LuAnne with her MasterCard. When she was done she asked her what to wear reminding her that she had never been in a courtroom in her life.

"Scream mother!"

Ivy looked at her blankly.

"Anything. Just make sure it has some green bean and carrot stains on it," she answered as if she was answering what day of the week it was.

Ivy said thanks and left the office. Her head was spinning the entire drive back to Misty Falls.

CHAPTER FOUR

Jeff was called up to the witness stand. Since he was suing, he was the lucky one who got to go first.

As Jeff climbed into the stand, LuAnne shifted to the left side of her chair to whisper in Ivy's ear while her right elbow pushed out and slid across the table, knocking over her stuffed briefcase, legal pad and pen. Everyone in the court-room turned to look at them, including Jeff. He glared from the stand, obviously not liking the attention taken away from him. Ivy's eyes caught his and quickly looked away. The moment sent her blood pressure soaring. LuAnne lifted the briefcase up off the floor and pulled out a stack of papers zigzagged this way and that. She squirmed as she tried to keep them from falling out again, then shifted her body to the right, which caused a loud fart-like sound to come out from the friction. "Remember, nursery rhymes in your head or stare at the clock while he tells his lies. Don't listen to him." Again the entire room looked at the two.

Ivy responded in her ear, "Okay LuAnne, I understand," in the most emotionally detached voice she could summon only to have it lapse once she got a better look at him. "He's a mess. The drugs have taken a toll on him. How could a judge let a baby be with someone like him?"

A "Shh!' was shouted to them. It was Jeff's attorney, a thick legged blond with designer reading glasses, a tailored dark blazer and skirt with sheer black stockings that revealed bruises underneath. Her nose reminded Ivy of a chicken beak and her attitude was just like Jeff's, she wanted all the attention on her. After all, she was the attorney with the celebrity client and it was their turn. Hush hush all you other nobodies.

As Ivy looked over at Jeff's attorney she noticed the back of another blond's head sitting where his witnesses would be. The hair was an ice blue shade of white that hung in long skinny strands. Ivy replayed her history with him and all the friends of his, who were really only admirers of his work when you got right down to it. Her mind scrolled through the years trying to recall if this person who's hair was the whitest she had ever seen, struck a chord of recognition. Ivy drew a blank. She couldn't place the woman no matter how hard she tried.

Ivy did her best to follow LuAnne's directions of not listening, but it was impossible as there was a microphone propped up in front of Jeff and he was sitting less than 10 feet away from her. Regardless, she hummed "liar liar pants on fire" in her head over and over but couldn't help but to stop breathing when she heard the words "alcoholic, cocaine addict, rage disorder, mood disorder and lesbian" being used to describe *her*. Those utterances caused Ivy heart palpitations and the walls started closing in around her. Fear of having a panic attack set in. She kept silent but could not help raise her eyebrows a few times or hide the fact that her jaw would go slack in looks of disbelief before she could catch herself. She thought she was going to faint, but LuAnne jabbed her in the ribs with her lime green covered elbow when she caught her paying attention and the sharp pain she induced jolted Ivy back to the land of the living. She had warned LuAnne of her panic attacks in case they were to reoccur of which LuAnne took no sympathy. Other than that Jeff mainly bragged about what a great writer he was and parroted the things he had heard great dad's say such as, "I have never known a love as deep as what I have for Olive. It changes your whole life. Someone else is suddenly the most important thing. There is nothing I wouldn't do for her. Nothing." The sound of Ivy's nerves, like frayed lightening crackling, could practically be heard by everyone.

More questions from his attorney followed such as how much money he thought Ivy was worth and wasn't her father the late great Beverly Hills plastic surgeon to the stars, Richard Weiss? It was obvious to Ivy why Jeff was pushing for primary custody. It really was all about money. He wanted her to pay him child support as he would pretend to be taking care of their baby. He claimed she was too busy working and in her ever-growing business and with other personal affairs. Ivy knew the judge could see through his ploy.

Ivy stared at Jeff's oily face in disbelief. This was not the person she had fallen so hard for. This was someone else. His pores were like wide open craters outlined with broken capillaries around his nose. His skin was no longer the tawny olive complexion it had once been. His body was scrawny, pale and weak. He was not the rugged movie star looking man he used to be.

Once Jeff was done being questioned by his attorney and then crossed by LuAnne, the judge called Maruska Czoborova to the stand as his first witness.

The blond stood up, erect, as if she had a plank tied to her back. She strategically placed the white strands of her thinning hair over her shoulders in a way that looked as if she had practiced in front of a mirror. The strands nearly matched the color of her face making it hard to tell where the hair-line began. Her hands were hard and lined without any adornments of rings or polish. Ivy thought to herself that she looked like a gold digger and those were in fact her claws. Her profile revealed a contrast of harsh makeup lining her eyes and mouth that otherwise may have had no definition as she walked to the witness stand. Her over-sized manufactured chest was stuffed inside a vest that looked like part of the costume from a 1980's hair band's keyboard player. Maintaining the posture looked painful, as if she would split in two if she tried to maintain even a modicum more of straightness. She was adorned with cheap gold chains around her neck and wrists of varying weights and lengths. Ivy tried to imagine who she was but couldn't think of anything but the possibility of her being a prostitute or a topless dancer. But far too old for either. She was the type men went gaga over, primarily because of her animal like sexuality, more than her beauty. A has been ex porn star. Her over-sized chest begging, "Notice me, notice me, with my platinum hair and the fact that I am bigger and therefor better than all others." Ivy thought about that. It had been four hours now since the case started. She felt as if her own butt was getting bigger and wondered if preparation H and hemorrhoids were a popular topic amongst judges and bailiffs.

The woman took a seat in the witness stand with what seemed like an attempt to look classy and gentle. The moves didn't fit the vibes Ivy was feeling about her. She knew it was some sort of an act. But who was she and why was she here?

Jeff's attorney, Rebecca Zolanowsky, questioned her after she was asked to identify herself. "What is your relationship with my client?"

"We are friends. We have been friends for over 15 years. Very close friends." Her voice was deep, *probably mistaken for a man's quite often if you didn't have the Euro trash Barbie image in front of you,* thought Ivy. But Ivy understood. The last line was spoken to her as a threat.

The woman, Maruska, continued to answer questions from Miss Zolanowsky about what a wonderful person Jeff was. A true and remarkable American talent. Someone worthy of notable prizes. Someone who in fact had had a best seller. A raw talent, world recognized. What a wonderful father he was going to be, how he adored Olive and couldn't wait for Ivy's prevention of seeing her be put to an abrupt end. How he had tried so hard to be a dad but Ivy would have nothing to do with it. She was a spoiled selfish girl who thought the baby was all hers, so he had been forced to take her to court. Something Jeff would have never done as he was far too kind of a human being. But Ivy had pushed him away from the one thing that was nearest and dearest to him. And how no, he was not on drugs and she herself had never ever done drugs in her life or had ever seen Jeff partake in them.

Ivy wondered what the appropriate term was for someone like this woman. She looked at the judge to see if she saw any signs of him wondering the same but he held his gaze stoic to the back of the room simply taking in everything with his ears and mind only. Ivy couldn't remember the definition of what a sociopath was, although she was sure the woman before her was one. She did recall the definition of what a psychopath was: a charming deviant who felt no remorse for their anti moral behaviour. She wished she could remember the definition of a sociopath. She wasn't sure which one better suited the pale woman but it was certainly one of the two. No one could tell lies like that so convincingly and have the nerve to do so on a witness stand unless they were one or the other.

Then it was LuAnne's turn to question her.

To Ivy's surprise, her first question was asking her for her address rather than questioning her about the validity of the statement she just made about her having prevented Jeff from seeing Olive. Ivy resisted the urge to pull on Lu Anne's pant leg to get her to when she saw the bailiff eying her intently.

Maruska was struck silent and stared at Jeff's attorney.

"What is your current address?" LuAnne repeated the question. "It's a simple question!"

"1610 LeVane."

The same address as Jeff. *Son of a bitch,* thought Ivy. She had no idea he was involved with someone. And with someone like her? She and this woman had nothing in common by appearances. Her image reminded her of the eerie legend of the White Lady; a tragic female ghost that was fabled to be a bride betrayed by her husband or a mother who lost her child, depending on what version you were told in what part of the world. The apparition apparently drove in her car along rural roads dressed in her Victorian era clothing. The myth ran amok from Washington to New Jersey to the Philippines, England and Portugal. Her appearance was world renowned and symbolized a death to those that saw her gazing at them with her cloudy eyes. Ivy shook the story out of her head. She looked at the woman and compared herself to her. Ivy was natural, wholesome, a little meaty, but the type that men said they liked as it gave them something to hang onto and this woman well, she was baseballs on popsicle sticks. A twang of jealousy zipped through Ivy, making her more confused, disgusted and pissed at Jeff.

"Miss Maruska. Is it okay if I call you that? I have no idea in tarnation how to pronounce your last name and I am sure you rather not hear what I come up with." With that the judge chuckled knowingly.

Maruska's pink and blue eyes appeared to blink nervously as they shifted from side to side.

"What do you do for a living?"

"I work at a publishing firm in Austin. I also promote writers. Some local stuff," she continued to answer, the accent becoming more clear. "But mostly overseas. Europe."

"So, not only are you very familiar with Mr. Hunter as it appears, but you are extremely familiar with him on a professional level as well? Familiar with his professional reputation here and abroad?"

"Yes."

"So why is it that his career, if he is so brilliant, has completely tanked?" LuAnne spun around and stopped dead in her tracks right in front of her.

"Excuse me?" Maruska looked from Jeff's attorney to the judge in hopes of gaining some sympathy. "I no understand question." Maruska continued to hold the puzzled look from the combination ballerina twirl and loaded question.

Jeff's lawyer started to rise but the judge waived for her to sit down.

Maruska had time to interpret. "His reputation is very good. Everywhere."

"Is that so?" LuAnne asked.

Ivy was finally starting to relax a little. LuAnne was taking over and making the other side nervous with her mighty Green Giant pantsuit presence.

"Then why, Ms. Maruska, did his publisher drop him six years ago?"

"That happens to almost everyone sooner or later. Is no a big deal. Not. Not. Not a big deal."

"Oh really. It's NOT a big deal to whom? You? Not a big deal to you? Wasn't it because his publisher found out about Jeff's drug habit and refused to give him any more advances? And you, I am looking at your criminal history sure'nuff right here in front of me." She fumbled around for a few seconds trying to find it. The culmination of how surprised Ivy was with LuAnne doing her homework and then her almost not being able to find the important information was making her feel as if her heart was going to explode.

"Six years ago you were busted for possession of cocaine isn't that right Miss Maruska?" LuAnne asked a few moments later. LuAnne had checked with the cops that had made the arrest. There was reportedly heroin in the mix as well but she was going to save that as a surprise for later. She hadn't even told Ivy of that good news. Unfortunately, the tactic didn't play out. The judge ruled before she could use it for ultimate effect.

A reluctant "Yes."

"Who was with you when this happened?"

Another reluctant answer. "Jeff."

Jeff's attorney jumped up and objected, stating that the criminal record was passée as it was before Jeff became a father.

Three hours later the judge ruled in Jeff's favor granting him weekly visitation, both overnight and unsupervised. Today was Friday. The visitation would begin on Monday.

Beaten down, Ivy could barely lift herself from the court bench once the ruling had passed. She willed herself to stare at the cold tiled floor and to not look at Maruska, Jeff or Jeff's attorney as she did not want them having the satisfaction of seeing her tears. Once they walked past her and left the room LuAnne got up.

"What's supposed to happen now? I just wait until he overdoses and forgets Olive is with him or something? Then we can come back and convince this judge this is not smart? When it's too late?" Ivy was on LuAnne's heels out the courtroom doors and down the hallway.

LuAnne parked down on a bench next to a busy water fountain. "I am so Sorry Ivy. I hate that fucking judge. He's back asswards. Plain and simple. Redneck county you live in too, Ivy, doesn't help not one wanker either. Don't worry though it's not over. You still have a final hearing. His weekly overnights are just under temporary orders for now. Hopefully he'll fuck up with the rope he's been given. That's what we need. So far in the system's eyes, he hasn't."

"What do you mean in the system's eyes he hasn't? Look at him." Ivy pointed out the window where he stood in a celebratory circle with his lawyer and Maruska. The lawyer hugged both of them and then went towards her BMW. Maruska and Jeff walked towards a small car in the parking lot and both got in. Ivy wondered how high they were going to get in their celebration. "It's obvious what's going on. Even I can tell now. He didn't look that bad when he left. And the judge is going to let a baby have overnights with him? I don't get it LuAnne. And you did tell the judge that he got arrested for cocaine possession with that strange woman, so it's not like they don't know." They both watched as the small car sped past. Maruska was driving.

"Yes, Ivy but it was a while ago. Every one screws up in life. The system has to be fair about those things and not hold people any more accountable than they have to be, especially on separate issues and occasions. Bottom line is he's the father. And the court thinks he deserves a chance to prove himself in that department. Neither one of you argued that he wasn't. You couldn't have possibly gotten knocked up by someone else could've you?"

Ivy looked at LuAnne with disbelief she was asking this question, now of all times. "No, I'm not like that. One person, one at a time is the way I do things LuAnne, obviously unlike others."

"Sorry Ivy, just thought I'd ask. Would be pretty cool if he wasn't. We could appeal with the new information and then the sorry mother fucker would be jumpy as spit on a hot skillet. Anyhoo, until he screws up you can't prevent his daughter from being with him. And by screwing up we mean something tangible Ivy. An arrest when they are together, abuse, proof. Bam! Not just you saying he's a creep on drugs. That's hearsay. Proof. We need proof. If he endangers Olive, you've got it made. But hopefully it won't come to that. Look. Look on the bright side darlin'. He obviously wants to be with his daughter on some level or he wouldn't have taken it to court."

Ivy just stared straight ahead without responding. She was listening though, LuAnne could tell. The concern was genuine and not just the typical drama between two former lovers that now hate each other more than anyone else in the world once they have a baby together. "Maybe the judge really is just giving him enough rope to hang himself."

Ivy thought about that. Jeff fucking up could be a blessing. But on the other hand it could also be a curse. It depended on what it would be and she didn't want to think about the options. She silently said a prayer for Olive asking the Big Man Upstairs to please, please, please watch out for her. To please not let anything happen to her. She remained seated next to LuAnne and together they stared at the paint chipped wall in front of them. Ivy sent a text message on her Blackberry to Punch whom she promised she would call with the outcome and to also give her a clue as to when she'd be on her way home to Olive. It simply said, "lost."

Ivy drove the long drive home by herself. It was almost six o'clock and the night was turning gray. Green County was one of the largest of all the 254 counties in the state, placing the court house considerable distance from where she lived and giving her lots of time to think. It would be over an hour until she was back home with Olive. She couldn't wait to get home to see her, to hold her and hoped liked hell there wouldn't be any new surprises waiting for her.

She had left the house in the morning, asking Punch to take it easy with the treats for Olive. The last time Punch babysat, Ivy had come home to a brownie poop explosion. It was all over Olive's playpen, enmeshed in the tiny netted holes of its walls and all over Olive. It also covered the playpen's floor in smears like someone had taken a paintbrush to it and brushed the bottom with large sweeping strokes. Punch had lit a butter cream scented candle in hopes of hiding what had just happened from her, but it failed only emphasizing the sweet sticky pungent odor. Ivy felt bad when Punch got a disappointed look on her face when she made the request. She felt like she was taking all the fun out of watching Olive as Punch folded over the unopened greasy brown paper bag she had brought over and placed it high on the kitchen counter out of reach.

When Ivy arrived home, Punch was holding Olive and patting her on her back to burp her. They were sitting on the front porch's rocking bench enjoying the balmy weather and moonlight with Wendy, Punch's new girlfriend. Punch had recently met Wendy at Austin's very first Lesbian and Gay, Bisexual and Transgendered Wedding and Family Expo, which was held at the Hyatt Hotel downtown. Punch had tried to get Ivy to share the cost of a booth with her as gay friendly wedding officiants, but Ivy had to decline as it was not good timing with everything else she had going on. And now after the gay allegations in court, whatever controversy they were meant to stir up, she was relieved she didn't. She could imagine if Jeff found out and what sort of twisted perverted picture of her he would have painted if she did. Not that it mattered. Gay people all over the world were raising kids and doing a great job. It was just hard to shake off lies told about you in court no matter how ridiculous or harmless they were. Punch had been very excited about the expo and was hopeful about meeting more couples and singles with similar sexual orientations that she had and was disappointed when Ivy had to say no. Ivy tried to recall the details of how the two had become acquainted there as she pulled into the driveway, but her brain was too fried.

She got out of the bug wishing she had Punch to herself like she used to but told herself to be friendly and welcoming to Wendy. It had been a long time since Punch had found someone who cared about her.

Wendy wasn't at all what Ivy had pictured when she first heard about her. She expected someone tall and lanky and boyish and natural (as in wore no makeup) and tattooed like Punch. Instead, Wendy was almost as short as Ivy. She had ringlets of silver frosted hair that framed her eternally red face, which was either from too much running in the sun or aggressive scrubbing or both. She only wore jet black mascara and ringed her eyes in a metallic blue eyeliner which she probably thought emphasized the blueness of her eyes rather than the makeup. She looked up expectantly and eagerly at whomever was speaking and never seemed to blink. She was athletic and a go getter in comparison to Punch's laid back demeanor. Originally from Minnesota, she liked to think scorpions were a blessing of the Southwest and looked forward to stepping on them with her bare feet for sport. She thought the sting healed certain ailments.

The only thing that had bothered Ivy about Wendy up to this point was the way she dressed. She knew it was trivial, but hated when someone so close to having it together sabotaged themselves with bad taste. Wendy perpetually dressed in running shoes, sweat shirts and track pants. Ivy liked to make her over in her mind smartly dressed in casual business attire; Jones of New York would do wonders and would put her meter rating way up on the richter scale. A hydrating conditioning balm for her hair would soften her and the eyeliner absolutely positively needed to be tossed out. Maybe someday she would give her the chance to give her a makeover, but she doubted it.

Wendy, Punch and Olive greeted Ivy as she got out of her bug and with arms around her, escorted her into her home.

Ivy immediately wanted to hold Olive once she made it to the shelter inside.

"Sorry Ives," Punch said as she handed Olive over.

"Yeah, sorry Ivy," repeated Wendy as she trailed them into the house.

They both sat on the couch that she and Olive sat down on not leaving any extra wiggle room. It felt good to Ivy. She was thankful to have the company and the ears to hear her hash out all the horrific details of what Jeff had just accused her of and in so doing had won.

Wendy mainly listened, taking it all in with her eyes as if she was watching a UFO hover above her while Punch interjected with personal opinions and cussing, which helped Ivy's morale tremendously.

Wendy seemed extra curious about the part about Jeff accusing her of being a lesbian and Punch and her could tell she was wondering if there was any truth to that. There wasn't, but both Punch and Ivy felt it beneath their dignity to have to explain that to her. She either liked Punch or she didn't, regardless. She knew Punch was gay. She described herself as bi-sexual. So, there were enough unspoken liaisons between the three of them to keep quiet unless they wanted to change the subject and ramble on endlessly about lovers for the next three days. All of them were too tired for that right now. Except for Wendy who seemed to have an uncanny way of changing the subject to suit interests that appealed to her curiosity in the sexuality department. More than once Punch and Ivy cast knowing glances at each other that perhaps there was more to Wendy than they had first recognized. But tonight was not the night to make waves.

Ivy called for pizza, her treat for the eight hour babysitting shift. Ivy ordered thin crust vegetarian with extra olives for herself and ordered Punch and Wendy a deep dish meat lovers pizza. Wendy insisted on getting a bottle of Cab and left Punch and her alone for twenty minutes. Ivy could tell something was on Punch's mind but she was holding back. Punch only held back when things concerned her about herself.

Ivy thought the meal wouldn't be complete without dinner salads, which she had failed to order, so she decided to prepare homemade salads for the three of them. Her mother had come from a long line of Italians, her maiden name being Gravada, and Ivy knew how to make certain treats as good as the best of them, thanks to her grandmother. Grandmother Gravada had been a huge inspiration in Ivy's life. She visited every other year with Iris as they were growing up. Her apartment overlooked the canals of Venice, Italy. Ivy was only eight when she had taken taken that first magical trip full of gondola rides, pigeons and gelato. Ivy would never stop talking about it while her other class mates were babbling on about Scooby and Mickey. She opened her refrigerator door and pulled out the greens, red pepper, goat cheese, fennel and prosciutto. She set them down on the kitchen counter and bent down to tickle and kiss Olive who was in her bassinet right along side of her, ready to call it a day.

She walked to the pantry to retrieve the cans of garbanzo beans and olives. "Thank you Punch for today. Is everything okay with you?"

Punch was lost in thought, gazing at Olive now fast asleep. "What?"she asked.

"I was wondering if everything is okay with you and Wendy?" She began chopping the vegetables quietly so she wouldn't wake Olive and could hear Punch.

Punch turned around to look at her. "Hard to say. Something ain't sitting quite right you know? I mean you are gay or you're not. You are bi like she says she is or you're not. You're straight like you are or you're not. You just are what you are, but she constantly wants to talk about it. I'm not used to talking about it. Even right now. I just want to be. Jesus Christ, I feel like I am being questioned by the CIA sometimes with her. It's stupid I know. I mean I like her a great deal, I know she doesn't mean any harm, but I feel like she's a reporter or something. Give me a fucking break already."

Ivy nodded. She knew what Punch meant. She had just witnessed it and had found herself questioning what Wendy was really all about. It wasn't always easy to tell with certain types but when you knew you knew. And nothing about Wendy spoke of not really being straight. But there was nothing to confirm otherwise either. Ivy, without saying it out loud, hoped it wasn't a repeat of Punch's last relationship when after seven months of dating, her girlfriend figured out she was really straight and abruptly broke things off and got married to a man she met online five months later. To make matters worse they called Punch to proceed over the ceremony which she not so politely turned down.

Ivy had an antiquated phone -not according to her, but to all her friends. It hugged the wall of her kitchen like an animal clinging to life trying to make a hasty get away up to the ceiling. It's long coiled cord drug down like a critter's tail. It was the same color as her bug, her favorite- a creamy yellow, complete with rotary dial. Ivy liked to hang onto things even if the rest of the world was far ahead of her. What was the point of keeping up with technology if you really didn't need it and it just kept draining your bank account just to be current? There was something comforting in traditional technology. She was the last of her friends to change over from eight tracks to cassettes to CDs. At present she loved to watch movies in her spare time, granted that they were on VHS. The phone in Ivy's kitchen had no answering machine attached to it either. She was either available to take a call or she wasn't. And if it was that important, whomever it was could call her back until they reached her and if it was an emergency, they knew where she worked and they knew Punch and the very few who had her cell number were strictly limited to Punch, the chapel staff, her mom and Iris and Jeff if he counted at this point in time. The phone had rung six times before Ivy was able to answer. If she would have skipped the hand washing after Olive's diaper change it could have probably been answered on ring number four. She almost skipped that important step to get to the phone before whomever it was hung up, but the old infomercial, it that's what they were called in those days, kept playing in her head: "Wash your hands after going to the bathroom. Wash your hands after changing baby too. Cause we don't want to get hepatitis. And we don't want hepatitis to get you. Who? You!"

"Hairyew?" the voice asked before she could say hello. It was LuAnne. Ivy shifted Olive over to her free arm so she could manage the cord without it strangling either one of them. Ivy had been so preoccupied with the care of Olive and work that the whole court thing had almost escaped her until now. *What did LuAnne want?* Ivy hoped it was good news.

"Ivy, the reason I am calling is because you and Jeff both need to get before the psychologist for the evaluations. You'll have to make the appointment yourself. Here's the number of the fellow that Jeff's attorney and I agreed upon. His name is Doctor Neetle. N-e-e-t-l-e. Phone number 512-329-0003. That's Doctor Roger Neetle. N-e-e-t-l-e. Phone number 512-329-0003." Ivy was glad that she was repeating it because she talked so fast and never asked if she was ready with a pen and paper, which she wasn't. She tried to memorize the doctor's name and number but the hepatitis song was still running interference.

"Oh, and Ivy don't forget you're court ordered to pay for both of them. Yours and Jeff's." The hepatitis song screeched to a halt. "Take it easy doll. Call back when you're done. I'll let you go now and get to that beautiful baby of yours. I'm sure he'll think Jeff is as crooked as a barrel of snakes." Ivy could picture her making the next phone call to tell some other client equal or less encouraging news. She hoped that this doctor was in the phone book.

The mention of the evaluations had sent Ivy's heart plunging down heavily to her gut. Why was Jeff so insistent on them? And worse, why did he think they were going to work in his favor? The reminder of the extra five thousand dollar expense nearly made Ivy throw up. She thanked LuAnne for the follow up call and assured her she would take care of it the next day. She was speaking to dead air. LuAnne was already on her next call.

CHAPTER FIVE

The next morning, Ivy hung up with Dr. Neetle. She felt good about things. He sounded young, nice, and had a sense of humor as he laughed with her in sympathy that she was the lucky one who got court ordered to pay for the whopping five thousand dollar diagnoses.

The following morning she went to her first appointment. Dr. Neetle's office was located in the most pretentious part of West Austin. A modern complex of three juxtaposed office buildings made of tan stucco with gray black tinted windows, fancy feminine landscaping of bright yellow esperanza and lantana and fuchsia bottle brush trees separating the lanes of traffic with plenty of parking in shade. Ivy parked her bug in front of Building B and then found Suite 109 by foot.

The suite led into a complicated maze of multiple unmarked rooms and hallways. She felt like a rat in an experimental maze being observed to see how she was handling the pressure so far. Finally she saw human life. An orthodox Jew was sitting on a leather couch. Ivy parked herself a couple of feet away from him and then asked him if she was in the right place. After several moments, he turned to look at her and said, while the bottom of his fuzzy rust colored beard brushed his groin, that the waiting room was the room next door and that she was currently sitting in Dr. Neetle's personal office space.

Panicked that she was already appearing cuckoo, she jumped off the couch before the doctor approached and reminded herself for the umpteenth time as she walked to the waiting room that she would not divulge the fact that she was a huge admirer of Sylvia Plath's writing to the psychologist.

Thirty minutes later Dr. Neetle called her in. He was tall, but short waisted, with a receding strawberry blond hairline and narrow eyes all pulled together by taut, slick poreless skin. He wore dress pants, polished loafers and a starched and pressed long-sleeved button-down cotton shirt. She guessed he probably didn't have any body hair. He took a seat next to Ivy and looked her straight on. He started with the cold hard fact that nothing would be off the record. The final report would be given to the judge and that ultimately he would be forced to say things about both her and Jeff that they would wind up using against each other. *What a positive profession* Ivy thought.

The psychiatric evaluation consisted of three, three hour crazy making sessions. And if it took longer, Dr. Neetle reassured her, it wouldn't cost her any extra, which didn't make her feel any better as she thought the money a waste to begin with, thanks to Jeff; money she thought should be going towards Olive. The first session consisted of answering T for true and F for false to a series of questions on a computer screen while she sat alone in a blackened room. The questions ranged from asking her if she had fantasies of being an auto mechanic to asking if she heard voices telling her to do terrible things.

The second session had her completing sentences. Finish the sentence to: Masturbation is:

Ivy's written answer: Something I think most people do. What she really wanted to say: One of the most fun things on the planet that you can do by yourself

Bed wetting is:

Ivy's written answer: Something I think young children do for the most part. What she really wanted to say: No matter what your age, diapers and Depends can help

Sex is:

Ivy's written answer: Wonderful if you are in love. What she really wanted to say: Something that can get you into a hell of a lot of unpredictable trouble

If someone offered you free drugs:

Ivy's written answer: I would not be interested. What she really wanted to say: I would save them for when this is over and I am completely broke to sell on the East Side

Gay people are:

The answer she wrote: People we should all treat with respect. What she really wanted to say: A group that I am waiting and waiting for marriages to become legal with in the State of Texas as it's nobody's fucking business who people want to have sex with. I could also use the money to help me recuperate the money I am losing answering these fucking ridiculous questions

My favorite day was:

The answer she wrote: A day in Fredericksburg eating peach ice cream with my daughter.

She really meant that one.

I like:

The answer she wrote: Being a mom, cooking, my work and eating. What she really wanted to say: all of the above and fantasizing that I am the killer in *Points of Passion* and Jeff is my victim

When nobody is looking I:

The answer she wrote: Get real goofy with Olive. If she was telling the truth: And pluck the sudden disturbing gray hairs that are making a presence down there

The questions continued for three more pages.

The third and final exam was verbal. Ivy sat in the waiting room waiting for the doctor to open the door that separated the waiting room from the corridor and his office suite. He was running late. In snippets she could hear some of the dialog going on on the other side of the wall that separated her from his office. It was the Jew who had the appointment ahead of her who was obviously called in for a psychiatric evaluation for some reason or another himself. Ivy tried to amuse herself with reasons why; perhaps he had committed a crime, perhaps he was only attracted to Catholic girls and committed a serious offense against one of them or someone in his own race, perhaps he self-administered the exam. Bored with her speculations, her mind drifted elsewhere. She wondered if she had the nerve to give Dr. Neetle the beaver shot like Sharon Stone did to her interrogators in *Basic Instinct* and if she did, if she would be let off the hook. She imagined with Dr. Neetle that it would probably be a guarantee to land her in a straight jacket. *But it would finally get me committed,* she mused. She glanced down at the coffee table at the magazine selection. On top of the stack of the tattered assortment was a heavily creased and torn *Cosmopolitan,* various pages hanging by a thread. Ivy caught herself reaching down for it and then retracting; *was it a trap?* What would reading a Cosmo say about her if the doctor walked in and noticed it? It might reveal that she was oversexed, which wasn't the image she wanted to give him. She stared around the room at the four walls and carpet and two other chairs. What the hell, she reached down and grabbed it and horrified, found the article "My Bi-Sexual Adventure" by Wendy Olenger advertised on the front cover. Quickly, Ivy checked her watch. The doctor was ten minutes late calling her in. She looked down at the magazine again, was it the Wendy Olenger she knew? She flipped through the table of contents to find the page number of the article. It was on page 67. Hurriedly, she flipped the magazine on its backside and went from the back pages forward searching for the article. Page 110. Page 97. Page 103. Page 54. Darn it! Where was page 67? As if a joke, she found every page past it and before it and just when she was convinced someone must have torn the article out, there it was. And next to the title was a cheery picture of the Wendy Olenger she knew and her husband Dave Olenger from the waist up with his arm wrapped smugly around her as they smiled for the camera. Ivy glanced through the article noticing quotes like Dave Olenger saying "I am very proud of my wife. A lot of people have asked me if I was jealous and I have to say no, I was never jealous. Our marriage has always been based on trust. Wendy had always been bi-curious and I felt in order for her to feel complete, I had to set her free and give her my okay to experiment. Now she realizes it's not what she wants and it's made our marriage even stronger."

The interviewer then asked Wendy how many liaisons she's had.

"Really just one. And I did enjoy it and the woman tremendously. But I feel I have gotten my curiosity out of my system and it's time to come home so to speak." The interviewer then told the readers about the loving proud smile that Dave Olenger just gave to his no longer bi-curious wife.

She heard Dr. Neetle's footsteps approaching as the Jew walked through the door and gave her an apologetic look. She slammed the magazine shut and threw it on the table. It slapped hard on its landing and slid askew from the rest of the stack. She prayed Dr. Neetle wouldn't notice. She crossed her legs and folded her hands around her purse.

The doctor opened the door to the waiting room and called her name which sounded like an unfinished sentence, the remainder being: "You have the right to remain silent. Anything you say can and will be used against you in a court of law. You have the right to talk to a lawyer and have him present with you while you are being questioned. If you cannot afford a lawyer, one will be provided to you at the government's expense."

Calling out her full name was unnecessary as she was the only one sitting in the waiting room. And momentarily Ivy wondered what the results would be if the doctor himself were to be put under a psychological examination. He led the way to his office as if she might get lost if he didn't and directed her to sit down as he himself sat in his seat. He told her that today he wanted the whole story from the day she was born to this very moment in time.

Ivy sat back in the sofa, tired from all the questions she had already been asked and her mind reeling from what she had just found out. She wasn't sure she had anything more to share with the doctor that would allow him to determine if she was nuts or not. Her elbow rested on the arm of the sofa and she rested her head on her hand. She wanted to talk to Punch, not him.

"I was born in Pacific Palisades, California at my parents house. They hated hospitals and wanted privacy. They had already hired a nanny who took over immediately as my mom and dad were occupied with their careers and social lives. I mean I had it good, I am not complaining. It was nice to grow up in a home like we had overlooking the Pacific, and my Nanny, her name was Bess, was the best there was and then my sister Iris came along so it was a lot of just us three..."

"What kind of work did your parents do?" Dr. Neetle asked as he scratched notes vehemently on a yellow legal pad.

"My dad was a plastic surgeon and my mom was a high fashion model."

He looked up from his pad as if the answer was startling.

Ivy was used to it. Most people looked at her funny when she said her mom was a model. Ivy didn't inherit the model look so to speak. Just good taste in clothing. She smoothed out the wrinkles of her blouse that fell in her lap. The blouse was Channel. A rare piece that had been gifted to her mother by the designer when she had done her first show in Paris.

"Is that how they met?" The doctor stared at her, waiting for an answer, with a look like the answer either way would be earth-shattering.

His reaction caused Ivy to reflex. She was now sitting up straight on the sofa's edge. "Yes, it's how they met. She went in to have a nose job and apparently at some point, not sure if it was pre or post schnoz, he fell in love with her and her him." The little snort chortle came out but she decided not to hold back and hoped her choice of words would get him to lighten up at least a little. He continued writing with intensity on the pad.

Ivy continued, "Anyway, like I said, it was all good. They weren't around much, but who's parents are perfect? So then..."

"What do you mean by that statement and how does it reflect your perception of you as a mother?"

Jeez, thought Ivy. Couldn't she just tell the story without him interrupting every sentence? She suddenly felt as if she was being interrogated for a major crime. She shifted in her seat and crossed her feet, looking down at the pretty shoes that she was wearing that had come with a variety of clips to be able to change their look- everything from tiny anchors to buttons. She had decided on two flowers, thinking it might help convince the doctor that she was feminine, a good example to her daughter with soft and pretty taste. The doctor stared down at her feet as his face twisted up. *What the hell was that for*, she thought. Did her crossing them mean she was being defensive? She uncrossed them as he took notice of her change of mind and then scribbled something. She decided she needed to reorganize her story if this was how it was going to be. He wasn't going to manipulate her into saying something regretful by making her nervous.

"Dr. Neetle, personally I believe almost everyone has a gripe or two about their parents and their upbringing. That being said, mine was very good. But my parents liked to work and got their identities through it. I have learned that I don't want to do that with Olive. It's my desire to be with her and if I don't get married or don't have the option to stop working to be more to the point, I plan on taking Olive with me to work and incorporating her as much in my world as possible."

Dr. Neetle placed his pen down on his pad and stared at her as if she had just grown a third eye.

What the hell, she thought. No answer was good enough for this jerk. The frustration was starting to eat at her. She wasn't much practiced at the art of lying but this was just too painful. She knew she was a good person, way better than the average Joe, so why was she feeling like she just committed an unspeakable heinous crime?

"Tell me about Olive's delivery," he said suddenly, taking on the tone of a near and dear friend as he crossed his leg over the other. He put down his pen and paper and rested his elbow on his leg, propping up his head with his hand.

Now Ivy understood. All the questions were aimed at getting her worked up for this one. They had all been calculated to get to this point to see how just likely to fly off the handle she might actually be. She closed her eyes momentarily and at first she pictured Olive with her round pale cheeks and pools of gray blue eyes that you could dive deep into, her rosy triangular lips; the upward one pointing to heaven in an upside down v, and her squeezable chubby chubby thighs. Her miracle baby with the smile that could heal the world she thought. Then she rewound as the events sped past going back to the beginning: the bleeding that wouldn't stop, the blood all over her and her bedroom, Punch racing over to help, the ambulance- her very first ride in one that was not the luxury ride she had imagined. It was a rickety rackety tin can ride while a paramedic swayed above her trying to find balance with his sea legs while holding an IV needle. Then the birth 24 hours later after everything conceivable had been done to make it happen including putting a balloon device up her; her cervix that wouldn't open and Olive being trapped inside, her life threatened as well, while mom was bleeding to death. And finally, the happy moment of Olive finally painfully sliding through. The astonishing relief right afterwards, like a giant pimple had been squeezed and all the infection had been drained out or like a giant lumpy turd had just finally passed but through the wrong end. That one *huge* second of relief. Then the smiling baby girl that was passed overhead. The very first sight of her baby and her baby was smiling! The joy abruptly halted by the sudden shrieks of the doctor still sitting between her legs, and the long rectangular fluorescent lights moving in fast forward sequence overhead as the stretcher was raced down the hallway with all the hospital's most authoritative and credentialed coming out of every nook and cranny and meeting up in one chaotic operating room. The final memory of the oxygen mask placed on her face. Fade to black. Wake up. The intense searing pain felt like her insides had been charred while someone was inside with tiny knives slicing away. Dr. Cherry informing her that she would never be able to have another child. Her hopes shattered. She so badly wanted one more. She had held hope of Olive having a brother or a sister someday. It wasn't fair. None of it was fair. Her face began to quiver and tears flooded her eyes much as Ivy fought against it.

"That! That! What's that all about? Talk. Now!"

The bossy tone jolted Ivy back to the psychiatrist's office. For a minute she couldn't help but just stare at him. That? "That" was private. No matter what, she wasn't going to share that lost dream with this prick.

She got herself together and told him it was just that things didn't go well during the birth and she wound up having a hysterectomy to save her life.

"That must be a terrible shock for a woman to face. The fact that you won't be able to have any more children."

"I only wanted this one. So it was fine," she lied.

She waited for the terse reaction she expected from him now. Any second he would call her bluff and she wouldn't give in. She was strong now. He had pushed out what he thought was going to be the crazy woman inside of her but instead he got something else. Obviously he was the expert and must have known she was lying. But much to her surprise he took no notes and didn't ask any more questions on the subject.

Dr. Neetle stared at his silver watch again. "Let's skip to what you do for a living. Tell me about that."

"I work as a non denominational wedding officiant. It's a strange career path I guess and I was really not intending for it to happen. But, well, it did. I do love it and am very busy. Very happy."

"Sounds interesting."

She couldn't help letting out the loud sigh of relief. "Yes, it is interesting. I get to meet a variety of people from all over the world with a variety of spiritual beliefs. My first job after I got my degree from religious studies and art at UT was working at an all black church, just assisting the pastor with concerts, baptisms, and other events that took place at the church. He was also blind, so you can imagine the help he needed." She smiled at the doctor waiting for him to smile back in the knowing of how lucky sighted people are, but got no response. The humiliation of not getting a reaction caused her to flash back to the infamous slogan of Reverend King: "Looky heeya, it not how you look, it how you cone duct yosowf," when he had become exasperated at times with her. Even though she got no reaction from Dr. Neetle she was sure he was taking note of her good Samaritan ways as he went back to scribbling on his pad. Usually the mention of someone blind, especially in this close proximity, had people asking more questions, but when the doctor did look up, he simply held his stoic gaze on her. "Anyway, he got sick one day and after ordaining me, asked me to perform a wedding. At his church." She recounted that day forever grateful that it spared her from going to seminary school, not that she would have gone to one anyway. She was tired of school. High school and college had both been arduous tasks to get through. She was naturally a very lazy person. Any accomplishments took a lot of coffee and peppy self talk. She wished that the world started at eleven in the morning rather than eight. Any classes or jobs that began before that hour she had with record failed. She also couldn't take the Bible as seriously as some of her other classmates that majored in religion at the university. It had become especially hard after Punch and she had a movie night and rented Religilous. It was the night before her final exam in Religions of the Middle East. The rental was Punch's choice who suggested it may give her the other's perspective. Ivy did have to give it some merit and had found herself laughing out loud when she wished she wasn't. "And it just sort of took off from there. Always had an interest in this type of thing I suppose because my parents were atheists while all my other friends growing up had interesting traditions and belief systems."

"Fascinating," he replied.

Ivy shifted in her seat again. Her body more relaxed. He was finally being fair.

"We're about out of time so let's just skip to how the exchanges are going with Jeff at Kid's Exchange. But first I need to use the restroom and get a glass of water. Feel free to take a .." He looked at his watch, "three minute break, too."

Ivy smiled at him, pleased at his sudden shift to a more pleasant demeanor again. She told him she was fine and she would just wait for him. He smiled courteously as he left her alone in the frigid office. She wondered if there was a spy cam watching her. Five minutes later he returned. "So, you were going to tell me how the exchanges were going with Jeff," he said as he shut the door behind him. He grabbed his legal pad and sat down while straightening out his slacks and crossing his legs.

"Yes. They are going fine for the most part. Sometimes I am concerned about the way he looks. Honestly, I feel he is still doing drugs but unfortunately I can't prove it." She wished she hadn't said the word honestly and wondered if the doctor now thought she was a liar.

He flipped through his legal pad. "Yes, I see here that you initially expressed that concern when you first came in. So, you still think it's highly likely that things haven't improved or stopped in that department?" He looked at her sympathetically as she nodded her reply. Finally, he was the doctor again whom she had first spoken to on the phone that day: empathetic and kind. She knew this was his real nature. She felt warm and fuzzy again knowing these exams were going to work in her favor. The doctor understood her dilemma.

The doctor stood up, placed the legal pad on a shelf, and turned around to grab something from his filing cabinet. His panty line showed through his khaki pants as he bent forward to retrieve it. The posture exaggerated the fact that his briefs were crawling up his crack. The vision reminded her of Mr. Kartwright, her economics teacher sophomore year of college whom she swore wore a sock in his front pant pocket as ridiculous as it seemed. Her friend Scott who sat next to her agreed and it was part of the fun of sitting next to each other, passing hilarious notes back and forth when he wasn't looking. He must have noticed Ivy and Scott checking him out because much to both of their amazement he rewarded the two of them with undeserving A's.

Dr. Neetle found what he was looking for in a bound manuscript, took it out of the cabinet and shut it with the bend of a knee. He turned back around to sit down. Ivy smiled at him and made sure her eyes were upward by the time he spun around so he wouldn't think she was checking him out. She had also checked out the time on her cell phone when his back was turned. Time was up. The psych exam was finally over! She felt pleased. Even though there were some rough patches, she felt she had done exceptionally well. She waited for him to acknowledge this as well before she stood up to leave.

Dr. Neetle looked at his watch and held his gaze on it as if in deep thought. He finally lifted his gaze, rubbed his eyes, and flipped open the manuscript in his lap. Without looking up he said, "One can't help coming to the conclusion that you have a psychological disorder."

Ivy didn't know what to say, her body was frozen still with this latest surprise announcement.

"Over the course of the evaluations, you gave me at least eight examples in your relationship with Jeff where anyone in their right mind would have left. No one would have ever stayed with such a person and not only did you stay and stay and stay for the equivalent of five years, you also got yourself pregnant."

"Yeah, well, love is blind!"

Dr. Neetle just stared at her.

"Doctor Neetle, I assure you that I wouldn't make the same mistake of dating him or anyone like him ever again."

"But you did and you won't be able to hide that from your daughter. What are you going to do when she does the same thing?"

Ivy rubbed her eyes in confusion as she felt her blood pressure soar. She reminded herself of a yoga breathing technique to calm her down. *Breathe in through the nostrils with 7 counts, hold for 14 counts, breathe out for, oh forget it,* she thought. *Why was he being such an asshole?* And why of all times was she thinking about yoga now? The last time she had taken a class the instructor had her in a shoulder stand and then grabbed both her legs simultaneously by the ankles, yanking them as high into the air that they would possibly stretch, which much to her and the instructor's surprise, let out the most loud gassiest longest winded fart that the whole class, including Ivy, had ever heard. In humiliation, she vowed to never return. She regained her focus. "Dr. Neetle, in my opinion I think it is good that I experienced someone like Jeff. Now I know how to sniff guys out like him. If I hadn't experienced what I have, I might think differently of someone Olive brings home in the future that is bad for her."

Dr. Neetle shook his head as if saying "Bzzzz wrong answer, but nice try." He continued, "Would you agree that alcohol has given you some problems?"

Oh my God, who hasn't had alcohol give them problems, thought Ivy. She took a moment to think of her answer and hoped it was finally the right one.

"Yes?"

"Thank you Ms. Weiss. I hope that the future will find you with better judgment."

What a prick, thought Ivy as he held the door open for her to leave.

She grabbed the Cosmo on her way out and stuffed it in her purse not giving a darn whether he caught her stealing or not.

After bathing and feeding Olive pureed spinach and spaghetti from a jar which Olive promptly spit up, and making a dinner of pasta carbonara for herself, she put in the dreaded phone call.

Punch was livid and wanted to sue. Ivy talked her out of it recounting the horrors of a courtroom in detail.

"She didn't mention your name Punch. Try to at least find peace with that if you can please."

Punch was silent.

"Punch?" As Ivy waited for her reply she thought about how Punch came to earn the nickname. She had punched a bully out in eighth grade who picked on all the kids with freckles, lisps, excess weight, glasses, and braces. She knocked him out cold and made even the teachers happy for finally putting the creep in his well deserved place. She was adoringly crowned the nickname by all her peers. It also served as a reminder in case the bully's intimidating tactics made another appearance. It worked and all the misfits befriended her and defended her as well when they all entered high school together. Punch's height alone made them feel safe, plus she was fun and the only cool person they knew who would give them the time of day. "It is terrible. I have to agree with you. Shame on her. But please don't retaliate. Just for yourself. She has embarrassed herself. No one here will ever talk to her again. Especially me."

"Yeah Ivy that's a fact. I am just humiliated. You don't just use someone like that. Why does this stuff keep happening to me?"

"I don't know Punch. Let it work itself out. I do know you believe in Karma. Remember?"

Punch was quiet again. Ivy could hear her thinking about karma. Maybe in ways she didn't want to imagine. "Punch let it go. To heck with Wendy. Live and learn."

"Yeah to hell with her that's goddamn right."

Ivy winced at the cursing on the other line.

Punch continued, "I thought I was living and learning with someone who really cared about me this time. Yeah, this time just like last time. What's the sayin? Fool me once shame on you. Fool me twice shame on me." Punch was on the verge of tears. Ivy could hear her fighting it in the cracking of her voice.

"Well that might have been true up to now to be honest but there is no reason why that can't change. Third times always the charm. Remember? Besides, you want the real deal even if you have to wait longer for it. Right? Wouldn't that be worth it? Or should I just hang up and let you run back to her and have her use you for article number two? Let's see what could she call that article. Maybe 'My Comeback as a Phony Bi'?'"

"Okay Ivy I get the idea. You can be crass when you love someone do you know that?" Punch had a smile in her voice. She was amused at her angelic friend's sudden bursts of dictating at the most unexpected moments. "You got any rehearsals coming up where you can save it for bossing diva brides around?"

Ivy was relieved to hear Punch lightening up. "Yes, as matter of fact I do. And if my being crass works in your best interest then it can't be that bad." She tried to sing the last sentence in the melody of the Sheryl Crow tune of similar words but it just came out as a pitchy whine.

"Okay. Thanks Ivy. I'll chill out. At least for tonight. Anything to stop you from singing. See you at the chap. Hugs and kisses to Miss Olive Oil."

"Goodnight Punch. We love you. Get some rest."

CHAPTER SIX

Things came to a stand still and time slowly drifted by. There was still no word on the outcome of the psychological exams. Rumor was that Jeff hadn't taken the last one and that was the hold up. The results of the two exams had to be compared to each other in regards to who was the better parent, so until then, there was nothing to do but wait it out until it was completed and analyzed. The exchanges continued without a hitch, but Ivy worried at the times she got a visual of Jeff. Sometimes he looked okay, like he was getting it together, only to be a complete mess the next time.

Thanksgiving had been a quiet affair with Olive, Punch and herself. Ivy had prepared a simple traditional meal of candied yams, blueberry pecan pie and an enormous roasted turkey with sage stuffing and two types of gravy; a clear broth one for her and a white creamy one for Punch. But Christmas was on its way and the notion gave Ivy a much needed lift. Olive's first Christmas was right around the corner. It would be the start of many traditions that she would immerse Olive in unlike how she was raised. There would be real Christmas trees adorned with ornaments they together would pick out over the years. Thrown on tinsel would hang in glistening clumps. There would also be eggnog with nutmeg grated straight from the nut. Ivy smiled as she imagined the sweet, spicy scent. They would attend Christmas Eve mass at any of the beautiful historic churches in Austin. There would be a traditional meal served-perhaps the feast of the seven fish? Maybe. But that may be too sophisticated to start with. Whatever it would be would be made right. Ivy had no tolerance for bad cooking whether it was her own or someone else's. She had plenty of time to consider what she would create in her Italian tradition, which depended on whether Olive wound up liking seafood or not. But something delicious and traditional would be figured out as time went on depending on Olive's likes and dislikes. And hers too. She was smart enough to know that the best intentions could sometimes fall to hell in a hand basket. So far the only thing Ivy knew that Olive liked that was Italian was spaghetti without spinach in it. But that could work. Perhaps a traditional meal of spaghetti topped with fresh basil and zesty pecorino and romano cheese, glazed with a delicate olive oil and a sauce of ripe roma tomatoes, chopped garlic and onions seasoned with fresh cracked black pepper? The thought made Ivy's mouth water.

There was a Target on the way to the exchange and Ivy pulled in the parking lot on a whim when she realized she had 15 quick minutes to spare before being due at the exchange location. The exchange place was only another two exits off the freeway. She felt in the mood to start some early Christmas shopping. A rambunctious

version of "Santa Claus Is Coming To Town" played in her head over
and over and over, which kept her mood jolly and her efforts quick-
paced. Ivy checked her watch one more time just to make sure
before jumping out of the car into the rain. Only one more minute
had passed. If she was quick, she wouldn't be late. She was going to
give Olive an early present tonight. Her very first doll.

She entered the building with the cold air conditioning blowing
from a ginormous unit that nearly knocked her small body down as
she passed through the automated doors. The toy section was just
ahead and to the right past the greeting cards. Ivy walked down
the predominantly pink aisle of girly toys when what seemed like
on cue, every fake plastic infant began crying, crawling or blinking.
Feeling as if she was starring in a Stephen King novel, she just as
quickly made her mind to leave the store as she couldn't bring
herself to buy any of the dolls. She also wasn't sure what freakish
one Olive would prefer. Maybe it was her nerves as she knew she
was pushing it with being late to the exchange. Whatever had come
over her, she decided she best be on her way.

Delores, the stout Guatemalan social worker, who decorated
her whole face in metal from the frames on her wire rim glasses to
her hoop earrings to her mouth full of silver and gold, refereed the
exchanges at her office and never passed comments or judgments.
But Ivy knew she knew the whole unspoken story.

It was a Wednesday evening in December and the weather
had turned overnight to gray skies and a biting cold harsh wind
followed by a downpour of icy rain. It was the type of weather that
LuAnne would refer to as a turd floater or frog strangler. Ivy drove
out of the parking lot to head back on the freeway to pick Olive
up. Her bug was like a ship at sea being knocked off kilter.

The exchanges took place at a building off the access road of
Highway 35, which if you were a convict on the run, you could

take straight up to Canada. It was a dismal building so nondescript that you had to really watch out for it, otherwise the turn would be missed. The building was five stories and built in the 1960's. It had enormous amounts of available parking and the building was set quite a ways back from the freeway's access road. The suite where Kid's Exchange took place was on the first floor and smelled like pee pee. Its thick dark blue carpet, which hid a lot more of its history, seriously needed to be pulled out.

Delores came down the hall to the waiting area after Ivy signed in. She was wearing her signature uniform of jeans that barely came together to snap at her waist and a work sweatshirt. Her tummy was out of proportion to her skinny legs. She had on brand new white tennis shoes and the dark blue sweat-shirt with the company logo. Surprised to see Ivy, she looked up at the clock, frowned and told her "No Jeff, Miss." Ivy thought it strange as Jeff was always there first, reminding her of how people could change some habits for the better only if the legal system was watching over them. Besides, the court system set it up that he was due twenty minutes before Ivy's arrival to have Olive ready and waiting for her mama without witnessing any confrontation between her two parents.

"Has he called?"

"Uh, no miss." Delores watched Ivy's reaction and then gestured that she would go back down the hall to check with the rest of the staff, which meant one or two other people, to see if they had heard anything.

A couple minutes later Delores returned to the waiting room. "No, no one know nothing," she said as she shrugged her shoulders up to her ears. She pulled up a mustard colored plastic chair with metal legs for Ivy to sit in. She patted the chair for Ivy to sit down in and began walking down the hall again. "No worry miss, he late. Just late."

Ivy nodded in agreement and smiled a shy smile that apologized for the overreaction.

She sat in the chair for twenty minutes with still no word from Jeff to her or any of the staff. She pulled out her cell phone from the Juicy Couture diaper bag her mom had sent as a gift and called him. No ringing. It went directly to voice mail.

The room started spinning in circles. She tried to stand but her legs were goo. She decided to call LuAnne.

"She hasn't come back from court Miss Weiss," her secretary said. "Do you want her voice mail?"

"No. Thank you."

Delores came back down the hall. "You okay miss Ivy?"

"No, no no. I am not okay. If it was some other guy and if we had some other judge in some other county it would be okay..," she rambled on nervously.

She called Jeff's cell phone again, the only phone he had as far as she knew, and still got no answer. She snapped her phone shut. "Delores, if he shows up or calls, tell him to call me too. I am going to his home Delores. Please don't tell him that though. Just ask him to stay here or wherever he and Olive are and call me. You call me too if he shows up or you hear anything. And make sure if he does show up and I'm not back yet, he doesn't dare leave with her again."

"Okay." Her slumped face and thick rubbery lips pulled down in a frown as she watched Ivy run out the door.

Ivy did not know exactly where Jeff lived. She only knew the address from her attempt to send him Olive's medical bills so he could pay half, which he never did, but the zip code told her what part of town it was in. She pulled up onto the highway and took it north past downtown and exited almost fifty streets later. Her nerves were making her eyes blurry and she could barely read the street signs as the rain had not let up either. She reminded herself she had to be cool if she saw him, to show no anger even though she was raging inside. If there were witnesses that saw her yelling at him like the crazy woman she felt like and everything turned out to be just a simple misunderstanding, it would not look good at the final hearing. Half of her didn't give a damn. She knew Maruska would make some story out of it to make her look like the star of an episode of Snapped even if she was sweet as molasses pie. She wondered if LuAnne ever did any criminal defense work.

Seven and a half minutes later the bug turned onto LeVane. The area was once a desirable part of Austin as little as five years ago, but the crime had pushed up and out in this direction. It was a pretty neighborhood with older homes and large trees, but it was now too close to the highway and was pocketed with criminal looking types in hoodies more for camouflage than weather, walking the streets looking over their shoulders before passing cars got alongside of them.

1610 LeVane was a modest home of brown brick and black wooden shutters. A large dying oak tree stood in the center of the front yard with dry broken leaves scattered around it. The rest of the yard was covered with patches of crunchy dead grass and long spiky strands of Bermuda, broken up with bald round mounds infested with ant hills. Ivy jumped out of her car and got to the front door as quickly as she could, hoping no one was watching her through the windows.

She knocked gently on the front door. No answer.

She knocked louder. Still no answer.

She looked back over at the driveway that led to a carport with a huge spider web hanging from its side that looked like baseball netting. There were no cars parked inside of it.

No one was here.

She tip toed to the front window not sure of why she was tip toeing when it seemed obvious no one would hear her, but nerves make you act strange and she couldn't help it. The window was covered with lacy curtains that hung unevenly with a small crack in between them that let her take a small peek inside. It was a view of the kitchen table for the most part. In shambles, a phone book propped under one leg that was cut off at the end. The table was smothered with old newspapers, junk mail, unopened bills, ashtrays, bottle caps, empty beer bottles, a couple of crusty dishes and a baby bottle. But there were no signs of life.

Ivy took a minute to contemplate her surroundings. It felt like the quietest moment on earth. There was no one outside and no sounds from any of the neighbors. Did she get her days confused? She thought about it. No, it was absolutely the right day and time to pick up Olive. *Did he just get his days confused*, she wondered. *That was a crazy thought,* she told herself as Jeff couldn't wait to return Olive to Kids Exchange so he could have his freedom. *Then where the hell was he?*

As Ivy opened the door to her bug the sound of her cell phone ringing brought her to a new reality.

She picked it up. It was LuAnne.

"What's going on?"

"I don't know. I don't know where Olive is or Jeff."

"You went to the exchange?"

"Yeah, but he didn't show up or call. Don't get mad at me but I am just leaving his house and there is no one here."

"Okay Ivy. Call the exchange place again and then call me back."

Delores had no news.

Ivy pulled out of the driveway and then pulled over on LeVane. For some reason she felt compelled to take a deep look at herself in the rear view mirror. She saw a different Ivy staring back at her.

She wasn't as pretty as she used to be, gray hairs had grown in. Lines around the eyes had settled in. She looked ten years older. Her eyes were dull. "No, no no no!" she screamed in fear. In fear of what she did not know and took a deep breath and sped down I-35 to the Austin Police Department.

The police drilled and drilled her while LuAnne was buzzing her like a maniac on her cell phone. A missing persons report was filed and an Amber alert was sent out immediately.

The good news, according to the police, was that her baby was with the father most likely and since he had no history of physical abuse or sexual abuse with her she was probably okay. Ivy wondered when all the so called authorities in her life were finally going to get it.

Punch drove down to the station to check on Ivy and followed her home about an hour later.

As they climbed up the steps to Ivy's front door. Ivy opened the screen door and turned around to Punch and said, "Well, it's as good a time as any."

Punch looked at her surprised and confused.

Ivy pretended not to notice and while she waited for Punch's reply which was still on delayed reaction, she got her keys out of her purse and unlocked the front door. She barely opened it and looked back again at Punch waiting for the answer.

Punch didn't answer but looked down at the ground and with her long arm and fingers reached out over Ivy's head to the door and pushed it open enough for them both to walk through.

Simultaneously they took off their rain and mud soaked shoes and placed them outside by the front door under the shelter of the front porch's awnings. Punch grabbed some of the cedar firewood that was stacked next to the fireplace, threw it into the fireplace and lit it with a long stemmed lighter. She then went into Ivy's kitchen and made two mugs of hot cocoa, out of complete nervousness. It was now at least 80 degrees outside. That was one thing about Texas weather-if you didn't like it, you could stick around a couple of hours because it was almost guaranteed to change. When she sat Ivy's mug of cocoa down on the coffee table, Ivy just simply stared at it.

Punch didn't seem to know what to do and appeared afraid to speak for the first time that Ivy could ever remember. Ivy stared at her for what seemed like an eternity. She was determined not to talk so that Punch would be pushed into filling the void. She watched Punch reach down for the cocoa, lift the mug to her lips as casual as could be but just before it reached her lips, she gently placed it back on the coffee table. "Okay Ivy, you asked so here goes. One summer me and my little sis were playing in the front yard, going berserk. Spraying each other with the watering hose, you know? Running around going crazy. It was hotter than hell. One of the hottest summers of Austin's history. I knew Jeff a little then cuz we went to the same high school-Waterloo High, and we were both worked on the school's newspaper. Well, I don't really know how to tell this story very well being that you are the only one I have ever told it to, but that day, Jeff came driving by in a baby blue Ford pickup truck and my sister and I well, for lack of a better way of putting it, we thought he was cute. He asked us to get in to go for a ride with him. Mom was too doped up to notice so what the hell did we have to lose? And well, then, one thing happened after another." She reached back down for the mug and took a sip.

Ivy turned her knees to point at Punch, which directed her eyes in the same direction. "What do you mean one thing happened after another?"

Punch pulled in the breasts of her corduroy blazer that were still damp from the previous down pour, as if she was embracing herself. "I mean one thing happened after another. Ivy, you know what I mean, the strawberry hill wine story, blueberry hill song, whichever you prefer. It was before I knew I was gay.

"Punch of all times, this is not the time to be evasive."

"Okay Ivy. I get it, yeah, I get it. We drove up to Mt. Bonnel." Punch looked at Ivy hoping that Ivy would just guess the rest of the story and she wouldn't have to say it out loud.

"Okay, so before you found out you were gay, you fucked the father of my baby? Yeah, okay Punch, again, not a great story but I am glad you finally told me because what a fool I must have looked like to you. Both of you. Filling you in on the details of our love life? Why in the hell did you let me do that? You already knew for Christ's sake what it's like to fuck Jeff! But thanks for sharing. Especially now."

Punch went silent and then blurted it out. "No, even then I knew I couldn't do that! It was Misty. He fucked Misty. He got her pregnant."

"What?" The revelation had Ivy's head swimming. Misty couldn't have been more than fourteen years old at the time. It also meant that Olive wasn't exactly his first child. The information was sickeningly overwhelming and Ivy fought the urge to kick Punch out of the house for holding it back for so many years and throwing up at the same time. She regained her composure and said, "Why, why Punch? I mean why now for goodness sake, are you telling me this now? Why not in the car on the way home from the bookstore? You knew darn well you had plenty of opportunity." Ivy took some time to replay that fateful day while she waited for Punch to continue. Punch didn't look like she was going to reveal any more. "Okay, so he got a minor pregnant who happens to be my best friends little sister. That's not a great story but why do I have this really strong suspicion that there's more to it than that?"

"Because there is. Oh for Christ's sake Ivy, I was hoping it would never fucking come to this."

"Jesus! What the hell is happening to me?" She redirected her mind to no longer focus on Punch's revelation but on her own dilemma with Olive. She was hoping Punch wouldn't continue any further as she got up off the sofa to go use the bathroom.

Just as Ivy shut the bathroom door, Punch said, "Misty had the child."

"What?" Ivy pulled her underwear and skirt back up before she opened up the door to look at Punch to see if what she was hearing was real. "What? I didn't hear what you just said."

Punch wouldn't look at her.

"Punch, I said I did not hear what you just said."

"I said Misty had the baby."

Ivy's blood was boiling catching up to the temperature in the rest of the house thanks to the rumbling fireplace. Her heart beat so loud she could hear it. Tears of confusion and pain filled her eyes. What had ever happened to Misty? Punch had barely ever spoken of her and Ivy couldn't remember all the details she had shared. Where was she living these days? She wasn't sure if she wanted to know the answer to her next question but couldn't help it popping out of her mouth. "Where is the child?"

Punch lowered her voice. "I don't know. She was adopted. Misty wanted to keep it and we figured out a way for her to have it without mama knowing. She told mama that she wanted to go live with Granny up in Tyler for a while. Granny was in on it. Mama never found out. Would have whipped the bejesus out of Misty. But Jeff got wind and was furious she was going to have it. He got up there fast as he could and talked her into giving it to some friends of his. I guess eventually she felt it was best to give in to the bastard."

Ivy fought another urge to throw up but knew there'd be nothing there; she hadn't eaten all day. The heat had suddenly reached the temperature of hell for her. She asked Punch for some ice water. Punch went to the kitchen and made her a tall glass of water and ice, putting out the fire on her way back to the sofa, embarrassed that she was the one who had started it. But Ivy still wasn't there. Further embarrassed she picked up the mugs of cocoa and poured out their contents and placed the mugs in the sink-washing dishes was not a priority, not that Punch would have thought of it anyway. She walked to the bathroom and found Ivy hovering over the toilet. She was ghostly white and Punch had to feed her the glass of water as she knelt on the floor besides her while she smoothed the strands of damp hair out of her teary eyes and wet face with her large porcelain hands. "Ivy, I am sorry. I was so damn confused about it when it happened. I just tried to not ever think about it again. Poor little Misty was never the same and then she just took off. I never saw her again. Ran off with some other guy of all things. And then we ran into the motherfucker at the bookstore. And you were so taken by him. I didn't know what to do. I hate to admit it, but he kinda spooks me and I didn't want to say anything. I guess I was hoping there'd be a happier ending. I am sorry Ivy. I really truly am."

Ivy gave Punch a look that said it all. She wasn't happy but forgave her. She hastily grabbed the toilet paper off the roll and scrunched it up to wipe her eyes. "It was a girl?"

"Yes."

"What was her name? Where is she?"

"Ivers" Punch tried to stay as calm as she could. She didn't like it that she was getting worked up over this now when she had more pressing issues. "Honestly, I really don't know. Like I said, she was given away immediately after Misty had her. Poor child was just a nameless hooligan as far as I know." She knew telling Ivy the story wasn't helping the situation, but she had a hard time of keeping her mouth shut for most of her life. "I don't know where she is. Friends of Jeff were waiting for her right when she was born to take her away. Misty shut me out of it after that. I understood. She was done. It was something between her and Jeff. I wasn't invited in on it after a certain point. Everyone became the enemy for a while. But you know how it is, it becomes a thing of the past and not such a big deal as life goes on. Mama got sick and died right about then and I didn't bother Misty anymore and lost track. I understood what she was doing. She needed to be away from all of us and the memories. Start over. I never felt like she wanted to see me again so I finally stopped trying. Wasn't what I wanted but who the hell cares? I got the impression she didn't want me around any more. I don't know why. Dysfunction runs rampant in my fam' Ivy. But come on Ivy, we can't worry about this now. We need to focus on finding Olive."

"I know Punch, but don't you get it? I swear sometimes you are so frickin' exasperating." She jumped up and looked at Punch who was now looking up at her with lost eyes still sitting on the bathroom floor. "Maybe Olive is with those people, too."

Punch thought about it. "Maybe. Jeezers, I don't know Ivy. I never thought about that. I hate to be the devil's advocate but I didn't get a bad feeling with where Misty's baby wound up although I didn't like the way things were being done at the time. You know lots of people adopt. But then the way they did it was kind of strange even for back then. I guess anything is possible. I don't know why I was so scared of Jeff. It wasn't about that so much after it all happened. I just don't like his writing. Something about it gives me...."

Ivy cut her off. "I can't believe you are going to play me for a fool now Punch with this rambling babble. His writing? Since when? You study his writing as if he was Yeats. Don't think I never noticed your collection hidden behind your other books. Second shelf about midway a little to the left." She gestured wildly with her hands as if she was standing in front of the bookcase. " And if that were true, which it isn't, what does it have to do with anything? You had knowledge and instincts about Jeff. You didn't protect me. Or Olive for that matter. You never told me any of this until now. Punch, I thought you were my friend!"

Punch was at a loss for words. She knew anything she said now to defend herself would just drive a wedge deeper between her and Ivy. She decided to just continue with complete honesty about the current situation, knowing that wouldn't help much either. "It's different with Olive. With Olive, I feel different."

Ivy stared at her a minute longer waiting for her to speak again. But Punch seemed to be done. She knelt back down to Punch. She couldn't afford this right now. She needed Punch. She thought about their friendship over the years, and yes, Punch was the one who sometimes set it on a precarious edge, but she wondered if she would have reacted any different if the tables had been reversed. It was impossible to talk someone out of being in love with someone and she probably wouldn't have believed her. Would have just thought it was some weird competition amongst the two writers in her life. She knew Punch was full of faults but regardless of her ways, her intentions, albeit sometimes misguided, were always, well more often than not, full of heart. She believed that she had hoped the best for her and probably thought Jeff was full of regret about what he put Misty through and that the past would never come to haunt them. Punch was tough as nails but was a big believer in true love and forgiveness. For the first time ever Punch broke down and asked Ivy to pray together for the safety of Olive. Punch didn't pray. The request was hard to make peace with for

Ivy. *What was driving her to do it?* Ivy told herself not to think too hard about it, perhaps it was just because she was trying to connect on a deeper level with her regarding the circumstances. Once the emotions had run their course, Punch promised to stay over and keep Ivy company, doing everything she could in her power to help until Olive was home again.

CHAPTER SEVEN

24 hours passed.

And then another 24.

The cops were evasive. Never revealing much of anything and Ivy knew time wasn't on their side anymore. She already knew that seventy five-percent of missing children's cases wound up with a deceased child if they weren't found within the first three hours. She was going on the third day. Ivy hired a private investigator who came to her home in Misty Falls to retrieve more pictures of Olive and to interview her further.

His name was Karl Muehller. He looked to be about thirty-five, handsome and clean cut with a shiny crew cut in that crazy in-between stage that was growing out like a long haired porcupine. He had bright clear blue eyes that must have been fed regular does of Visine given his profession, and a tan, long muscular build. He was the type most people would refer to as a red head with the ruddy complexion, but in reality is a brunette who spends a lot of time outdoors. He wore a dark blue polo shirt tucked into his straight-legged jeans with some very torn up looking cowboy boots. He seemed the loner type and a quiet, "Yes ma'am, No ma'am" kind of guy. Ivy had gotten his name from her younger sister Iris. Iris was currently living back home in Pacific Palisades with their mom trying to save money to open up a beauty salon and she promised not to tell her of Ivy's dilemma. The first thing their mother would do would be to blame Ivy, and then she would use the media attention to distract from the real story and use it for her cause du jour, which typically varied from rants demonizing Democrats to reliving her glory days of starring in Breck hair commercials and how models just aren't the same these days - what with their substance abuse issues and the public being unable to discern if they are a male or female? They both knew this without acknowledging it out loud. Iris had lived in Dallas briefly, working as a third grade teacher after she graduated from UCLA. She wanted to be closer to Ivy. She had dated someone in the Dallas FBI unit who had worked with Karl. Iris assured her sister that he was a workaholic, bright as could be, and determined.

Ivy gave Karl more pictures of Olive and described the sudden custody case, how Jeff hadn't shown up on time to the exchange and then never showed up at all or called and had never been heard of or seen since. She assured Karl that the police were aware of everything she was now telling him, but they hadn't found any traces of Jeff or his whereabouts as far as she knew. She couldn't be certain though because even while she called at least ten times a day, no one seemed to want to talk to her or have anything new or old to share with her when she did get someone on the line.

"Jeff Hunter, you say his name is, correct?" Karl took some notes as he questioned her. He looked back at her after looking at the name on his note pad."Sounds familiar."

Ivy nodded."He's an author. Has several published pieces but the most famous one was a best seller that came out many years ago called *Points of Passion*."

"Yes, think I read it." He took more notes. Ivy wondered if he was going to check the book out from the library to see if there were any clues. She didn't know if private investigators really did things like that in real life but they certainly did on tv and in the movies. "He ever not show up to any of the exchanges? That at all typical behavior for him?"

"No, it's not typical because there is a legal system watching over. But before that came into place I would say this type of behavior was extremely typical of him."

"Who does he hang out with? Any criminal background? Anything or anyone whom he may have gotten into some trouble with?"

"He has a substance abuse problem." She almost laughed at the surprisingly overly polite way that sounded. "He's a cocaine addict to be more to the point. He lives with this woman named Maruska." Ivy thought again about how shocking that revelation was in court and still questioned herself about why it upset her so much. "I don't know a lot about her. Honestly never saw or heard of her until we were in court. But fool that I am, I think he's been seeing her all along and was definitely involved with her before I came into the picture. She's Slovakian. Not sure if that's the right word. Slovak? They got busted together for cocaine possession. My lawyer has the papers."

Karl made a note and asked who her attorney was. He nodded knowingly when she told him it was LuAnne Dalton, which gave Ivy some comfort although she wasn't sure why. Karl then proceeded down the hall and continued to take notes as Ivy told him any tid bits she thought might be helpful. He stopped in each room he passed but spent the most time in Olive's nursery. Ivy wanted to see what he was doing but thought it best to stay put. She knew that as much as Karl seemed to believe her, he was looking at her as a potential suspect just as much as he was Jeff. She knew the rap with missing children's cases. How could you avoid it? It was on the news every night. "Missing two year old walks out of the house in the middle of the night. Daddie's drugs found in his back pack." "Mother sells child as sex slave to repay drug debt," "Mommy kills baby then parties the same night and brags to party goers that she is now a 'free woman'," "Step mom drops child off at school and no one ever sees him again" and on and on it went. Yes, parents were looked at as the first suspects and for good reason because in most cases they were the last people to have seen the child.

As Karl poked around the nursery, Ivy made a deal with God that no matter if she was wrongly thrown in prison or executed, that would be fine as long as Olive was okay.

Karl quickly came back out of the nursery and walked down the hall to the living room where Ivy was waiting. He told her he had all he needed to get started, apologized for the misery she must be feeling and in an attempt to do what he could in case she was innocent, said he'd work on it day and night until it was solved.

"Detective, before you go there is something else." The cops really don't know everything. But only because I just found this out." She waited for him to verbally respond but he simply looked at her expectantly to elaborate. She wondered if he thought she was a liar. Even though she wasn't one, the new turn of events were sounding unbelievable even to her. "I just found out that Olive's not his only child."

He continued to look at her with anticipation.

Ivy searched her thoughts for a good starting point to make the strange story that was just revealed to her clear to Karl. "My best friend, Punch, well she was over here last night. She's staying with me now until this ordeal is over." Ivy thought that sounded a bit wrong or maybe she was just paranoid after court. "We're just friends." Karl stared at her blankly, wondering why she felt the need to qualify that remark.

Ivy realized that he never had a reason to assume that they were anything but friends and continued. "She left right before you came over to give us some privacy. Anyway, she told me her sister was impregnated by Jeff too. But it was a long time ago," she added dismissively. Ivy regained her composure still feeling paranoid and embarrassed by her behavior as she smoothed out her crumpled floral print robe. Karl had arrived a half hour early, not giving her time to get dressed appropriately before he knocked on the door, and she forgot to politely ask him to wait while she got dressed. "Never mind. It was just a shock to hear it. That's all. I don't know why I am telling you. Guess because I feel like the biggest fool ever," she gave him an apologetic half smile.

"No Ivy. It's good. It's good to tell me these things. I need to know everything. Did she say anything else that stood out to you?"

"Not really. Just that the child was given to some friends of Jeff's right when she gave birth. I guess her sister agreed to it by then."

"Who are the people that adopted her? The friends of Jeff?"

"I don't know. Punch doesn't know. Her sister, Misty, ran away right after it or that's what the whole town thought according to all the rumors. She was really young, a minor. It's just so confusing. I really don't know the details. Doesn't seem like anyone does for sure. Just a lot of small town gossip for the most part. Well you know what I mean. Austin was a small town back then. Just thought maybe you'd like to know about it. I didn't tell the police. They don't seem to be doing much anyway. And like I said, I don't even know if it matters one way or the other." Ivy took a deep breath and stared out the window at her backyard's jasmine vines and peach and pear trees that were drooping and withering with neglect.

"Thanks Ivy. Of course. All these details help. I will start searching for the child's whereabouts. You never know Ivy, this could be it. If anything else comes to mind, you give me a call with no hesitation, got it? Like I said, you never know in these cases. The more information the better. Sometimes things mean something you would never expect." He bent down to give her a couple of taps on the knee for encouragement before he departed. He wanted desperately to speak to Punch to get more details, but she was out buying Ivy and her dinner and he didn't have time to wait. He would call her.

Ivy thanked him, buried her head in her hands and heard him help himself out the front door.

Forty-five minutes later Punch returned with the Chinese food just as her cell phone wouldn't stop ringing. Punch threw the containers of food down in their white plastic bags on the counter before scrambling for the noise-making machine buried deep in the recesses of her hemp purse.

"Hello?"

"Punch?"

"Only one here by that name."

"Detective Karl Muehller. How are you? Do you have a couple of minutes? I'd like to ask you a few questions if that's all right with you."

Punch stared at the plastic bags wondering how much longer the food would keep warm and not turn into a cold soggy mess then remembered the built-in microwave Ivy had installed last year, finally. "Yeah. What's up?"

"I was there earlier tonight while you were out, questioning Ivy."

"Yeah, I knew you were coming over, that's why I high tailed it."

"Ivy said your younger sister had a baby with Jeff. That the baby was given up for adoption. You have any idea who adopted her, or where your sister is these days?"

"No and no."

There was a long silence on Karl's end. "Um. Okay, if anything comes to mind please call me okay?"

"Yeah, okay."

"Thank you Punch. By the way, what's your real name?"

"Gloria. Rivadiera."

"Okay, thanks Gloria."

"No prob."

Click. Karl hung up first. Gloria still hung onto the receiver in a haze before hanging up. She wondered if she would ever see her sister again. And if she would, if it would only be because of this mess.

CHAPTER EIGHT

Karl was on it. He wasn't sure about the story about the first child. Something about it rang irrelevant to him but he learned in his career that feelings meant nothing-facts and forensics were the ball busters these days. But you never knew. His feelings about the whereabouts of Olive could be completely wrong. She could be with her "sister."

First call of order was to search the vital statistics for a child born with the last name of Rivadiera or Hunter around 1989 or 1990. Karl had built a friendship with Kathy Cavanaugh over the years while working on missing persons cases. She was a clerk at the vital statistic office at the Travis County Court House, but she confirmed no little girls were on file of either last names born in either year.

Karl was at a stand still. Time was of the essence in a missing child's case and statistically things weren't looking good for Olive. As a matter of fact they were looking very bad indeed. He hated to think like that but it was clear he had to make a choice: *Does Olive's sister's whereabouts have anything to do with her own? Or is is it a totally separate issue?*

He decided in part by intuition and part by statistics as so many years had passed between each child's birth that they were two separate issues and to treat it as such in his mind. But that was just his intuition and what was taking place in the space between his ears. Regardless of what he thought, he still had to go by protocol and that meant following through on every lead. *Shit.*

First, where was Misty? According to her classmates who attended Freshman year with her, rumor had it that she bailed to Oregon after giving birth. Further rumor had it that she was working on a cattle ranch just outside a town called Jacksonville taking care of a couple's horses, pigs, cows and twins. According to the school counselor who reluctantly revealed the information, Misty had met a boy her age who had taken sympathy for her situation with Jeff. His uncle and aunt owned the ranch and they ran off together, dropping out of freshman year of high school.

Karl booked the next flight from Austin to Portland, also known as the "City of Roses," the airline reservationist informed him with a certain amount of pep and pride in her voice. He guessed it was her home town. Jacksonville was a four hour drive away from the airport and the ranch another twenty or so miles deeper into the wilderness. The drive was beautiful with giant red woods, clean fresh air and pretty parks and rivers. Karl made a mental note to put on his "to do" list a scenic drive up the coast from Northern California to Oregon some day, maybe even going up to Seattle or Canada. It was too bad he couldn't have taken the flight to San

Fransisco and then driven up to Jacksonville, but this most direct route was already taking up too much time.

Karl found the signs directing him to Jacksonville on the I-5. Luckily, he got to drive through downtown on the way to the ranch. It was a quaint historical town bustling with an old West camaraderie of nineteenth century shops, bars, galleries and romantic bed and breakfasts. As he drove through the main thoroughfare he noticed the Olivia Union Restaurant and Saloon. He prayed this was a good omen as he sped past in his Ford Mustang convertible.

Four and half hours after Karl's flight landed, Karl drove up a remote gravel road. It's destination unclear except for the mailbox on the dusty roadside that indicated he was at the right place. It was late afternoon. The air had suddenly taken on a quick chill as Karl rolled up the roof before finding an inconspicuous place to park. He did a quick take of the property as he walked his way toward it. It wasn't palatial but it wasn't run down either. Somewhere in the middle. Misty was living in good conditions.

He found her walking a copper penny colored thoroughbred around a corral. She was clearly surprised to find a stranger pulling up in a car other than a work truck, and and even more mystified when he got out to walk up to her and started asking questions about her one and only child.

"Misty Rivadiera?" He asked as he quietly shut the car door and made his way up to the corral.

"Yeah," she answered stopping in her tracks, waiting for him to get nearer, looking up at him once he got close. Her eyes squinted to make him out against the setting sun. Her hair was in two long straight braids, a smattering of freckles across her face, her brown almond eyes devoid of eyelashes staring up to him. She still looked no more than 20 years old. But by Karl's calculations, she had to be at least 32.

"Detective Muehller. Austin, Texas. You have a couple of minutes?"

Misty looked around her but was not sure of exactly what she was looking for. Apparently pleased with what she did or did not see she visibly loosened up. "Guess so."

"I am an acquaintance of your sister Punch and have been hired by her best friend Ivy Weiss. Do you personally know Ivy?"

Misty answered that she didn't know of her but Karl could tell he had a liar on his hands almost immediately.

"Let me ask you this. You familiar with a Jeff Hunter?"

Misty turned her back to Karl and led the horse to his watering trough. She then tied the horse, shut the gate to the corral and came out to the other side to join Karl. She put both hands in the pockets of her jeans and leaned her back against the fencing. She bent one leg back, her boot tucked in the gaps of the fence with her foot resting inside on the other side of the rail. "Nope."

Karl now even further convinced he had a real character on his hands had to resist the urge to chuckle. "You mind telling me in your own words how that's possible?"

Karl watched her body language closely as he gave her time to think if she was going to embellish her lie or leave it be. At least thirty seconds went by and she didn't say another word.

"Misty, this is important and I need your cooperation. There is a missing baby. Jeff Hunter is the father. I know that you had a child with Jeff some years ago and gave it up for adoption to some of his friends. I need to find these people. They may have another child that doesn't belong to them. Are you following me?"

Misty nodded her head but said nothing else.

"You wanna go somewhere else to talk about this. Are you uncomfortable here?"

"Naw, here's just fine," she raised her left hand out of her pocket to her forehead to shade the sun out. She looked back at Karl with a half grin as if to explain her odd behavior. A large gap between her front teeth showed. "If Jimmy sees me leave with another man, especially one as fine as you, I'll be up a shit creek."

"Who's Jimmy? The one you left Texas with?"

"Yep."

"Listen Misty." Karl thought about her name. Why was is that the name Misty seemed to produce girls who got into trouble? "Everything you tell me is just between you and me okay? I need to find a missing baby. And I need your help."

"Well my daughter would at least be 18 by now. Surely you must have figured that out before you came a visiting. She got the right to live like she want to. I don't know where she is and I intended for it to be that way. Now if you'll excuse me, I have work to do by sundown." And just like that she walked back up the hill to the main property as two rambunctious tow headed twins came running down to greet her.

Damn, thought Karl as he slammed the steel point of his boot into the dirt for emphasis, nothing like wasting time in a missing child's case.

CHAPTER NINE

Maruska Czoborova had a plan. She had always been quick to think on her feet and it was always her greatest asset: turning unforeseen misfortune- especially that of others, into opportunity. She started at an early age, growing up in the slums of Kosice (pronounced Ko-sheets-seh) in Eastern Slovakia. Her family was only one of three other whites who resided there, the rest being gypsies. Kosice was the second largest city in Slovakia. Bratislava being the first. Her father was a good man, earnest and hard working. He was also very shy and kind, which her mother took as opportunity to abuse him both physically and verbally. She forever blamed him for their lot in life-the squalid living conditions with the Roma and the despicable spawn that he had produced. She often reminded him of this as little Maruska sat on the floor watching her pet hamster run in his spinning wheel.

Her mother would often kick her in the back while she was laughing at the little beast. Mr. Czoborova worked at an industrial factory as an assembly line man while her mother stayed home and drank Borovicka, a gin like alcohol straight from the bottle and Slivovika, a plum brandy when she was especially cantankerous with stomach aches. Her spare time was spent belittling little Maruska, her very unchildlike daughter who was at once stunning and repulsive. Both of Maruska's parents were very fair in skin and hair and eye color but neither was an albino like little Maruska.

Her mother's drinking had become so bad that eventually she became delusional believing she had given birth to a real life witch, which added to her violent tendencies.

Then one day her father, without warning, left them both behind. He simply did not return home after work. People from the factory told little Maruska the secret that she was to never tell her mother. Her dad had met a Polish woman at the factory from Krakow. She worked in the office handling secretarial work and she was also married to an abusive alcoholic. They fled together to live with her brother in a small Hungarian town. The people told little Maruska it was time for her to go away too if she wanted a better life. But she mustn't let her mother know they told her.

The following day, after a particularly bad beating by her mother, Maruska set her mother's bed on fire while she was passed out. She had grabbed the bottle of alcohol that had rolled underneath the bed, which much to Maruska's surprise was vodka. She doused her mom with what remained in her bottle as the flammable, getting rid of both of their demons once and for all. Now, left to her own devices, she had to survive. She had just turned ten. She began working as a child prostitute, which eventually led her to being under the control of a particularly vulgar pimp whose name she never knew and never cared to find out. In order to escape from being smothered under his thumb, she kidnapped a girl from her old village and ransomed the child but only took the money without returning the child. She gave the child and the money to her pimp with the deal that she would be let go. She wanted to go to Bratislava. Some of her clients had been men in the drug trade and she was ready to move up in the world. But that was none of his business. The pimp was happy with the trade. The other girl was only six.

Maruska made a run for the capitol city the second she was able. She had seen the jewels on the fingers of the men that had come from there and the cold hard cash they used to pay for her services. She didn't know any of them personally and wanted to keep her background hush should she ever come across them again. No need in them thinking of her as a piece of meat. It would be hopeless to change their perception if that started again. And if they recognized her which she had to be highly aware of, for her hair and skin made her stand out more than she could help, she could say something that they would never know to be true or not; that she had a twin. She would never be able to be a chameleon. To others she would always look like a ghost. Her only way to get ahead was to outsmart and out power. That was how she had survived up to this point. No one would know she was lying or not about a twin sister if it came up. Maruska had spent most of her years in Kosice with dyed black hair. She had now let it return to its natural white.

She had enough cash to take the bus to the city where she wandered around the streets aimlessly searching for a sign for a place to start. At first, nothing and no one piqued her interest. Some of the men eyed her lasciviously and it was tempting to go back to her old tricks as money was running thin, but she knew that would be just the same old same old routine. She was ready

for bigger pay and bigger challenges and bigger risks to get them.
From now on, she would be the one in power, not the other way
around. She knew she was as smart as any of the men that had
screwed her literally and figuratively, and the fire that blazed inside
of her taunted her to once and for all to put it to use and make
something of herself. She cared for no one or nothing and nothing
and no one would stand in her way.

She saw the sign one day after checking out of the motel that
had raised their nightly fee in the midst of her stay. She had been
forced to prowl the streets by foot in the harsh sunlight. Her
eyes were sensitive to light, for her blood vessels shown through
her irises that otherwise centered around her eyes that were the
color of blue topaz. It was a strip club located on the outskirts
of the city. It was a business. Not the type of business Maruska
was used to, but it was close enough and could lead her to better
things. And, for now, it would get her out of the harsh rays that
felt like laser beams going through her. She took one last drag
from her Marlboro cigarette, stubbed it out and walked in and
asked to speak to the manager. The young hostess, taken aback by
her abrupt business like tone, jumped off her stool and strutted
quickly to the other side of the room to knock on a back door.
Her g-string now facing Maruska, revealed a flabby butt riddled
with cellulite. Maruska turned away in disgust. But it was a start
to her list. The front door needed someone charming, pretty and
clothed flirtatiously-not half naked. Why were they giving it away
so soon and with such a beastly girl? She had a lot already she could
teach this establishment. A bald man with a shiny head that beamed
like a flashlight every time he moved it, peaked his head through a
crack in the door to see what the hostess was bothering him about.
As he did, two skinny blonds slithered out. The hostess pointed
to Maruska with a serious look on her face. The man nodded and

closed the door. The hostess made her way back to the hostess stand, the strings of her tassels, which hung from her dry looking nipples of her sagging breasts, brushed against her belly button. She stopped midway to stomp out a cockroach's life. When she got back to the stand she motioned for Maruska to make her way back to the manager's office.

Maruska walked in confident long strides across the room. In the dark and from a distance, Maruska looked stunning. She glowed in the dark and everyone turned to see who she was. Most of the dancers hearts sunk as they wondered who the tall skinny platinum woman was who was about to steal their loyal customers away. Maruska felt the stares and scoffed to herself at the petty jealousies young girls had. *If they only knew what she was really here to do.* She had to keep herself from laughing out loud at their soon to be fate. She deliberately did not keep time to the ridiculous Mickey Mouse music that played overhead as she was watched and made a mental note that the music would have to be changed too.

Without knocking, Maruska stormed into the office and introduced herself as a former manager of a strip club in Kosice that had burned down. The move had forced her to seek other options and she welcomed the change. She informed the manager of her success in revamping the former strip club, which resulted in a revenue increase of fifty percent. She spoke confidently, selling herself for a job that both parties knew didn't really exist. The manager was confused by her sudden bombardment and informed her there was nothing, no openings at the moment but if something were to change he would let her know. He asked her for a card more out of formality than interest, which she was thankfully unable to produce, and then he asked her to please excuse him as he had work to do.

Maruska could feel the humiliation raging through her body. She stood up and suddenly smiled with her mouth closed. She had an idea. They always came to her rescue. But she had another job she had to do first. This would be her first claim to power. She smiled to the man and shook his hand and thanked him for his time anyway in the sincerest way she could muster.

The manager watched through his surveillance monitor as the mysterious blond who just tried to take over his job without seeming to have the tiniest modicum of respect left the building. He had an uneasy feeling about her. He had never heard of the club she mentioned, the one that she previously worked at, and that was unusual; so many of the girls in the business were from Kosice. It bread trouble, particularly in the form of drug addicted strippers and prostitutes and they all went back and forth from one club, one city, and one profession to the other. And they talked about it — a lot. Except for the prostitution. No one ever talked about that.

Maruska kept walking. Something would come up. She didn't pray. She didn't believe in any type of God. It was one man, or one woman for themselves. Survival of the fittest or some other bullshit that she had heard on an American television movie. Someday she would get there too. Texas always appealed to her. Lots of crazy stupid beautiful girls to exploit and millionaires with oil in their backyards. Yes, that would become the goal in time. She lit up a new cigarette and kept walking and dreaming. She felt a new electric energy surge through her. She would find her way. And it would be today. She felt it. She checked her watch. It was three o'clock in the afternoon. The anticipation was making her more excited. She quickened her pace as if it would make the time go by faster. She had a rule. No coke until six at the earliest. That way she could make it last. She also liked exercising control games on herself. It made her aware of her power. She had control over the drugs that she chose to take. She wiped the sweat off her brow and pulled her jeans up around her shrinking waist. She pulled her zebra style tank top out and then pushed it back down her pants, smoothing it as she did so. She dug in her purse and sprayed on the cheap cologne as she sucked on the remaining butt of the cigarette. The cologne made her feel more cool when she wasn't able to shower-even though the scent was a thick cheap musk. One of the heels of her pumps got caught in a crack in the sidewalk and she held on to the wall of a store front to remove it and then wiggled it back into place on her foot. As she did, she looked up, and ahead in the distance she saw a sign high in the air. It wasn't large but it was what most people would call pretty, if they dared, regarding its subject matter. It had tiny pale pink twinkling lights surrounding it and a night time background of various shades of blue with a topless woman swinging on an old fashioned porch swing. Her figure was robust and minuscule in all the right places and she had the classic beauty of someone from the 1940s. This could be the place where she could wave her magic wand. She quickened her pace and within a matter of a minute pushed open the thick front door, which let out a blast of cold air that sent her hair flying backwards and nearly knocked her skinny body over. No one was at the hostess stand and she couldn't get a good look inside unless she paid the cover charge that was also good for one free drink. *Nice touch,* she thought. This place already had their act together far more than the first club. She contemplated her agenda-would she check it out as a customer first having a drink? No one knew her here. It wouldn't matter what they thought. Or would she rush right in to do business? She would rush right in to do business. She needed money to stay ahead of herself.

This time the hostess was an attractive slim figured brunette. She wasn't exactly pretty in the conventional sense, but that didn't matter because she wasn't a dancer and she had enough of a certain something to intrigue most curious men to venture on into the club, thought Maruska. She told the woman the same thing she told the last hostess and a few minutes later a middle-aged man came out to greet her. He was handsomely dressed in a light tan suit and tie. His body revealed his past as a footballer with a thick, tan muscular neck. He smiled at her beneath his thick brown mustache and motioned for her to follow him. *Very charming.* But behind the facade lay a snake, thought Maruska as she trailed behind. It was almost always the case. She knew how to read people well in the sex trade even if this wasn't a part of it she had ever worked before. The man led her back past a kitchen that was preparing steaks, baked potatoes and placing live lobsters in large pots. The classy surroundings were starting to take Maruska aback. Perhaps she was out of her league her? *Silly thought,* she told herself. A place like this was less likely to be under the radar of the police like the last dump she was just at. This place was perfect.

The man led her into his office which was small but busy with blinking phone lines lit up like tiny Christmas lights and video surveillance monitors and "to do" lists and phone messages pasted haphazardly on the walls and taking up space on his disorderly desk. He sat down on a puckered leather chair, placing his feet carefully on the desk as to not knock any papers down-putting his boots on top of them was obviously acceptable, however. He took a cigar out of a drawer. Maruska was directed to sit down across from him. In front of her was a bowl of matches that had the club's name on them, which she hadn't taken note of before, "Swingers." *Now that is a start,* she thought. The name had to go. She reached into the bowl and struck a match.

She leaned over the desk towards the man with the flame glinting from atop the small stick. "May I have the honor?"

He bent forward, his thick body restrained by his jacket tightening around him. His cigar lit, he took a long inhale and then when he was ready, asked what he could do for her.

"You could give me a job. That is *what* you could do."

"You're too old to dance."

Maruska didn't react. She was only 25, which wasn't too old. But she knew she didn't look like it. "No, I don't want to dance. I want to work for you. With you."

"Doing what?"

"Making this place a million times better."

The man choked on his smoke, her words catching him by surprise; he had the most successful strip club in the whole city. "Excuse me?"

"Yes, I know you think you are successful because you are compared to everyone else. But I am talking about really making a difference. I work strip club in Kosice as manager. Unfortunately there was fire and everyone lost job. But before, I improve profits fifty percent."

"What was the name of the club?"

"Lollipops." *Damn,* she thought. She resisted the urge to get up and leave, explaining that it was clear there were no openings. She rarely fucked up, but the name she came up with was hideous even though there was a strip club in the States that had it. She realized that was where the name came when it seemingly popped out of her mouth from nowhere. But luckily he didn't know about it. She told herself to stay focused and not to trouble her mind over the stupid answer she just gave. She would not bring the name up again.

"Excuse me?"

"Yes, I know is stupid name. We working on changing but fire beat us ."

The man stared at her not sure what to do or say next. She was strange- electric, and intense. Somewhere between a saint and satan. He could picture her being run out of the Catholic Church in Medieval times based strictly on her appearance. The vision of her running out of the cathedral dressed in white, her silver hair splayed out from the fear and wind, its parishioners chasing after her with their own fires set on the end of sticks. Her hair and her skin were almost a perfect blend with each other. The whitest white person he had ever seen. He felt she was hiding something, not being entirely upfront, but he admired her balls. She reminded him of the aggressive ways of his past that came to a screeching halt once he had children.

"Listen. What's your name?"

"Maruska Czoborova."

The man swung his legs off the table and onto the floor. He sat up straight and spoke seriously. "One thing you need to understand in this business is the girls bounce back and forth from club to club. What the hell do you think we ask them when they want to come work here? We ask where they have worked before and none of them has ever answered 'Lollipops'." He broke out in laughter.

Maruska did not laugh. She waited for him to get a grip on himself before she explained. "It was a new club. So not many girls there yet..."

"Maruska Czoborova, now either get the hell out of here or have a drink with me and tell me what you really want." He started chuckling again repeating the name Lollipops as he punched a set of numbers on an intercom and ordered two whiskeys on ice.

Maruska leaned back into her chair. She wasn't used to not being the one in control and was feeling the heat rise up inside of her but knew she had to play it cool. She sat silent. *Make the fools talk,* she told herself. *Make it their idea.*

"I've never had woman come in here like you who didn't want to just be another nameless dancer. To be honest, business has been good but I could use some help." He stopped talking hoping she would fill him in some more. This was the strangest interview he had ever conducted. She stared back at him. Her face blank but supremely serious. Her mouth was tight and she didn't speak. "I am still confused. What exactly is it that you say you do?"

There was a light knock on the door that then opened gently and a young androgynous looking person in black pants and a long white shirt set their drinks down.

The manager thanked the waiter and waved him or her out of the room. He continued to stare at Maruska sizing her up. He had a story about her in his own mind and in that story he knew what she wanted. He was hoping she would say it out loud so he didn't have to. He was also hungry for more. More of what? He did not know. But not anymore of the steady boring business, the demanding wife and boring children. He needed a shake up. Something to wake him up, bring him back to life. Something to inspire him. He needed someone exciting like this woman sitting across from him to help him push the envelope a little further. He clanked his glass to hers and said congratulations. Congratulations to what he wasn't really sure of, but he could feel it in the air. The electricity of the woman with the long platinum hair was sent to save him.

Maruska began work the next day as Roman's assistant. Immediately upon arrival she rushed to his office removing the list inside of her purse and telling him of the changes that would have to be made immediately. The first order of business would be a change to the venue's name. The sign outside could be kept but moved inside. She liked the idea it would give the men in subliminal messages: Swing; do what you came here to do and don't hold back. She kept that thought to herself for now.

And then to Roman's surprise he let her take over renaming the club to Lone Stars. It was Maruska's way of paying homage to her future. Then one-by-one Maruska called each dancer into the office and ordered them to bring all identifying documents to work with them on their following shift and if they failed or mentioned it to anyone, they would suffer consequences that they'd rather not know about. Suddenly the girls weren't jealous anymore of this woman. It was fear and anxiety they felt towards her. And then they built the back room.

Arnost was the first back room customer. He had been a regular at the club since Maruska started working. When he wasn't throwing money down girls g-strings and having them grind his lap, he would have a drink and a smoke with Maruska at the bar. Eventually it led to the sharing of lines in the back office and from there she decided she would hit him up first. And he went for it. The girl was in the back room waiting. This one went without a problem. Maruska and Roman agreed to let her keep the pay without turning over a percentage to them. They needed someone to go first to show the other girls it was okay and that they would make a lot more money by being agreeable to it. They also didn't have a choice.

Most of the other girls weren't so easy and argued that it was not what they had come to work to do. Maruska warned them repeatedly until they were worn out. Word had spread in underground circles that Lone Stars was cheaper and safer than finding a girl on the street and tourists and locals were packing the place nightly. But the amount of customers to "dancers" was out of proportion and Maruksa had to order some of the girls to do as many as four back room shifts in a row most nights. Arnost suggested that Maruska recruit from the streets but Roman would have nothing to do with that. Maruska argued vehemently with him saying it would make no difference, the girls ultimately were all the same whores no matter if they started by working the streets or the clubs. But Roman wouldn't bend. He had wanted a change but the back room was starting to make him uneasy. Not only was it making him feel nervous but his wife was becoming more and more suspicious of what he was up to at the club spending every waking hour there with some mystery woman he had given a job to who had come from out of nowhere. And although his wife was accepting of the topless dancers parading around him all day and night, that was how they had met when he was in college partying with his team, prostitution would have been out of the question even though it was legal. But Maruska's ways crossed the lines of what was legal and what wasn't. She was forever crossing the boundaries, blurring the lines. Roman became ever more fearful of his wife finding out about the prostitution in the back room. He feared it would result in her divorcing him and taking the children away. Suddenly she wasn't so demanding and the kids wholesome ideas of fun were a lot more appealing. He also was paranoid of the ever increasing amount of cocaine he was doing with Maruska and Arnost. It seemed as if in the blink of an eye his life was moving deliriously fast and felt as if he had totally lost control. He was becoming someone he had never been up to this point, and he did not like the slippery slope he felt he was sliding down. Maybe it wasn't a slippery slope because Maruska was so confident and nothing bad had happened, yet. Regardless, he was losing control and that was something he would never accept of himself as a man. Almost as soon as the change occurred, Roman was ready for a new change: there would be no more cocaine. It was making him agitated and paranoid. There would be no more back room and no more Maruska, the instigator of it all. It had become all too much for him. He couldn't keep up with her and her never ending ideas and he felt as if he was going to explode any moment from all the sudden stimulus in one giant bloody red burst of a heart attack. He had to stop her and the whole set of wheels put in motion before it was too late.

Maruska had worked the club a total of six weeks. Her last day of work she returned to the same sign she had first seen; the one of the topless woman on the porch swing. Incredulous, she stormed into the club and demanded to know what was going on. Roman did not waste any time telling her she was fired. He told her he was happier with the way things used to be and he wouldn't be needing her anymore. Arnost was sitting at the bar smoking and drinking, watching the scene. As Maruska exited the building, he jumped off his stool and trailed her outside.

They settled at a quiet coffee bar for an espresso and smoke. They were the only customers. Maruska was seething inside. After all she had done for Roman he had the nerve to tell her to go shove it up her ass? His profits in six weeks doubled, she told Arnost. Who knows what could have happened in the future? She could have been wealthy and now she had nothing to show for all the hard work she had done but a measly paycheck.

Arnost reached across the table to hold her hand.

"No worry, Maruska. Your dream still can come true. Come to work for me."

Maruska pushed his hand away. She did not like physical contact. She looked away from him and then back at him. "What do you have in mind?"

"You'll see. Come with me."

Maruska didn't get up. She finished her cigarette right down to the filter and drank the rest of her espresso. When she was done, she got up from the table. Arnost slapped some Korunas down on the counter as they passed it to pay for their espressos. His car was parked less than a block away and without another word they both got in.

It was a sunny day with bright blue skies and white clouds and a cool breeze that would drift through the car windows, making the ride very comfortable. They drove to Vajnorska street. Maruska's rage was calming down, although the bright sunlight was killing her eyes. Roman would have to pay and that thought comforted her.

Arnost pulled up to a house at the end of the street and opened the passenger door for Maruska to exit. He walked up to a gate that surrounded the house and punched in a code. He let Maruska go first as he held the gate open for her and he carefully took in his surroundings. He saw no one on the street. It was too early.

Inside, loud music and strange moans of human life, which sounded more like pain than ecstasy, could be heard from upstairs. Maruska looked around. The house was not what she expected of Arnost. She thought him to be at least a little more sophisticated than this. The walls and floors were filthy and the furniture torn and mismatched. But she could tell he thought he was impressing her. She looked at him and waited for his explanation of why he brought her here.

Instead, he directed her to follow him upstairs and he opened the door to a room with a girl who looked to be about fifteen, naked and sprawled across a mattress lying on the floor. "Zuzana," he said as he smiled a sly smile.

Maruska wasn't sure if she was asleep or stoned, but judging by Arnost's expression, guessed the latter. He closed the door and proceeded down the hall and opened the door to another room. His brother Andel was inside polishing a gun while humming to the Wang Chung song, "Everybody Have Fun Tonight." It played from the portable radio perched up on the shelf across from him.

They made quick introductions as Andel set the gun down and then turned the radio off. Arnost asked Andel to come downstairs to talk.

The three of them proceeded back down the stairs and took seats in different chairs in the living room. Maruska looked around, taking in what she could of her new surroundings, trying to get a reading on where she was and what this was all about.

CHAPTER TEN

Arnost explained to her that he and his brother dealt mainly with a Russian group of men with cocaine, heroin and the selling of girls. Business had been good, even great at times. But things were not so good right now. There were at least four other gangs in Bratislava that had stolen their girls and the only girl they had left was the one upstairs. Andel insisted on keeping a regular job as a baker, something he had excelled at and had a passion for from an early age. It also helped to keep up appearances of looking like a normal working person in the household, while Arnost handled the traveling and details of the business. But what they needed now was someone to help with the girls. Someone who girls would trust and follow to the house. They needed more and they needed variety. And they needed to make sure the girls stayed. They needed great girls, the best.

The Russians were demanding them and business was coming to a halt if things didn't change soon. There was someone in particular whom only trusted Arnost. This someone was very powerful and life would be great. But he needed help. Simple as that.

"What about it Maruska? Seems you are perfect," Arnost asked as he took out a cigarette and smiled at her. His teeth were gray and crooked with black in between that looked like mold creeping up tile grout. His face was angular and tan and the skin around his mouth had folds and deep lines. Maruska realized that today was the first day she had seen him in natural light and if wasn't for his teeth he could almost be called handsome. His gaze fixed on her with his heterochromia iridis eyes; one was green and the other was brown. Another genetically defected person. She thought about the coincidence and wondered if that somehow had brought them together. She shrugged the thought off. Thoughts like that were a waste of time. They were for people with nothing but too much time on their hands who tried to make sense of the world they lived in. The world made no sense.

Maruska didn't respond. She wanted to know more. Specifically about the money. Money up front had to be mentioned before she would consider anything. He had to mention it first. No exceptions. Very first rule of the game.

Arnost was puzzled by her silence but didn't show it. "Look around Maruska. You have nice home to live in, too."

Maruska looked around. The home was lit by naked bulbs with a yellow and brown dinginess that hung from unraveling cords. Specks of dried blood were splattered on the ceiling. She wasn't impressed. He needed to keep talking.

"I understand Maruska. You tough woman. You business woman. You get paid every girl."

"I want money up front before I start. And I prefer not to live in this pigsty."

"In time Maruska. In time."

Maruska did not smile. But inside she was getting excited about the prospects. The job sounded easy. She would know how to manipulate young girls without a problem. She would know exactly how to do it. Her past had magically presented her with the opportunity she had been waiting for. She envisioned what headquarters would look like once she took over. It would be sprawling, immaculate with marble floors and lush hidden suites, and filled to the brim with every type of girl one could imagine on their way to Austria, the Czech Republic, Western Europe and Japan or anywhere else that paid the right price for that matter.

"I want to work with the other part, too, Arnost. Not just girls. I want percentage of sales from the drugs." What she really wanted was full blown control and she was going to start with as much of it as she could get. It would be harder for them to take it away from her if that's where she started. So why waste time doing anything but? She may be a woman, but she wasn't stupid.

Arnost wasn't prepared for this. Dealing drugs was a man's business. Women had no place there with the men in that scene.

Maruska saw the shift in him.

"I help you with girls but you let me in with the drugs too Arnost, otherwise, forget it."

Arnost stood up from his chair and scratched his chin that was rough from not shaving the last three days. He paced the room, thinking. He wasn't sure he could trust someone who obviously had the start of what was looking like a serious addiction. With the girls, yes. The money would motivate her. She would need it to buy the drugs. But he wasn't prepared for her to want to deal. That was risky. His intentions had been to keep her separate- sort of a customer and a colleague at the same time. He would have the power that way through her dependence on him with the drugs and she would be less likely to turn on him or cause any other type of trouble.

Andel was silent. He had not said one word the entire time. Maruska curiously looked over at him, she secretly in her mind referred to him as the "muffin man." He seemed totally worthless to her but she knew better than to insult the bosses brother. She wondered if he was as stupid as Arnost. It amused her that Arnost didn't seem aware that she was seeing right through his ploy.

"Okay. Maruska. We try once. If it goes terrific, you will continue. But if not, you are out. *Completely out* you understand?" He gave a look to Andel that Maruska took as a warning.

Maruska stood up. "Where is my car? I need a car to to do my job."

Arnost liked her down to business attitude. It amused him. She should have been born a man. There was nothing besides the way she looked that was woman. He showed her to the front door and took a set of keys out of his front pocket. He fished around for the right one and removed it from the chain. He opened the front door and pointed to a pale gold four door American sedan parked across the street. "See, you can put many girls inside." He laughed and handed Maruska the keys. She held out her other hand. In it, he placed 3,000 Korunas, which equaled about $200.00 in Texas money she calculated. It wasn't great but she would let it be just this once.

Maruska walked across the street to the car that fortunately had tinted windows. She'd get to what Arnost wanted soon enough, but first she had two other problems she had to take care of.

The car took some getting used to. She had barely driven in her life. She finally got a rhythm about ten miles into it. The car was large. *Like a boat,* she thought, and she liked to think of herself as a captain sailing, dodging swerving surfers-the pedestrians that crossed streets randomly in front of her, risking their lives.

First order of the day was Lone Stars. Or was it called Swingers now? Either way it wouldn't be called anything soon. She pulled into a space a block away and sat in the car dreaming of the things she wanted to do to the establishment. Would she burn it? Would she go in with a machete and slice and dice? Would she bomb it? The possibilities were endless and she enjoyed the fantasies tremendously. They took her mind off her dwindling high. But the easiest thing to do would be to shoot. She wished for a moment that she was unrecognizable. But that was not something she could help. Her albinism was the first thing people noticed. She sat low in the car and watched girls arrive for work. She had an idea. She could take them out one by one as they walked towards the establishment. Roman would suffer the consequences of his deed. Yes, that is what she would do. But, he would know it was her. Not if she played her cards right. The story would be that he took out his staff and then took his own life. Gossip would have it that a cocaine addiction and a shaky marriage along with his recent involvement in some immoral ways at work had eaten at his soul and he couldn't take it any longer. Yes, that was it. She knew where all the video cameras were and would keep out of their sight or better yet, turn them off. The timing was perfect. There would hardly be any customers, maybe none yet, since it was early on a weekday. The kitchen staff wouldn't be inside as dinner was only served on the weekends. There would be no Dee Jay as on the weekends. During the week, it was the bartender's responsibility to cue the girl's songs up. She got out of the sedan and bolted across the street. One-by-one she took out the hostess, six dancers, two customers, and the androgynous weirdo. With her gloved hands, she placed the gun in Roman's hands. He was the only one she would let live, his gun shot wound wouldn't be lethal but would look like a lame attempt at suicide. The plan was last minute, but deliberate. And when she was certain everything looked as if he would be accused of the crime, she would leave the scene.

Most of the dancers had been huddled in a group gossiping about customers and comparing notes to other clubs and cities they had worked in waiting for the night to kick in. The silencer had been an excellent choice. Roman hadn't even noticed anything by the time she got to him. When she walked into his office, his back was turned as he was just about to make a phone call. He turned around and was surprised to see the apparition like figure of Maruska standing in his doorway, gun in hand. Maruska had hung up the phone for him when she had gotten closer to him. She got behind him and took his hands in hers, the gun aimed perfectly. It was meant to be. *But it is too easy,* thought Maruska. She liked things to be more exciting. She wanted struggle, she wanted the rush of adrenaline it produced in her like when she had taken the screaming kicking little girl in her village. No, it was the coke she thought. The buzz was dying. She needed more. That was what was missing.

She went around the club a second time making sure all the doors were locked and went into the bathroom to clean herself up. Some of Roman had splashed onto her and she wanted no traces of it. She looked at herself in the mirror. Her white skin had a yellow tinge to it under the fluorescent lights. The baby blue tiled walls were unflattering as they surrounded her in the mirror. She paused for a moment and looked at herself. She was just a person but she didn't know what she was looking at or who. She was just a person staring back at herself in the mirror. She felt nothing but the high slipping away. She saw an open locker that one of the dancers must have forgotten to lock. In it were a pair of jeans and a black t-shirt stuffed inside a plastic bag. She undressed, replacing her clothes with the dancers and took the bag with her to the car. She would get rid of it later.

CHAPTER ELEVEN

Onto club number one. Maruska drove the seven blocks to the first club where she had interviewed. This would have to be different. *All policemen were idiots*, she thought, but there was no use in giving them anything that could point the finger that both crimes were committed by the same person. The first job was too easy. The disappointment washed over her like a bucket of liquid dread. She pulled over into a parking lot across the street from club number one who's name she was still unsure of. The sign outside was simply the address in a neon sign. But perhaps that was the business name, which she thought was a lazy attempt at looking hip. A couple of Roma girls were walking towards the club. That was one area where Maruska did not have an entirely cold heart. She had some empathy for the gypsies. She could make their lives better. They would be perfect recruits being more exotic for the European market. The Slovak government hated to admit it, but much to her benefit, a lot of the Roma girls were sterilized, which would take care of one pesky problem in her business. She watched the girls as they giggled entering the building. Their dark eyes, hair and skin made them more valuable. Rare. Yes, she would take them. But not today. Lead up to it. Everything is illusion. Perception. She would start with someone else and then give Arnost the impression of her constant never ending improvement on the job once Roma girls were brought in. If she impressed him too much today, she would have a hell of a time living up to the standard in all the days to follow. He was an idiot but she had to admit that he was the one with the connections and the power. For now. She would have to impress him to get anywhere.

Maruska drove off. She hatched an idea by watching the Roma girls; it was some version of payback for not giving her a job. She would let it be-for now.

Maruska was tired. She was out of coke and wanted to get back to headquarters soon to see if Arnost would help her out. She remembered the two hundred dollars he had given her and groaned internally. It wouldn't look right if she came back empty handed. But she needed a pick me up. Coffee wasn't even close to the wonders of what she really wanted but for now it would have to do. She cruised down the street slowly looking left and right for a coffee shop or a bookstore that housed one. She saw everything but. She was on the wrong side of the tracks for something that sophisticated. She would have to get closer to the old town square on the other side of the river which was on her way back to headquarters. After crossing the bridge over the muddy Danube, she at last came to a small bookstore that had a picture of a frothy latte painted on its window. She cruised the one way streets until she found a place to dock the tank. The car's size was a nuisance with parking, but she wasn't going to complain.

The store was tiny and full of wood and dusty, smelly books with yellowing pages. She went to the counter in the back corner and ordered a tall glass of espresso straight. She paid the cashier and with glass in hand abruptly turned around walking straight into the man standing behind her and spilling the dark hot liquid all over his light blue cotton shirt. Maruska furious, looked up at the man and cursed at him in Slovak under her breath. To her surprise he just smiled at her and nodded. She cursed again, this time more loudly but he did not speak. When she turned back around to the cashier to replace her empty glass, the man stepped in front of her and in English told the cashier he would pay for her drink and anything else she wanted. Maruska was now standing enough distance from the man to get a good look. He was tall. Rugged. Dark blond. He was as good looking as any American movie star she had ever seen. Maybe he was one. He spoke perfect English. She told him thank you for the refill and apologized to him in English.

"Oh, so you do speak English," he said. "I was beginning to think that I was only going to be able to speak to old Kornel here during my visit," he gestured at the cashier with the long black hair pulled out of his face with a baseball cap who smiled back at the famous author paying him mind. The cashier couldn't wait to get off work to tell all his friends. It had been an interesting day at work for once.

Maruska watched as the American man pulled out a wallet from the back pocket of his jeans and gave the cashier a wink. He handed over money to the cashier, enough to buy the entire display case of sweetbreads and scones. He pointed to the seeping dark brown stain on his shirt. "Another one of these and a large black coffee."

Maruska, not used to being charmed by anyone, had to mentally tell herself to be cool. She thought it funny to herself that she hadn't even thought about the murders she committed until just now. She wondered if the man would be talking to her if he knew what she had just done. She liked what was happening. *You never really knew anyone, did you?* Here was this unassuming lonely tourist looking to her of all people for chit chat. She had to turn away for a moment to wipe the grin off her face at the absurdness of it all. She also did not want the man to see her teeth. She had learned how to speak without showing them, but laughing and smiling were something she managed to do rarely and only when others weren't looking.

Both drinks ready, the American asked if she cared to join him. Maruska couldn't think of a reason not to and hoped that a small conversation would give her some new energy simply by the challenge of it. She didn't have idle chit chat with people. She could care less about others and their silly hopes and dreams and fears. Or worse, the mundane details of their family and work lives. Her body was heavy and pins of anxiety and dread were poking her everywhere. She'd have to get back to headquarters soon. The espresso wasn't going to do a thing. She deliberated whether to initiate the conversation or not. She couldn't think of anything to say. Then she noticed the silver Rolex he wore on his left hand as he grabbed the sugar container.

"Where are you from?" She asked the man.

"United States," he said as he poured what must have been a cup of sugar in his coffee.

"You like it sweet I see?"

He looked up at her with a playful look. "Yes, I like it sweet."

"Where in United States you from?"

"Texas."

Maruska couldn't believe it. Maybe, after all, this was going to be her lucky day. Roman was taken care of, she had a new job, and she was now sitting across from one of the most handsome men she had ever seen who just happened to be from Texas, wearing a Rolex.

The man stirred the sugar aggressively into his coffee and then looked back at the woman he thought looked like Johnny Winter's twin sister. She was staring at him taking him in. She was unusual he thought. Mystical, magical, witchy? He couldn't exactly find the right words, which made him curious.

The woman finally spoke after drinking her tall glass of pure espresso in one full swig. "What bring you here?"

"Oh, I wrote a book and am doing signings for it at six tonight. This store is one of the stops along the way. European tour." He looked up and around his small surroundings implying that he was surprised this was where he was.

Maruska wondered what his book was about but wasn't going to ask. Reading was something for boorish people and she did not do it and she did not want the conversation going there. That could get tiresome. She looked around the store. It was charming but it was small. Whatever he wrote must be stupid and unworthy she thought. Her eyes caught a splash of color behind her and to the left. It was a poster of a dead man and blood splashing from stab wounds on his body. The poster read *Points of Passion* with a Slovak subtitle. It sounded familiar, maybe she had heard about it on the news or saw posters for it before.

Jeff caught her looking at the poster. "Yep. That's it. Bestseller in America. Slowly catching on here. Doing very well in England though."

Maruska smiled. Jeff saw her teeth; fragmented like a small fish's, jagged and sharp like a small saw, the color of beige. He could tell she was humiliated that he had seen them but was trying to be cool. He knew he had witnessed something that wasn't shown to most people. Others weren't supposed to see. The sight made Jeff excited. He was bored out of his mind in Europe. He longed to get back to Texas. The tour had been too long. Most of the women had boyfriends, and usually it was the boyfriends who had read his book. He hadn't been lucky once, which was unusual and he also hadn't been offered any drugs, which was unusual too. And boy oh boy could he use some he thought. Maybe this strange woman sitting across from him could alter that.

Maruska had recognized the knowing look in the man's eyes when he saw her teeth. Writers knew more, were more observant about things than most people. They knew the real reason behind things. That was their job. She wasn't going to pretend anymore. She had showed her hand. He looked like the type that was intrigued by hard drugs but only smoked weed and drank beer. The espresso was kicking in but it was making her more jittery and nervous than awake and confident. She really had to get back to headquarters to see if Arnost could help her out. Then she had the reoccurring sinking reminder that she had been paid but had not done anything to earn it yet. She looked at the man sitting across from her and thought about the girl, Zuzana, in the upstairs room.

"Do you want some fun in Slovakia after your book signing?"

The man eyed her curiously, hoping she would offer the meth, the coke, whatever it was that made her teeth the way they were. A tingle of excitement crept up his long, lanky body. "Hell yeah I want some fun. What do you have in mind?"

"I pick you up here. Seven o'clock I surprise you. But I tell you now fun is not free."

"Hey, nothing in this world is free. I hear you loud and clear." He had a mischievous twinkle in his eyes.

Maruska smiled not caring anymore about her teeth showing. "I go now. See you in couple hours."

"Hot dog!"

The man's name was Jeff. She saw it on the poster as she made her way out.

CHAPTER TWELVE

Arnost and his partner Pavol, had flown into the United States to pay a little visit to Maruska Czoborova. The trip was long overdue and Arnost slept soundly on the plane as he felt a sense of peace wash over him for the first time in years. As he slept on the plane, he dreamed about who he was and the ambitions he had left. The final traces of a larger than usual binge before the flight left Vienna gave him some last lingering delusions of inflated self-esteem. He named his dreams "Consolation Soldier" in which he was the star. It was also the loose English translation of his real life gang, Vojtech, that he led out of Bratislava.

These days Vojtech consisted of a very small but very violent and therefor very powerful group of Slovak men who had histories ranging from narcotics, grand theft, pimping, passport fraud and identity theft and trafficking. Some of the members had a cross tattooed on their forearm that was really a switchblade if you looked closely. In his dreams he saw himself in a mosque-like setting leading a mass of young aryan men to their destinies. A harem of young girls danced before him. After the meetings, the men would watch as the young girls did anything Arnost told them to. He felt himself becoming aroused just thinking about it.

A long stretch of sweet and bitter syrup ran down from the inside of his nose to the back of his throat. He swallowed hard. He knew the buzz was about to die, just about when the plane landed. But he tried to stay positive and upbeat. What he was up to was worth it and it would produce more highs for him and everyone soon. It was time to get Maruska to come back home. It had been somewhere around sixteen years. She was the best and her expertise and cunning style had long been missed. The young girls in the sketchy city of Bratislava were much more trusting of a woman than of a man especially when Maruska had frequented the strip clubs and the streets of Vajnorska and Krizna to recruit. Her results always exceeded his expectations. Not once had she ever let him down. She had a great technique, promising the young girls respectable jobs such as waitressing in other European countries for three times the pay than Slovakia, so naturally most were interested. However, their world would soon enter a much darker reality when they were drugged and taken to Vojtech headquarters where they were forced to sell their bodies and were repeatedly raped and beaten. The best ones got sold for the highest prices overseas. Arnost shifted in his seat as he smiled a drowsy smile in acknowledgment and thanks to all the naïve girls of the world.

Maruska was working as an assistant manager at a strip club when she met Arnost. She was the first woman Vojtech had let in. But they let her go just as fast when she wouldn't stop talking about moving to the United States, Texas to be specific. And her cocaine problem had gotten out of hand. She had begun bringing her use up a notch by mixing it with heroin. But her work had been exceptional. Vojtech housed thirteen beautiful young girls. Twelve of them had been "discovered" by Maruska, as she liked to call it, as if she worked for a high fashion modeling agency. But she had become bored quickly and needed a change. She needed a clean break from Arnost and his brother, Andel. They had been at it longer than her and watched her every move and held tight to the power they had, not giving up the connections as easily as she thought they would. She wanted independence and would get it one way or another. She had her sights set on the United States now. There she could be out from under their thumb and do her own thing. A clean slate. Be her own boss.

They didn't know of her using relationship with Jeff. She had managed to keep that mum. "Maruska wants a fucking American Cowboy," Arnost and his brother, Andel would joke behind her back humming the "Lone Ranger" theme. Eventually, they simply didn't trust her, the paranoia ate at them the more she talked about wanting to go to the land of the free and the home of the brave. She gave them the impression without words that sooner or later she would rat them out unless they gave her what she really wanted, which were papers to live and work in the U.S.. So they created the paperwork that she wanted with a promise in return to never speak. If she did, well, she knew what was coming.

As the buzz wore off, Arnost realized just how much he had really missed Maruska's business savvy. He looked over to his left and saw Pavol sitting next to him, the little grunt. He was snoring, his mouth gaping and a pool of drool gathered at the corner of his lip. He watched him in disgust. Lately he had to rely on Pavol to do the recruiting and Pavol wasn't exactly an entrepreneur and didn't have the eye for quality like Maruska, who was able to scope out real beauty, not trash. Pavol's tactics were also much more gruff and impulsive, raising eyebrows more than a few times unlike Maruska's natural and believable ability to con other women or to simply not be suspect because she was a woman. Pavol forcefully convinced the young girls that he was a customer, got them in a private location, usually his Volkswagen bus, knocked them out physically and then with chloroform as an extra precaution as he dragged them back to Arnost's house in the heart of the city- a square cream colored two story stucco house that looked like a small prison with only a couple of windows.

Arnost had kept in touch with Maruska from time to time over the years. She had told him she had met a famous American author after she got work at a very small publishing firm in Austin, Texas that specialized in Western fiction. She did not want Arnost to know he was the first customer she had brought to the house. He would become paranoid about that. She did tell Arnost that her boyfriend had a bit of a cocaine problem though. But other than that, she was happy. Arnost chuckled to himself when he heard about the boyfriend having "a bit of a cocoine problem though." Of course Maruska would hook up with a coke head. Took one to know one.

Arnost remained curious about her activities — if she was into drugs as much as she used to be, she would eventually need more and more money. He could promise her three times the amount of money she was making working for any small time publisher. Time was on his side.

The plane landed on time at 10:25 a.m. at the Austin Bergstrom International Airport. They had traveled light-only bringing carry-ons. They went through customs and then made their way quickly to stand in line at the Hertz Rent a Car station. Ten minutes later they sped away from the airport in the rented Ford Focus. Twenty minutes later Arnost and Pavol checked into the Melody Inn off Highway 183 in the North East part of Austin. Pavol was going to have his last meal there as far as Arnost was concerned. His plan was to knock him off before heading home. Maruska would know what to do with the body. And hopefully, if all went well, Maruska would be flying back home in his place.

Arnost and Pavol got situated in their rooms, then walked next door to the International House of Pancakes, the name sounding like a safe comfortable bet, and had a late breakfast for their first American meal. Arnost excused himself shortly after ordering the New York cheesecake pancakes. He was going to go outside for a smoke and call Maruska.

She was surprised to hear from him, especially calling from only 10 minutes away. He told her he was only in town for a couple of days and wanted to see her. She agreed for old times sake but said she was happy now and not interested in anything but a little "hello."

Arnost agreed. He saw this coming. He told her she could bring her boyfriend. He'd have some very special exotic "coke a cola" for them to celebrate with. He told her it would be fun, just a little visit, and asked: "Where is the Southern hospitality Maruska? You learn nothing in your new country? How often do you get to visit from someone from your past, from your country? Of course just a hello. That's all." He could hear the reluctance in her voice but at the same time he knew that she knew the consequences and risks of not being agreeable.

Maruska thought about being with Jeff who was now in possession of Olive and considered seeing Arnost alone. But she knew it was impossible to hide anything from him. She didn't like the feeling she was getting but quickly convinced herself Arnost had simply caught her off guard and there was nothing more to it.

Besides, she had been silent. Texas was not the out of control land she imagined it to be and she was now viewing her new home as a temporary vacation that may or may not turn permanent. She didn't care about anyone anywhere so she reasoned with herself that she could move at free will to wherever suited her best. Jeff's daughter had sent her heart fluttering once- but it lasted half a second. And that was more out of rage that he would do such a stupid selfish thing to have a child with that pathetic creature Ivy than any motherly instincts. Jeff was definitely the person she had felt closest to in her life, but it was only because of their mutual love of the same drug and there were no secrets there. There never had been since the beginning at least on his end. *They were kindred spirits,* thought Maruska who then laughed at the mere thought of that. She hated any kind of talk about spirits or souls connecting people. But she had felt safe with Jeff. He had a reputation as a writer-nothing that was questionable. It made her feel more at home in the strange land of America. Particularly Texas, which was more than double the size of Slovakia, but hadn't produced even close to the number of people with her same values as back home had. She saw in the news recently that Slovakia trafficked anywhere from one hundred to two hundred persons a year.

CHAPTER THIRTEEN

She flashed back to the night Jeff had come to Vojtech. She couldn't remember just how much Arnost had taken notice of him. It was too long ago and so much had happened since then. She shrugged it off. He wouldn't recognize Jeff. He was no longer the handsome beefy movie star looking man he was that night. She would also call him a different name. There was nothing to worry about.

She went into the kitchen where Jeff was seated feeding Olive a bottle of sour milk. She told him she had an old friend from home visiting who wanted to meet him too.

Jeff asked who it was but Maruska knew all she had to do was tell him there'd be a prize waiting to get him to stop asking questions. She knew he preferred what he didn't know of her past being kept a mystery, especially after Ivy who was such an open boring book. Ivy and her designer wardrobe that made her look like an overdressed puppet. Her skin that spoke of no life whatsoever and the ugly car she drove like a lot of girls her age who thought they were being cool. Those days had passed, hadn't they figured it out? They were so unimaginative all they could do was go retro. She was so silly and boring. Yes, she could cook she had been told, but so what? Cooking was a pathetic occupation that only prompted weight problems as Ivy so clearly exhibited. *She looks like a balloon ready to pop*, Maruska thought. And her stupid hypocritical career. What business did she have marrying anyone? She herself had never been married either, but she wasn't trying to live vicariously through it with others like Ivy so clearly was. Why would anyone even consider hiring her? It was clear she didn't know what she was doing. What a desperate lonely and pathetic girl. Naïve as they come. Too bad she wasn't better looking, or had some sex appeal. Then she may have at least made something of herself, Maruska's thoughts rambled on. Maruska could have pointed her in the right direction. But no, Ivy was utterly useless. The despicable child who stole her boyfriend. The Ivy she knew of would do anything to hang on to Jeff, which Ivy made obvious by allowing herself to be impregnated by him. *How obvious. How cliché. How utterly stupid.What in the world had Jeff ever seen in her?* Ivy came into the picture when Jeff had decided that he wanted to go straight after a particularly bad withdrawal when the cocaine and heroin mix had disappeared. Maruska had told him repeatedly that it wouldn't last long, that she could easily score again, but Jeff had his mind made up to never ever feel that miserable again. Maruska knew better than to hold herself to such imaginary fantasies. But she was the stronger of the two and she had believed she had endured more of what most Americans would call "pain" in life. The small lapse without was a feeling she had been acquainted with. She too would become consumed with the thought of when it would appear again, but she could deal with the lack of drugs, knowing they always came around sooner or later. Jeff couldn't. She liked seeing the difference in the two's reactions. She hated the whining trembling ill man he became in the midst but loved to see how self controlled she was in comparison. When the drugs finally reappeared, Jeff was unable to resist temptation. Disgusted with his own lack of self control, he moved out in an attempt to self rehabilitate. Living with Maruksa was the equivalent of an alcoholic on an extended camping trip in a well stocked bar. He had been gone many long years. During that time he met Ivy who showered him with no white snow or anything close, just lots of adoration. She was the opposite of Maruska and just what he needed at the time. Unfortunately for him, he had shared that sentiment with Maruska on one occasion. Eventually his old ways had come creeping back; the pregnancy was the straw that broke the camel's back. Ivy, who earned a decent living, almost immediately started hinting to Jeff about earning more money-finding a supplementary "real" job on top of his writing. Jeff didn't know what to do. He had liked things the way they were. He didn't intend to bring a child ito the world and he didn't want to do anything but write. The pressure was building. He returned to Maruska whom he never had told Ivy about. Maruska knew he would return and waited it out for all those years. She saved a secret stash supply of the finest heaven dust for the day when he finally came back. Occasionally she entertained thoughts about killing the two of them, but she would rather have Jeff back and she knew it was only a matter of time. In the meantime she took on what she learned from Andel by keeping a straight part-time job at a small publishing firm to keep her reputation as the foreigner down the street in tact, as it seemed people in America were highly suspicious of Eastern Europeans.

She supplemented her income by dealing small quantities. She stayed very busy, which made the six years fly by. Her fantasies about prostituting Texas beauty queens had been put on hold. She had a lot to learn still about the States; living in them and reading about them were two different stories. The police were more on the ball here and it wasn't as easy to find as many kindred spirits as their were back home. Yes, she hated Ivy and everything she represented and was glad she would be getting a fix soon to take the ugly duckling off her mind.

Jeff agreed to go with her and they decided it was best to take care of this sooner rather than later. He strapped Olive in the recalled car seat in the back of Maruska's old Toyota and crawled into the cramped front seat. Maruska always drove. It was an unspoken rule.

In less than twenty minutes they pulled into the parking lot of the low budget motel. Maruska had second thoughts about Jeff coming into the hotel room as she drove. Olive would be her alibi. She told Jeff to wait in the car and went inside to the front desk. She had the desk clerk ring up Arnost under his alias. She had guessed right. He still hadn't changed it.

Arnost wanted to talk to Maruska. The clerk, a quiet, plump black woman, handed the phone over to her.

Maruska held the light receiver to her ear and gave the clerk a look that threatened her not to listen in.

"Maruska, you come by yourself?"

She knew he was looking out the window when they pulled up and saw Jeff in the car. He was testing her.

"No. There is a baby. So they wait in car, no?"

"No Maruska." He chuckled for a moment at her indicating that he was the boss, the one controlling the situation. "I told you I want to meet your new family. Have nice suprise for your new man, too. Please. For old times sake. Maybe I never come here again, no? Come on Maruska. What you scared-y cat now? Don't be ridiculous. Just a hello. No worry, okay?"

Maruska hung up the phone and pushed open the the glass front door of the building. She motioned for Jeff to get out of the car and come in. She watched his frail body barely able to maneuver his child in her car seat out of the back of the car. She watched the scene from the point of view she was imagining Arnost was seeing it. It would be fine. Arnost certainly would not recognize him.

The walk from the parking lot to the motel while carrying Olive in the car seat had Jeff breaking out in a sweat and hyperventilating. Maruska, exasperated, met him half way and took over the car seat in order for him to expedite things. The three of them made it inside and took the elevator to the second floor.

Room 210.

Maruska knocked.

The door opened, revealing a room with a large window overlooking the noisy highway and parking lot. *Not a place you could really understand the true essence of the city,* thought Maruska. This was not good.

Arnost was hiding behind the door in some form of strange humor or simply to show off the lines laid out like train tracks on the cheap plywood coffee table staring at them the minute they walked in. As they stepped into the room, Arnost jumped out from behind the door and motioned for them to help themselves while he cooed to the baby who was placed on the cigarette burnt carpet.

Arnost looked the same to Maruska but older. Tall and wiry with the same stubble of white hair on the face and head. Same brown eye, same green eye, gray crooked teeth. The teeth looked worse.

"You no tell me you have baby," Arnost said teasing Maruska.

Maruska replied back in English that it was not hers. It was "Chris's" from a previous girlfriend; she hoped Jeff caught on to his new name.

Arnost stared at Jeff who was enamored with the "coke a cola." Arnost fed him some more while he looked down and studied him.

Maruska, mainly to break his focus, bent down in between the two and did another line through the worn straw that she hastily grabbed before Jeff could get his hands back on. When she came back up, Arnost asked in Slovak if he had ever met the man before. He told her he looked familiar.

Maruska laughed. "Not unless you have been to Texas before today without telling me which I don't believe you would do."

Arnost looked back down at Jeff trying to place him but wasn't able to. He never remembered meeting an American named "Chris" even thought he knew it was a common name. He turned back to Maruska.

They finally exchanged a belated hug. Then Maruska sat down on the tattered sofa after some encouragement.

Jeff who was still preoccupied with whatever crystals remained, sat on the floor, his legs straddling the coffee table's legs as if they were one.

In Slovak, Arnost slowly broke into his desire to have her come back to work for him. Arnost knew how to play her and told her she was the best they ever had. Things had never been the same since she left. He would pay her at least three times more than what she made in the past.

Maruska laughed inside at that one. It was another familiar line. She looked over to see if any more cocaine had mysteriously reappeared. She was getting nervous. The mix was stronger than she was used to and it wasn't making her confident, it was making her jittery. She did not want this to happen. No matter how bad the high, you always wanted more as if more would balance the feeling out.

Arnost got up, opened up one of the plywood kitchen cabinets, and grabbed a plastic baggy so full of powder that it looked like it was going to pop. He then took out a soup bowl and dumped the contents in it. He pulled out a razor blade from a sticky kitchen drawer, placed the items on the coffee table along with a couple of crisp one hundred dollar bills, one for each person to use as a straw to snort the powder through, and gestured for Maruska and Jeff to help themselves to the treat.

Jeff scooped the powder in two uncut handfuls shoving it up his nose while it powdered his entire face.

"Pig." Arnost said in Slovak.

Maruska, realizing she had placed herself somewhere she didn't have to, got up to leave.

Arnost walked to the door and pressed his back against it. He pulled a gun out of his back pocket.

"No, Maruska. We not through with our discussion yet."

"I am through Arnost. We had deal. I keep promise. This is no good. This no part of plan."

He looked back down at Jeff. He knew the man. He looked different but it was him; the first man she took back to the house. He was amused at his memory knowing that he was remembering back as far as fifteen or sixteen years ago. She had lied. He couldn't remember the man's name but it wasn't Chris. She had not kept her promise.

"Who is this man? I know him. You bring him to house before. I remember Maruska."

"That's ridiculous Arnost. He's an American."

"What, like no Americans ever came to house? First man. I have great memory Maruska, you forget much when you do drugs.

You have turned into crazy bitch Maruska. You no keep word. The baby is mine now," he pointed to Olive with his gun.

Maruska looked at Jeff who was watching but unable to pull himself away from the bowl.

"No, Arnost. We done with hello now. Goodbye." She pulled Jeff up off the floor, grabbed the car seat with Olive in it and hooked the handle over her other shoulder. With all her force and the mass of Jeff and Olive she banged into Arnost, hoping to knock him away from the door.

He didn't move.

"You give me baby," he said in Slovak. "Or I kill you."

Suddenly out of nowhere a man appeared. He was coming from behind them. He was short and stocky with black shoulder-length curly hair. He walked fast with heavy footsteps.

He knocked Jeff over by bumping forcefully into the back of his knees. Jeff crumbled backwards and the man dragged him off to another room.

Arnost, still pointing the gun at Maruska, insisted that she calm down. He spoke in an even tone and waved his gun like it was a flashlight, directing her toward the couch. His face became red and sweaty. A large light green vein in the pattern of a small tree with scrawny branches surfacing from below the skin in the space between his eyes grew up into his forehead.

"Sit down," he said.

Without knowing what else to do, she sat back down on the sofa next to the purse she had almost left behind.

Arnost started in again. It was the same thing she had just said no to only moments before.

She let him try to convince her while her right hand casually fished around the contents of her purse. It was a large bag. Bohemian hobo style. She had bought it in Flagstaff, Arizona on her way to

Texas on Route 66 where she got many kicks after she had landed at LAX. Thick woven fibers of purple and white Navajo patterns hid the movement inside.

She found it.

"What do you think Maruska?" You don't want to say no now do you?" he laughed at her mockingly.

"I need time to think," she said.

"No. There is no time. You get pay. Three times pay. What you want? Stay with this fucking American loser? You're lucky his brain is fried. I trust he has no memories of Vojtech?"

Maruska nodded. It was true. Jeff had never talked about the day or night they had met at the bookstore or the trip to headquarters. He had blacked out that night.

Arnost continued, "You have big career back home. You make history. First and only woman ever in Vojtech! Give your fucking American friend something to write about!"

She sat silent, staring at him, waiting for the other man to appear again. Where was he? What was he doing to Jeff?

Finally she saw the short thick legs wrapped in the tight black jeans plodding towards her from the bedroom.

She grabbed one of the worn pillows on the couch with her left hand, slid out the .38 as smoothly and quickly as she could out of her purse with her right and brought the pillow in front of the gun, wrapping it around its barrel and shot Arnost and then Pavol. She thought about Jeff for a quick second, then grabbed the car seat and casually left the motel.

CHAPTER FOURTEEN

The pounding happened around 3 am. At first Ivy thought it was Bookababa the road runner that Olive had named that took residence at their home and delighted in banging his beak into their windows at the most inopportune times, usually when Olive was napping or when Ivy was bathing, making her think some neighborhood pervert was on the loose and after a cheap thrill. Ivy who had not been able to fall asleep at all, got out from under the sheets and turned the dimmer all the way down before flipping on the main switch to add the light. The house was built in the 1950's but when the wedding business took off, she added modern amenities one by one. Bookababa wasn't at any of the windows. And he or she (she was pretty convinced it was a she after she had recently witnessed it with two babies) normally only appeared in the early afternoons anyway. The pounding happened again, this time louder. It was knocking at the front door.

She peered through the peephole but no one was there. Now, she was convinced she was going nuts. She had experienced so much insanity the last few days. She headed to the kitchen to make a cup of hot Earl Grey tea to calm her nerves so she could think rationally and hopefully fall asleep once she got back under the covers. According to Kirk, the tea which they often drank together, was named after a British Prime Minister. Legend had it that a Chinese noble had given the secret recipe to him after saving his life. Kirk always delighted in small factual stories and silly bird jokes. She had saved one in her mind to share with Olive some day: "Knock knock." "Who's there?" "Owls." "Owls who?" "That's right, owls hoo!" She smiled, thinking about him. He was a good guy, no doubt about it. She wondered where she would be today if she had stayed with him and contemplated giving him a call. He would be just the right person to comfort her. That was, if he was willing. He hadn't been happy about her breaking up with him. In fact he'd been downright pissed. She wouldn't need the tea if she could get him on the phone. She looked at her watch. It was a little after three. Calling was out of the question whether he forgave her or not. She grabbed the box of tea from the pantry along with some honey and sliced up some fresh lemon. She put the teapot on high on the gas stove. As she waited for the whistle, she had a funny feeling. Yes, things may have been better or different if she stayed with Kirk. But Olive never felt like a mistake and it took Jeff too to make Olive who she was, which although was a strange notion, not everything, like getting pregnant with Jeff, was for better or for worse. Some things had a mysterious place in the middle.

As the water began to boil, Ivy thought she heard a voice.

"Ivy. Open up!"

This time it was for real. This was no imaginary voice in her head. Her heart jumped and she saw her hands trembling as she turned the burner to the off position removing the teapot before its shrieking would scare her even more.

Ivy crept on her tip toes, her back against the walls, leading to the front door. She looked out the peep hole again but still saw no one. She opened the front door slowly, not sure who if anyone was standing on the other side of it. She made a mental note that if she lived, she would need to get a burglar chain. It was so dark outside she could not see him even though the small porch light was turned on-her only version of an alarm system. She justified to herself that once a couple finally admitted that someone objected to their marriage, she would get a real one with the works: codes, bells and whistles. Up until this moment, she had liked the simplicity of the light. She had never felt unsafe in the house since she bought it. She finally saw the outline of his shirt at her feet just as she was closing the door sure her mind was playing tricks on her. He was in fetal position. She grabbed him under the shoulders, hoisted him up and dragged him inside. He was so slippery she almost lost him a couple of times. She propped him up on her sofa where she got a good look at him, his hair was oily, there were several abrasions on his face and mouth, and stains on his clothes that had the rank combined smell of drugs and body odor.

"Jeff, what's going on? Where's Olive?"

"She has her," he said agitatedly.

"Who?"

"Maruska."

"Maruska? Why? Where? Oh my god what is going on?"

"Ivy, you need to call the police."

"I have, they already know she's missing Jeff!"

"No, you need to call them now and tell them Maruska has our baby. Dammit! Do it!"

Ivy went into the kitchen and called the police and then Karl.

Thirty minutes later, the police arrived first and interviewed Jeff. As they began to interrogate Jeff, starting off by questioning where he had been all this time, which he couldn't seem to account for, Karl came through the door. He was quite a contrast to the pudgy cop with the beer belly who was going out to his car to make a call to Interpol and the FBI.

The thinner, taller policeman that stayed behind asked Jeff where he thought Olive was. Karl hung in the background but was listening attentively not missing a detail.

Jeff began to sob. "I think she is in Slovakia."

"What makes you think that," the policeman probed.

Jeff sobbed harder. His entire body was shaking. Everyone knew it could just as easily been a side effect of his withdrawal.

"I think she took her there to sell...to have money to pay those guys off or something. Keep them out of her hair. I don't know. I just know she never came back to the motel or the house."

The cop asked who he was talking about.

"Maruska, my girlfriend. We all went to this man's motel room last Wednesday I think in the morning around eleven I think. Some old friend of hers from back home. Her and this guy named Arnold, or something like it, got in a fight. They hardly ever spoke English so I couldn't understand what was going on. What was being said. But then this guy he was..." He clutched his side for a moment and winced. Then continued, "Tall, thin, shaved head, had a tattoo of a cross on his forearm started pointing his gun at our baby."

"Who's baby?" the policeman interrupted.

"Her baby and my baby" He pointed at Ivy with agitation annoyed the cop wasn't paying attention. "Then this other guy came out of nowhere and knocked me out and taped my hands and legs and gagged me and pushed me into a closet. Oh, god I can't really remember what else. It gets kind of blurry, but I heard what I thought was a gun shot and then another one. I couldn't get the tape off my hands or feet for like two days and when I got to the living room there were two men dead lying on the floor and Maruska and Olive were gone."

The police questioned Jeff where he had been for the remaining five days of which he couldn't account for.

The blood was evaporating in Ivy. She sat on the sofa speechless, empty, immobile, full of vile for this pathetic creature. A new cop on the scene, a female, started coming towards her for what at first looked like some kind of consolation but before she reached her, Ivy screamed, "You fucking son of a bitch!" She kicked Jeff as hard as she could in his chest and grabbed fistfuls of his hair, banging his head on the edge of her coffee table. And then she sank to the ground. A part of her missing. All their voices becoming static.

Three hours later, Ivy's mother phoned.

"Hallo Ivy darling, how are you?" Ivy tried to read into the voice. Had Iris broken down and told her? And who was she going to be tonight? Was it the Joan Crawford or June Cleaver version? Her mom had always shifted from scary self obsession to harmlessly crazy. And there were other times when she was just plain sweet.

Her mother didn't know yet and she debated telling her. "Mom, it's late. I mean early." She looked at the clock hanging on the wall that indicated it would be 4 a.m. in California. Why are you awake at this hour?"

"Dr. Shmidl has given me the most wondrous medication my dear." Ivy flashed through the various medicated stages of her mother's life: her first memories were those of her as a health nut and the only drugs in the house were aspirin and cough syrup.

Then she was discovered by Nina Blanchard. Her mom was even more beautiful at this stage, the competition of the business not rearing its ugly head yet. Men drove cars into the back of other cars as they craned their necks checking her out. Some simply walked into doors. The glass ones they walked through. Slowly but surely, the medicine cabinet became more full of complicated names with warnings as her mother took on various plummeting body weights and personality transformations. "I have more energy than I did as a teenager," she continued. "Did I tell you about the new conditioner I bought? Leaves your hair ravishing my darling, seriously you must try it, but the trick is to wash your hair upside down."

Ivy knew the advice well and sighed heavily as she let her mother continue to ramble on. Her mom, even if she knew crises were being attended to, continued to solicit beauty tips. Washing one's hair upside down was a must at all times in her book, which Ivy had learned well as a teenager. Not that washing her hair upside down, bent over the laundry room sink made her hair shiny or bouncy, as her mom had promised, but it did give her self-esteem some shine. It was Junior year of high school and Ivy bent her waist over the laundry room sink flinging her hair upside down into it. She turned the water on and while it ran over her hair, she pawed for the Jhirmack orange creamsicle smelling shampoo and conditioner in the cabinet above the sink when she found the stash of pill bottles. Not just one bottle, but one after the other after the other. She supposed they had been there for some time but was particularly hip to it now as someone at school had recently given her a black beauty.

Rumor was that Laura Long, the most beautiful girl in the whole starlet filled Pallisades High School (who was also the vixen for many hair bands on MTV those days) was on them. Laura wasn't only gorgeous, she was the type that could fit in with anyone: jocks, stoners, the cheerleaders, the straight A students. She was the epitome of cool. Part American Indian with long silky black hair, olive skin and vivid blue eyes. Ivy heard she was part Chinese too, somewhere down the line. Anyway, Ivy wasn't nearly as popular or cool as Linda even though she liked these kinds of highs too. Suddenly exams and staying up all night studying weren't so intimidating and food didn't have nearly the same pull on her. She was shocked the first day after she took one. Her weight had gone down three pounds overnight!

Ivy wasn't sure after her first ecstatic high that she would ever be able to lay her hands on another pill again. Now it didn't matter because now she could just swap her mom's stash with some Dexatrim from the local drugstore! Her mom would be too looped out to notice. But she did notice. Ivy didn't remember her mom being too too crazy back then, but the rage she flew into when she found out was unforgettable. Ivy guessed it was probably a withdrawal or maybe just the tension created by the stimulants. It didn't seem to be so much about concern over her daughter turning into a drug addict as it did about her stash disappearing. Ever since then, Ivy learned to walk on eggshells around her mother. And she vowed to never touch another pill for the rest of her life and even threw her Accutane prescription as well as a bottle of Bayer that she carried in her purse for her menstrual headaches down the toilet. The outburst had scared her that much. Even though this crazy conversation was now happening, Ivy was relieved to hear her mom more subdued and sounding more in control than usual. And as out of it as her mom was in a hyper way, there was something comforting about hearing her voice on the other end with all the pain she was feeling about her own daughter.

Sometimes when Ivy talked about Jeff, without being very clear, people often thought she was talking about her mom. As her mom rambled on she tried to find comfort in the wise decision she made of not marrying him. The only smart thing she ever did when it came to Jeff. She scanned her living room at the scene of police inhabiting it as she numbly listened to her mom's beauty tip monologue drone on. What it really came down to was that she never had enough courage to marry Jeff, she thought, *thank God*. But neither could Jeff seem to muster up the courage to marry her. She suddenly thought that odd and subtly amusing. Maybe the biggest mistake he made was not marrying her. Would have been a whole lot easier for him to get what he wanted out of the lawsuit according to LuAnne if he had. Ivy knew Jeff was full of shit for the most part when the subject had been brought up. She wondered how her intuition could have been so right about that but so wrong about so many other things about him. She thought about how she loved the idea of marriage and how much she loved making it happen for other people. But she inherently knew it wasn't the right answer for everyone. She was sure she and Jeff would have wound up divorced after that first hour and a half of their first magical love making session when they first broached the subject, only to get re-married then divorced again and again and again. Their relationship was always volatile. Just like her moms and hers. And then she saw something she would never forget. One of the Austin police officers read Jeff his rights and handcuffed him and led him out the front door.

"Ivy, are you still there? Who are all those people? Don't tell me you had a party on a week night?"

"No mom. It's not a party. Mom, I've got to go. I 'll call you back in a couple of days." Ivy hung up the phone before she could hear the protests.

Ivy awoke to Karl sitting at her bedside a few hours later. When all the cops had left and when she finished packing, she had started to second guess herself as she sat on her bed staring at her suitcase. She and Karl had discussed the details after everyone was gone. *She was going to Slovakia?* It was almost unbelievable and the circumstances made it even more difficult to wrap her head around. She wasn't sure she had ever heard of the country before all this. Czechoslovakia for sure, maybe even the Czech Republic, but Slovakia? She didn't even like the way the name sounded. It had a sloppy and negative tone to it, like a lot of words ending in "ia"; anorexia, bacteria, chlamydia and Cambodia, dyslexia, malaria, paranoia and washateria, she thought as she rolled down the alphabet with words she could think of.

The wannabe writer in her always came out in her in the most stressful situations. And now just before they were to leave together to the strange sounding country, Karl still wanted to make it very clear to Ivy that she was just accompanying. "This is strictly my job and my responsibility." Ivy understood he was telling her to stay out of his business. "I'm not going to allow you to do anything but stay in the hotel and keep a low profile," he said as he sat on the edge of her bed self consciously.

"I don't want to seem like a hard ass, but you have to remember this is for the most likelihood of a safe return home for Olive.

I don't mean to be impolite about it, but your coming could serriously botch everything. Do you understand?" Karl looked her straight on.

"Yes, I understand perfectly. I won't, can't have it any other way. I need to be near Olive. If she's anybody's responsibility, she's mine." Ivy looked back down at the floor. Her sense of duty had weighed in on her heavily all night making it impossible to get any deep sleep.

"Karl I'll tell you so you know what it is like. All the dreams and memories I have of her so far. The excitement of being pregnant. The ultrasound revealing I would have a girl. Her birth. She came out smiling. The first time I got to hold her three days later. The little hat she had on. Pink and blue. The first time the nurses let me feed her. Her six month birthday party. Banana pudding everywhere. The first time she laughed. This gut busting laugh when I was drying my hair and flung it upside down." Ivy had to regain her composure. "Never knew that could be so funny. The laughter I heard when I flipped my hair back up. She thought it was hilarious. Her first laugh. And that was only half of what I thought about. The other half was realizing I had taken so many things for granted, never thinking for a second I might not see them happen. Her first day of school. Her first dance recital and crush. The first time she comes crying to me because a boy broke her heart. Her wedding. And her children, my only grandchildren. The guilt I feel for being the fool to get her in this mess. Please don't ask me or tell me again Karl. I can't stay behind."

⚜

CHAPTER FIFTEEN

She sat up, swung her legs around so her feet hit the hardwood floors, scooted her toes to scrunch her feet to fit into her slippers that lay a couple of inches away, and rolled her head and shoulders around trying to relieve the enormous amount of tension that had been wracked up.

Karl sat still on the edge of the bed wishing he didn't hear what he had just heard. She was coming and he couldn't talk her out of it. Time to accept that. "You are to act and be just like the rest of the population of Slovakia. We will see more of what that means once we get there. But blend in is what I am saying. You are not to speak to anyone for any reason. You should not be noticeable. Most of the people of the country are overly formal and reserved. They value their privacy above all else." He looked up at her to make sure she was listening. Her eyes were locked on his. "Do not show any emotional displays. Ivy, that is something you are going to have to particularly keep in mind in this situation. Do not call anyone by a first name. And if you dine in public, your napkin is to remain folded on the table. Do not put it on your lap."

Ivy was still standing above him, staring down, doing her best to retain and absorb the information. She excused herself, saying she needed to get ready.

"Not yet. I need to give you a brief rundown of some everyday expressions. *Dobre rano* means good morning. *Dobre noc* means good night."

At that point, Ivy couldn't help giving Karl a look. She wasn't going to be able to retain anymore than that as much as Karl tried, especially with his Southern accent. It was just impossible to stop her train of thoughts and pay attention. Plus he sounded as if he was reciting rules from a traveling book for those visiting during the Communistic era circa 1950. Every feeling, every thought, every emotion was on Olive, not on Slovakian protocol past or present.

"Karl, stop. I promise to rigidly obey all orders and not talk to anyone. Under no circumstances. I will stay in the hotel and wait it out. Don't worry."

Satisfied with the promise she wouldn't speak to anyone, Karl left the room in order for her to get ready. Their first plane would take off in a little under two hours.

The three flights left on almost perfect schedules, the first one from Austin to Houston and the second one from Houston to New York and the third one from New York to the Vienna International Airport. It was customary to fly into Vienna as there were no direct flights from the U.S. to Bratislava, and if you were in a hurry, to take the small ride from Vienna to Bratislava by taxi (as opposed to the train). Ivy read a brochure on the flight to Vienna about Bratislava but her focus drifted often as fatigue prevailed. She did learn that it was the capitol of Slovakia and was situated along the Danube river, the second largest river in Europe and that the city bordered Austria and Hungary. But that was about the most information she could focus on.

She put the brochure back into the pocket in the seat in front of her and turned the knob of the small overhead light until the light faded out. The skies were like a gravel road pocketed with pot holes. Again, sleep was out of the question. She had never cared for flying even in the best of circumstances. Her mother always described her as a white-knuckle flyer, ever since she was a child making the routine visits to Italy and back. But the transcontinental flights were responsible for Ivy having a current passport. Her grandmother had passed away a year ago, just after Ivy had renewed it, thinking she would be taking Olive to meet her great-grandmother. But as bumpy as the plane ride was, her mind was more riveted with thoughts of Olive.

Ivy checked her watch but was too delirious to do the math. She craned her neck backwards to look down the aisle of the plane for Karl, but he was seated too far back to make him out without standing and making it obvious that she was looking for someone. She reclined her seat back, pulled up her thin wool blanket close to her chin and closed her eyes.

Almost a full day after leaving Texas, the final plane began its descent. The pilot's smooth voice awakened her and Ivy attempted to open her eyes. Miraculously she must have slept a little, but her eyes were as heavy as bowling balls and peeling the lids back off them felt like an iron woman endeavor. When they must have been no bigger than two slits narrowed with sorrow and so little sleep in the last few days, she got a look out the window. Vienna was blanketed with thick dark clouds, which obscured any real view of the city. She wasn't a superstitious person. She didn't believe that lit candles going out meant evil spirits were lingering, or that a bride's torn dress would symbolize the end of a marriage through death. She didn't believe that rain on a wedding day would promise fertility or many tears shed during a marriage, or in the Slovakian belief system that it symbolized great wealth. But something about the gloomy conditions outside spoke ominously to her. She thought about the tradition that some countries, including Slovakia, had of the bride being kidnapped on her wedding day, which she found painfully ironic.

As the plane landed and Ivy reached into the bin overhead to remove her carry-on and a backpack full of some small gifts and cards others had given her in the previous days that she hadn't opened yet, she thought of the gifts and advice she had been given since Jeff sued her. Punch had given her a voodoo doll. And Iris, her younger sister told her to put Jeff's name on a piece of paper, crumble it up, wrap it up in tin foil and stick it in her freezer so as to forever freeze him. The staff at Chapel Desidireo (thanks to Punch's big mouth) wrote her a card of sympathy basically suggesting that she just pretend that he was dead and carry on. Ivy had liked that one the best for a while. But it was kind of hard to believe after a week. It was her belief that superstitious beliefs were simply a business and a waste of time to those who weren't earning a living off of them.

The elderly taxi driver was eagerly polite to Ivy. He introduced himself as Bohdan and reached out to shake her hand. She introduced herself as Ivy. *Crap*, she wasn't supposed to use her real name. *Oh well, he was just a taxi driver. How detrimental could it be?* He acted as if he had won the lottery, that of all fifty possibilities, he got a genuine Texan. She wasn't supposed to let that cat out of the bag either. His eagerness to get to know her as they traveled to Bratislava didn't mix well with her exhaustion and emotional state of wanting to be left alone with her thoughts. She sat in the back quietly recollecting all that had taken place so far and followed Karl's orders to keep quiet.

At least Karl wasn't around to catch her goofs. He probably would've shipped her back home on the next plane if he had heard her, she thought. Luckily he was now separated from her until the end; he in a rental car, her in taxis and different hotel rooms and maybe flights home, but she vowed to herself that was the last talking to a stranger she would do. *So what? I made a mistake with the first Slovak person I met. Everyone makes mistakes.* She vowed it wouldn't happen again. She could always call Punch back home for emotional support if she needed it or just needed to talk to someone. She watched out the window as they drove the forty-five minute, thirty mile drive into Bratislava. The bucolic landscape was contradictory ranging from pre-war, post war to modern architecture. Some of the ride was especially bleak with public housing of Communistic tower blocks marching in formation with laundry strung outside under the gray skies. Occasionally, the black graffiti that decorated many of the buildings was broken up with some orange and green scribbles. Just before arriving in the old town square, Ivy caught a glimpse of a golden oriole flying in tandem with the taxi. The sight reminded her of Kirk, the ornithologist she had gone out with before Jeff. It was only because of him she could name the small bright yellow and black bird- a male. Something about seeing this familiar sight made Ivy catch herself yearning for his comfort again. But it was too late. Too many mistakes had been made. Life had taken too many drastic turns since she left him.

Her mind drifted back to the memories of their relationship. She had actually been jealous of his love for birds. She realized how petty that was now. He was the only one who had ever seriously spoken of marriage in the three months they spent together. But it was always about the wedding they would have, not about them. Kirk would talk obsessively of how birds would be the theme of it. There would be bird cages decorated with ribbons as the table center pieces at the reception, birdseed put in envelopes as small party favors, an aviary behind the minister and the two of them full of colorful finches, and her processional song would be a birds mating call. She came to believe he loved birds more than her and put an abrupt end to things. She thought of his bumper sticker that said "I break for birds," which was all too true.

When he first told her what he did for a living the snort chortle came out but instead of him looking at her appallingly like so many of the others, he laughed with her in an equally bizarre fashion. In fact, he told her once they were finished laughing, it was very cool what he did. He informed her of how naïve she was in a gentle way. After all, Bond, James Bond, was named after a very famous ornithologist as the author, Ian Fleming, was a keen bird watcher living in Jamaica when he came up with the idea. Ivy found herself smiling for a second. Kirk had always been full of trivia, especially concerning anything to do with birds. She pictured his house with it's eccentric collection of binoculars and cuckoo clocks hanging from the walls. His backyard was a mish mash of hummingbird feeders, bird baths and other various bird things. He hated scarecrows, snakes, cats and anything and anyone that scared or ate birds. Ivy had promised him early on that she would not eat chicken in front of him,which she had found to be far more difficult than she originally thought.

She wondered what he was doing these days and figured he had probably settled down with a nice girl with similar interests and accepted that probability with a trickle of guilt and regret. The bird was out of sight now and she had bigger and more pressing things to concern herself with.

The taxi pulled into the town center, which was quite a contrast to what they had just traveled through. The old town was riddled with winding cobblestone streets. More than a few climbed up to gargantuan castles perched on thick hilltops. The main roads were lined with placid historical buildings awash in soft pastels. For a minute Ivy thought she might be in a faux European village in Las Vegas; the buildings were so immaculate they didn't seem all that old. There were many handfuls of colorful actors on almost every corner, dressed up re-enacting the city's history in quite a loud and forceful way, as if the people were afraid the city might relive its ugly past unless reminded. Occasionally they would pass a group of British tourists who wore loud clothes that matched their loud voices. The taxi driver waved his hand in irritation as they passed a group. "They come here for weekend. More cheap fly here for weekend than stay home with pub with Guinness." He looked back at Ivy to see if he could register any understanding in her. She was in a daze as she stared out the window. For reiteration he exclaimed, "Is cheap, Slovakia, for English drunk obnoxiousness…"

As the taxi driver was going on and on about the down side of the English tourists, Ivy was noticing the undeniable and surprising beauty of the locals wandering about. Some carried paper bags of vegetables, milk, wine, and long loaves of bread sticking out the top. Some of the younger couples were out on romantic strolls. An assortment of all ages sat outside cafes smoking and drinking coffee. She could tell Maruska had the bone structure but she didn't inherit the rest of the classically stunning raw looks she saw passing outside the taxi's window. Chiseled high cheek bones and icy pale blue eyes seemed to be the norm. It looked like the land of the super model, the old part of her thought, a city put together by Nazis, the new part of her thought. *And a place where the bawdy Englishmen were coming for more than cheep beer,* she thought.

At last, after a mini traffic jam that had them cramped up on a one way street between two other cars and a stone wall on either side of them so close you could touch it if you tried, the taxi finally pulled into the open and made its way to the circular driveway of the hotel.

Hotel Pressburg was a three-storied off-white and bamboo green Viennese art nouveau building that over-looked the river. It was built in the early part of the twenty first century but had been upgraded to include a gym, spa, indoor pool and other modern amenities that Ivy had no interest in as she checked in under her false name.

Karl was surprised that this was where Ivy had wanted to stay. True, it would be more expensive than other places she acknowledged but perhaps more safe as well. And it was close to everything being so nearby the town square. She told him it was for morale and, that she felt their surroundings should be somewhat uplifting given what they were there for. He had been impressed with her fortitude. And the fact that they wouldn't be staying in a dump.

Karl had instructed her to look different too once she arrived since there was no time to work on it before the hasty decision to fly out here. He did not know where Maruska was or if her people had their eyes on them, Karl told her in earnest on the way to the airport.

Karl had also assured Ivy on the way to the Austin Airport that he had great leads on the case. It had been confirmed that Maruska had arrived in Europe three days earlier. For some unknown reason, she had arrived in Budapest from Austin instead of going the typical route to and from Vienna. Perhaps she thought this small glitch could throw things off enough if someone was watching her, or perhaps she had business in Hungary. He was certain he knew what was going on and he had a plan. His words were always spoken with such conviction they tended to put Ivy's spinning out of control mind more at ease, at least temporarily.

Karl explained to her that the two dead men found in the motel were from Bratislava and had links to prostitution rings and trafficking along with arrests for counterfeit IDs and passports. And although there hadn't been any links to kidnapping infants, of course many of the prostitutes and trafickees had been kidnapped to begin with. He wasn't one hundred percent sure how Maruska was tied in, but assured Ivy it would most likely be revealed sooner rather than later.

Ivy sat her luggage down on the hotel bed. The room was modern in contradiction to the hotel's exterior. The bed was low to the ground and dominated the room with its black comforter, gray sheets pulled tightly over the mattress, and pillowcases with their modern prints of gray, black and white triangles and circles overlapping each other. The window was open, letting in the chill of the outside air. Ivy quickly closed it after scanning the view, which mostly consisted of the hotel's driveway and customers walking in and out. It also provided a picturesque view of the river. She remembered Europeans always liking their windows open. To Americans the air would be freezing, causing sniffles and tickling coughs. The Europeans perspective was that it was healthy and fresh and made one strong. Ivy unzipped her suitcase and took out a see-through cosmetic bag that she carried with her to the bathroom. She leaned into the shower stall and after a couple of minutes figured out how to turn the shower on and get the water to warm up and spray. She stripped out of her cold damp sweater and jeans, letting them fall in a clump on the floor. As she looked back up she caught a sudden frightful glimpse at her new gaunt body staring back at her in the bathroom mirror. Her stomach was now scooped in like a bowl and her cheekbones were prominent for the first time in her life. *Great,* she thought. She imagined the headlines when she got back home: "The New Stress Diet: How Ivy Weiss lost 10 pounds suddenly, and you can too! Warning: You must risk losing your child to some unscrupulous former Barbie doll who is fucking the father of your baby who decides on a whim to take your baby to some freezing cold planet to do God knows what with."

She wondered what the most popular religion of Slovakia was and then remembered it was Roman Catholic. *Of course,* Ivy surmised. But she reminded herself it was not her place to get worked up about Catholicism or to suddenly become judgmental. She made a living off of a lot of people who had turned their back on the faith, especially when it was time to get married. Unlike Catholic priests, Ivy wasn't a stickler for the no premarital shacking up rule; she thought every couple should live together before marriage. After all, all marriages were happy, it was the living together afterwards that caused all the problems. It was only one of many jokes about marriage she had heard through the years.

Yes, this country was like another planet, Ivy thought. And then the helplessness jolted through her gut again, like bolts of lightening branching off and charging through the rest of her. She fought the temptation to bury herself in the bed and cry herself to sleep. Instead, she sat atop it waiting for the temperature of the water to be ready. She got up from the bed, her body heavy and tired, and made her way back into the bathroom. The shower was ready, the hot water steaming up the bathroom mirror, erasing her image. Carefully, she stepped into the tiny stall. The steam and hard deodorant soap eventually revived and masked the chill of the night air. She stepped out of the ridiculously small space and grabbed the bottle of black hair dye out of her cosmetic bag that was sitting on the counter, her only import from Misty Falls. Inside the shower stall again, she squeezed out the liquid and lathered the dark inky gel through her hair. Her wet fingers ran down the length from her scalp to the ends careful not to miss a strand. After twenty minutes she rinsed the stains from her hands and shampooed the excess out. Her feet made way to the electrically heated bathroom floors once again. She threw on a monogrammed robe that was hanging from a silk hanger behind the bathroom door, blew her hair dry, called room service for a pair of scissors, gave herself a trendy jagged euro style haircut, got dressed, and then viewed the results.

One more change needed to be made and she was already ahead of the game as she stared at her fresh face in the mirror; no makeup. Too American.

She left the hotel.

It was now close to midnight, but the city was reborn with an aliveness that had escaped the earlier part of the evening as Ivy made her way into the bustling town square. The town square was awash in golden light, emitting from gas lamps that lined uneven streets and alleyways and cast long colorful shadows up the sides of many of the buildings. A laser show played out from the top of an old theatre at the far side of the square that cast a dancing green and yellow neon shadow on the floor of the plaza. Disco and techno music thumped from passing bars. In the quieter corners were cafés that were still buzzing with customers. Couples out for a stroll filled in all the nooks and crannies.

Ivy didn't know what she was looking for. But staying in the hotel room and sleeping were out of the question.

CHAPTER SIXTEEN

arl had purchased two international cell phones. One for him and one for Ivy. Ivy found hers the next morning under her hotel room door in a manila envelope along with a note scribbled with the numbers. She called his but just got ringing on the other end.

It was becoming unbearable. She had no idea what to do with herself but felt almost too numb to do anything anyway. She questioned herself as to whether it was smart that she came here. The thoughts that she had been trying desperately to not let seep into her mind were breaking through, thoughts that perhaps they were too late, that it would take a miracle to find Olive and another miracle that Olive would be okay if they did.

She hugged her knees to her chest as she sat atop the bed. Room service had brought two more kolaches — one with prune filling and the other with grape filling along with thick, muddy brown, and sickeningly sweet Turkish coffee. Now there were four pastries on her bedside table. She stared at them ready to throw up and wondered if there would ever be a day to indulge in fried olives again and if she would even do so if there was.

Then like a lightening bolt she shot up. Something had happened. What exactly she wasn't able to explain to herself. A flicker of recognition, a feeling, a memory out of nowhere? *Deja vu?* She remembered seeing a box on Jeff and Maruska's kitchen table. It was an old grease-stained bright pink pastry box that lay flat on the table. There was a wax like wrapping paper next to it, it seemed as though it had been sent as a gift. It was littered with crumbs and ants hoisting them away to feast. It had the name of something Slovak on it. Pecar? Pekars? She couldn't remember, but it had the name Kvapil on it, too. Ivy had married a couple with that last name not too long ago.

Ivy could still hear the bride telling her over and over again, that at the end of the ceremony she would be introduced as Mrs. Kvapil to her guests and that her last name would be pronounced like Kwah-pil. Before Maruska entered Ivy's life, and before the Kvapil wedding, she hadn't been very aware of the Czechoslovakian population in Texas. But it was a well-known fact that they immigrated to Texas before the first World War because of its rural appeal as Czechs looked at farming as the ideal way of life and Texas soil could grow a nice cash crop for them in the form of cotton. Before a Czech wedding could take place, a couple had to have land on which to farm. It was one of those things that once you were aware of it, you saw things for the first time that have always been around, like kolaches in hot dog warmers at most Texas gas stations.

Ivy raced downstairs and asked the concierge if he knew about the name on the pastry box. She prayed that the bakery was located in Bratislava as he took a moment to look to the heavens to think about it. Ivy looked the odd character over as he did so hoping that he was going to come up with directions to the right place and not send her on a wild goose chase to some pub thinking she was English.

He was rail thin, dressed in a sports jacket with a name tag that said his name was Jozef, and matching slacks with a maroon, white and blue striped tie. He was distinguished, with cotton like hair that took the shape of wings on both sides of his egg-shaped head, with a landing strip running down the middle. His face was mottled with age spots and he stood with a hunch. His mannerisms were elegant, suggesting perhaps he had worked for a king in a past life.

He nodded as Ivy attempted to pronounce the name of the bakery again and asked, "Walk, yes?"

Ivy nodded.

"Novy Most," he said while gesturing for her to follow him to a window that gave a wide picturesque view of the river. Like a show man informing her that she had just won a fabulous washing machine, he used his entire large hand to point out one of the three bridges that hung over the water. One had a weird flying saucer tower thing at the end of it. He extended one outrageously long finger to point out this detail.

On the other side of the river from where Ivy was standing, she could make out a park and very little else other than some people roller blading and walking along the river bank. There were some signs of industrialization in the background but no bakery in sight. With no reason not to, she decided to trust him as her tour director to the bakery. She decided this was as good a time as any to practice her Slovak. "Dob.." The man looked at her quizzically and she gave up. She nodded instead and winked as a last resort to be kind and polite for the gentleman's help.

The concierge thought she was a strange young woman as he watched her hurriedly leave the building. He smiled perplexedly to himself at her charming oddity. He watched out the window as she made her way just to make sure she had understood him. Yes, she was going in the right direction. And then, just like that, she tripped over Cumil. Cumil was one of four quirky statues that the citizens created after the fall of Communism to lighten things up a tad. He was a bronze statue that poked his head out of a manhole, resting his head on his hands. If you weren't looking down it was a fun way for the locals to see who were the tourists. Locals liked to contemplate whether he just cleaned up a sewer or was looking up women's dresses. The concierge turned his back and sighed.

Ivy, embarrassed, got up from the ground. At first she thought it was a real man and got spooked. When she realized who he was she couldn't help but to laugh a little at herself with the rest of the square.

The other side of the bridge was further away than what it looked like from the hotel window and almost an hour later she was asking people on the other side of the bridge the same question. Where was the bakery? Most people didn't understand her or her them-it's location wasn't exactly obvious.

As her fast gait pounded the pavement she heard sounds coming up from behind her. Whirring sounds of small wheels rolling towards her. She turned to look back. It was a teenage boy with most of his hair parted to the right, hanging in his eye. He was riding a skateboard directed right at her. He had headphones on and one hand in a pocket and was looking at the water as he rode the board. Ivy hoped she wouldn't get run over by him and jumped over to the side of the walkway. As he passed her she saw a familiar logo on the back of his sweatshirt. It said SRV. She wracked her brain. What did it stand for? She knew but couldn't place it.

The boy now fifty yards away in front of her plopped his left foot down abruptly on the back end of the board causing the front end to pop up in the air like a teeter-totter. He briskly jumped off, caught it with his right hand, and turned the skateboard around to go towards Ivy. As he got near her she waved her arm to get his attention. Slightly annoyed that his cruising was being interrupted, he stopped the skateboarding and looked up at her expectantly while removing an ear piece. "Do you speak English," she asked.

The boy smiled at her and proudly told her that he did.

"Where is the bakery, do you know of a bakery around here?"

Ivy could tell he was about to ask her if she was from America. But thank God he didn't. She could imagine the conversation taking a lifetime to an enthused Slovak teenager especially when he found out she practically lived in Austin. It wasn't time to get into Stevie Ray Vaughan reminiscing, as much as Ivy loved the blues. The song "Pride and Joy" was already infiltrating the space between her ears as she thought most of the songs lyrics could just as easily be her singing about Olive: "*She's my sweet little thing, she's my pride and joy.*" The boy animatedly explained with his arms and hands where the bakery was located, the left turns she would have to make and the right ones too. She smiled at him and winked her wink that usually elicited a favorable reaction from whomever she gave it to. Little did she know how goofy it looked. The skateboarder skated off chuckling to himself about the funny American woman with a sweet tooth.

She marched up the river two more blocks, turned left, and then another quick left and then saw the building a half block up to the right and set quite a ways back from the street. Pink, like a gigantic cake box. No wonder she couldn't see it from the hotel or when she got to the other side of the bridge. It stood amongst itself like a sore thumb in the midst of a small park like forest. Climbing vines of what were once bright pink, red and white roses snaked their way up and around the building, their browning and dying limbs now looked like a cage around the building.

Her heart beat like a metronome set at 200. Again, she wasn't sure of what she was looking for, but she knew she had to be exact in her actions so as not to cause a scene, another one of Karl's rules. No calling attention to oneself or looking like a tourist. She pushed through the blackened glass doors slowly and was engulfed in a warm sticky aromatic cloud of cinnamon, sugar, and vanilla that mixed in a heavenly perfume with the musky and sweet smelling rose vines from outside.

In front of her stood rows and rows of blueberry and plum bublalinas, Hungarian cream puffs, yeast bread rolls with walnut fillings, Polish cheesecake, dobosh tortes with caramel toppings, chocolate crepes with mounds of whip cream, strudel, cheese danishes, vanilla and nutmeg custards, braided sweet breads, dumplings bursting with poppy seed, plum, apricot and cherry fillings and rows and rows of chocolates in the shapes of castles and the funny UFO looking building and some x-rated ones too. It was enough to make you want to break the display case and roll around in all the dough and clouds of whip cream.

Overwhelmed, Ivy did not notice the young girl at the counter waiting on her. She pointed to something although she had no idea what it was. The girl said something in Slovak, pointed at one of the very few tables for Ivy to sit at and then went back to the kitchen where she talked to a tall blond man who appeared to be the baker.

Ivy took a seat at the white table top, still damp with wet streaks from being sponged off after its last customers. In what seemed like only seconds, the counter girl returned with a warm pillowy powdered sugar dusted pastries. She gently placed them down in front of Ivy. Ivy nodded to her in appreciation, unfolded her napkin, placed it in her lap, then took a bite of the delicious treat. She looked up as she wiped the powder from her lips, catching herself making the mistake with the napkin. The baker was staring at her. He rolled up his sleeves with his large thick hands covered with flour and rings. Silver rings. Crosses. Skulls. He tilted his head to the side as if she was edging him on. Or was he stretching his neck? Ivy pretended she hadn't noticed him and looked away pretending to be at one with her pastry. But just before she did, she saw the cross tattoo on his forearm. Ivy thought Jeff had said one of Maruska's victims had this same tattoo.

Ivy nearly fell out of her chair. Was there a connection? *Stay cool* she told herself. Even if he was somehow involved and had seen a picture of her, there was no resemblance to the old Ivy whatsoever.

The young girl came back to the table to check in on Ivy who pretended she was suddenly full with a patting motion to her stomach. The young girl smiled while taking the plate back to the counter and and then returned with Ivy's order in a neatly creased white bakery bag and said slowly chopping up the words "Fo-you-fwesh" and smiled again in part at her bravery for speaking English. Her cheeks turned the sweet side of red.

Ivy nodded, smiled, paid and left as fast as she could. The baker had been eying her curiously. She was sure of it. And how in the hell did the girl know she was American? Fo-you fwesh? It was like a bad Natasha Kinski movie. Was Natasha Kinski Slovakian? She had met her once at the Bel Aire Hotel at a party her dad took her to while she was in high school for some famous clients of his. Natasha was very beautiful in person and sweet too. She was certain though that she had heard Andy Warhol was Slovakian now that she was thinking about it. *Who cares?* Why was she thinking about Natasha Kinski and Andy Warhol now of all people? Maybe it was some safety net the brain was throwing around her organ making sure it strayed every once in a while before it got locked up in one crazy thinking zone about real things in moments of stress. *Get focused Ivy, for Christ sake, if not now in your life, when?!* But the bottom line was she hadn't spoken a word. To blame it on the napkin was a waste of time Ivy justified to herself. Hell, Slovakians had to have learned the conveniences of placing a napkin on their lap. What if a table was covered to the hilt with food and plates, wine glasses, water glasses and there was no room anywhere else? Surely some did it. Where had Karl gotten all of his information from anyhow? She knew she had put herself in a precarious situation however, and vowed to not leave the hotel room again. From now on she would follow Karl's rules. But first she had to tell him.

Ivy took an indirect route back to the Hotel Pressburg. It wasn't exactly a marked trail. She kept the hotel in her sight once her eyes first latched onto its whereabouts as she left the bakery. It was just a zigzaggy route meant to confuse in case anyone was watching. Once in her room she threw the bag of pastries in the trash can without thinking, dead bolted the door with one hand, and called Karl as fast as she could with the other. He answered this time.

"Karl? Oh my God, you're not going to believe what just happened!"

There was no reaction on the other line but the tension could be felt.

"I just got back from this bakery I remembered seeing the name at Jeff's and Maruska's house and there was this man that worked there with this tattoo of a switchblade." What was wrong with him, wondered Ivy. He wasn't acting excited or interested. He wasn't saying anything.

"Karl!"

Finally he responded. "Ivy, stay calm. Stay in the hotel and don't leave again. You hear me?"

Deflated, Ivy said she understood. The unspoken message of him wanting his freedom to be left alone to think about what she just told him was loud and clear. They hung up. She checked the hotel door to her room again. It was as locked as it could be.

CHAPTER SEVENTEEN

Karl Muehller was making headway. In fits and starts. The rental car did not work out. He had gotten pulled over three times already. The first time was simply an alcohol checkpoint. Karl had been swerving by default into the right lane. Luckily he hadn't been drinking. Twenty minutes later he was pulled over again for using a cell phone while driving, which was outlawed in Slovakia. And the third time, he had made a right hand turn on a red light. Another traffic violation. The last thing he needed was to start calling attention to himself or wind up in jail. He had never been out of the country and too many years of following rules of the road in America made him a shitty contestant for doing the opposite. The driver's seat on the left side and the driving in the left lane were two rules he couldn't seem to remember and his body just seemed to naturally resist it. Luckily both times the cops had laughed it off. The third time they weren't so nice. They let him go eventually, but he wasn't going to take any more chances. He had the concierge return the rental car, a maroon Ford Focus and now he was going to solely rely on his feet and professional drivers, notably taxi drivers. Now, he just had to come up with a plan that wouldn't give him away. He knew that as long as Ivy remained still and calm, there might be a chance of getting Olive back. Her little private snooping could be seriously detrimental to the cause. He wanted to kick himself for letting her come along. How many times had he told himself not to let it happen? But she was persistent. And he was always a sucker for pretty girls. And she was more than just that, she was a good person who did not deserve this. Karl had seen a lot in his time. His work began as a policeman with the Fredericksburg P.D., but he soon transferred to the Austin Police Department where he had seen it all: pedophiles, rapists, ax-murderers on campus – you name it. Austin did a good job of keeping its precious Live Music Capitol of the World image in tact, but he knew only too well the crime that took place behind the scenes of many of the bars. Various club goers and a crazy musician here and there, not to mention the rest of the population harboured all sorts of deviants. But he'd never been in close personal contact with a mother who had lost her infant. Ivy was holding up well, all things considered. He couldn't imagine the real pain and torment she must be feeling. Or maybe he could. While Karl was growing up, his father had owned a history museum in Fredericksburg that largely focused on World War II holocaust relics and original photographs. One night when the cleaning crew didn't show up, he opened up the janitorial closet to take on the job himself and was met with a white supremacist who proceeded to strangle the life out of him. He and his father had been close, his mom had died when he was nine from breast cancer. When Karl found out about his dad's murder, instead of grieving, he made up his mind right then and there he would do something to protect the good from the evil. He knew he would become a policeman. He knew it since he was 17, the age he was when his father died.

The police work was rewarding. Karl had been recognized by his peers with many awards and other adulations. However, the red tape of the bureaucracy drove him crazy and he didn't fit in with the rest of the beer drinking macho men he worked with. It seemed to Karl on more than a few occasions that they didn't have their hearts in the work the way he did. And perhaps as a result, he did his best work alone, so he decided to quit the force and work independently.

He knew where the baby was. He was almost certain of it. That was if she was still in Slovakia and if she was still alive. The information he was retrieving was touchy with a client so nearby and potentially threatening. But he was almost certain he found the ties that connected Maruska with the two dead men. Many years ago, there was a woman involved in a particular gang here, but her stint was short lived and it was strictly hearsay with the local police. It couldn't be proved, and there were no pictures or credible witnesses. Just a bit of an urban legend for lack of a better analogy Karl thought. But he believed the woman really did exist and very likely could have been Maruska. He told Ivy what he could without revealing too much while still maintaining honesty. He knew Ivy was a strong woman, stronger than she herself knew, but he didn't want to tell her what he thought worst case scenario was. Not yet and hopefully never.

He had spent the last two nights trolling Vajnorska Street. He had picked up two prostitutes- one per night. But instead of having sex with them, he paid them to talk to him. He had cruised the streets quietly and carefully picking them out. The most important thing was that they come from the house at the far end of the street.

Casually, he gave them his bogus story of losing his beloved wife recently to a brain tumor. How she became deathly ill in a matter of weeks and then one day he found her dead lying in bed next to him. And how the shock and loneliness drove him to this country for a small vacation and companionship. He explained to them that it was not legal in the United States like it was in Slovakia to hire someone like them. So he had to come here to fill his void. He and his wife had wanted a baby so bad....and from there he would let them talk in hopes of mentioning a baby for sale. Neither one of them mentioned a baby for sale, but they both mentioned that one of the other girls had suddenly appeared in the home with a baby in tow out of nowhere. They had never noticed that she was pregnant or had stopped working the streets. He could tell they were scared when they told him of this. He wasn't sure if it was because they had been warned not to mention it or if it was the fear of themselves becoming pregnant by one of their pimps or clients. Usually the pimps made sure the girls weren't in the position to become impregnated so Karl was surprised to hear of the girl with the baby.

He was surprised and elated. His instincts were possibly correct this time. As he had made his way into the brothel with the second girl, he had seen the aforementioned girl in the kitchen with the baby. Both nights Karl had noticed the stunning girl with the infant whom she fed from a bottle holding it cradle style in her arms. She normally came out of the house and walked Vajnorska Street between midnight and one in the morning. She had come out of the same modern home with the high wire fence around it at the end of the street that he had gone into with the other girls. The home that housed Vojtech. At first he didn't think she was a prostitute. She looked too self-assured and did not seem strung out like the majority of the others, including the two he had spent time with. He had tried to approach her both nights, but she was in high demand and someone always appeared from out of nowhere and beat him to the punch. That is why he had settled on the other two. Karl's plan was to be the first to get her the next night, which would be Christmas. He set out the plan in his head to get there earlier in the evening, just in case she had an earlier shift when there weren't so many johns vying for her attention or if the routine around Vojtech was different on a holiday.

CHAPTER EIGHTEEN

Ivy had been in the icy slush of Bratislava for three days but it felt more like thirty years. Tomorrow would be Christmas. The few people on the streets were uncommonly jolly. She had noticed the people never seeming so happy until today. It made her feel worse. Especially with the harsh reminder that she and Olive might not be celebrating her daughter's first Christmas together. She wouldn't allow herself to think past that thought today. But then it happened. She simply couldn't control her thinking like she used to and the realization of her baby being gone, possibly forever, hit her like someone wrenching her insides out.

She had stayed in the hotel almost the entire day except for one small meal of Hungarian goulash stew with thick chewy sour dough bread at an Irish pub called The Dubliner and a small stroll to burn off some of the anxiety afterwards. She was doing her best of leaving Karl alone to do his job, but the lack of contact made the situation even more upsetting. This caused her mind to go places she was ashamed to think about. She had never been so alone in her life. She sat on the edge of the bed clutching her cell phone in her pocket awaiting his calls that came in randomly and never revealed much. For the most part Karl would just check in with her to see how she was holding up. When she asked how things were going and if anything new had happened or if he knew where Olive was, he typically abruptly ended the conversations with the reminder to her to follow the rules-sometimes going over one rule in particular emphatically, the one she had just broken. She felt like a prisoner in the hotel even with its luxurious surroundings. Her prison guard forever giving her timeouts.

She decided to put a call into Punch. She thought it might make her feel better. The hotel operator took down the number and connected the call.

Punch picked up after eight rings.

"Ivy! Oh my God, it's so good to hear from you. How are you? What's going on!?"

Punch's speech was so effervescent and fast it took Ivy a second to readjust herself to the cultural shock of it. "Oh Punch. It's so great to hear your voice. Um..." There was a long moment of silence as Ivy swallowed back the tears. "I don't know how I am doing to be honest. It's hard. I don't know what's going on. Karl wants to be left alone. He hardly tells me anything. I don't know if I should have come here or not. I am so lonely and miserable and scared and I can't stop picturing Olive. There's nothing to do. He wants me to just sit in this hotel room. How am I supposed to just sit in this room and do nothing? I have to do something. I am her mother! Doesn't he understand that? I can't just sit here and watch the hours tick away. I have these terrible thoughts. I try to control them and I just can't. I just don't know."

She burst into tears after she had done her best to hold them back. She wanted to talk and hear what Punch had to tell her, not spend the conversation crying. She regained her composure after Punch's silence on the other end. "I don't know what I am doing here. I feel so hopeless, helpless. I can't make sense out of anything he does. He doesn't tell me anything. I hate it here. I want to be home with you and Olive like we...." She lost control again.

Punch took a deep breath on the other line. "Ivy, this, if there ever was a time, is a time to have faith. You of all people should remember that. Stay positive. Sounds like you're in good hands with Karl even as redneck as he is. But seriously Ivy, hang in there. Okay? We're all praying for you. Yes, even me. I am praying too. I haven't stopped since that night at your house. We love you. The staff at Chapel Desiderio is anxious for you to come home and to see Olive again and even the Digest just ran an article about you. The whole town not to mention the entire state of Texas is besides itself with this story and while I have you on the line..."

"What? The Digest what?" Suddenly the tears dried up and a new emotion was settling in. "Oh no, you told them about this? It wasn't supposed to get out there." It was another one of Karl's rules that her friends weren't to talk to the press yet about it. She forgot to tell Punch of all people.

Punch hemmed and hawed a bit and Ivy knew she had her answer. Punch just couldn't keep her trap shut no matter what. "Punch, no more, okay."

"Okie dokie. Just thought the more people who knew the more could help. That's all Ive."

Punch always called her Ive when she was at her most heartfelt. She knew Punch's intentions weren't malicious in the slightest, that she really did care. But it bothered her that she took such liberties sometimes. Anything to get her name in print for writing and the Digest was a respected local paper in Austin. "You were going to say something else before I cut you off." As usual Punch monopolized the conversation but Ivy welcomed the distraction for once.

"Yeah, well, I know it's not really the time or place to bring this up but lucky me gets to take over all the religious ceremonies while you're gone and they're killing me Ivy. I don't think I can say 'God bless you' one more time with a straight face or recite Corinthians one more time without puking. We need you home for so many reasons. I just know you are going to come home with Olive. All the signs are here."

Ivy wasn't sure what she was talking about with the mention of "all the signs are here." If it was just simply because she couldn't handle the religious ceremonies, that wasn't what she wanted to hear. That wasn't the kind of talk she was used to from Punch but she decided it was best not to ask any questions. "Punch I am sure you are doing a great job." Ivy said blowing her nose hard into Punch's ear. The tissue never left her side. Ivy hoped some of the good sorts of people Ivy married were rubbing off on Punch and she wouldn't be so hard headed from then on about doing the religious ceremonies. Besides, these days even when people said they wanted a religious ceremony you could hardly tell it was once they were through putting in their own two cents in about it.

"Well I did get a big tip the other day."

Ivy smiled. "Just promise me I will have a job when I come home." She rubbed the excess wet off her face with the tissue.

"Amen. No worries cuz I don't know if I can take it much longer."

They hung up with the promise they would be in touch every day from then on. Punch told her she loved her and Olive Oil too and she couldn't wait to see them soon. And she knew she would.

Evening fell sooner than usual Christmas Eve and Ivy's restlessness was making her want to jump out of her skin. She had spent the day bundled up in the bed for the most part with depression, boredom and helplessness overwhelming her. She was glad she had Punch's calls to look forward to from then on. It was a great morale boost for her to hear the familiarity of her voice even if she was up to some typical shenanigans. Ivy thought of all the things she could do while keeping her promise to Karl to stay inside: she could watch television, she could stare out the window, and she could call room service. Her mind drew a blank for what else. She had packed a bright red journal with a heart and a key on the front cover. Punch had given it to her before she left. She took it out of her backpack for the first time. She groped for a pen that she knew hid at the bottom. She wrote for the first time on the first page: "Waited for the sun to shine and the day that everything would be okay. Instead never knew anything and the skies stayed gray." She reread it and slammed the book shut and threw it and the pen back in the bag. She jumped up from the bed, pacing the room and taking in the sounds that surrounded her. It was so quiet she wasn't sure she was hearing the inside of her ears buzz or the chirping of a million crickets in a low decibel hum. She looked at her watch. It was slightly past six and as cold as it was outside and without a plan Ivy bundled up for what she told herself was an "intuition run." And if Karl caught her, well then that was just too damn bad. She would remind him of the fee she was paying him and for what? And of the fact that it had gotten her nowhere fast.

There was a street called Krizna. And another one called Vajnorska. She had not seen them yet but had overheard some young Englishmen in the pub when she had grabbed the bowl of beef ghoulash comparing notes about their seedy reputations and comparing the girls on them to those on the streets of Amsterdam.

One of the men, the homelier of the two, thought Amsterdam took the lead and the other who was quite attractive and Ivy found herself surprised that he would even be talking about such things as clean cut as he looked, was arguing that he was out of his mind. The conversation became more and more difficult to understand the louder and more drunk they became. Something was calling her to go to the streets, to have a look around. But was it the good forces or the evil forces she wondered. She came to the conclusion that it's always hard to tell.

As she walked out the front door of the hotel, her soul absorbed the ominous stillness. Everything seemed surreal. She turned around to go back to her hotel room but then turned the other way.

The streets outside were quiet, but as she made her way up the square, a new life was happening.

The cafés and boutiques were buzzing with intimate customers. Small Christmas trees lined the walkways, naked to the American eye because of their simplicity, without the overcrowded ornaments. People sipped on hot cabbage soup in the cafés in part for warmth as much as custom. Churchgoers dutifully walked to the Blue Church for midnight mass. Bakeries merrily displayed oblatky, gingerbread and candy cane cookies in their store front windows as Ivy strutted past. People eyed her strangely. She couldn't help but feel it. It was as if they knew.

Ivy decided not to make any more eye contact. A detail Karl had mentioned but she had forgotten. He just had too many rules. It was impossible to remember them all let alone obey the ones she could remember. The last time she thought about his rules she counted how many there were. She could recall fifteen but she knew there were more. Maybe the people thought she was a hooker. Of course they did. Why else would a girl be alone at this time of night on Christmas Eve? Unless she was on her way to meeting someone. Yes, that was the air she would put on. She was off to meet someone. But who? Why, her daughter of course. She had forgotten what it was like to smile as her mouth took on a new form. She did her best to squash all the negative thoughts and to completely let her intuition take over but it wasn't easy. An empty feeling came towards her as she hit Krizna street. She walked up and down it a couple of blocks but something didn't resonate. She didn't know whether to keep listening to herself or not, but decided she didn't have much to lose at this point.

She made her way back towards Vajnorska street instead. The sky darkened and the holiday atmosphere that she had just passed seemed to be slowly dissipating as she made her way to the infamous street.

The street was a hodgepodge of filthy looking Chinese food restaurants, strip clubs, sex shops and t-shirt and souvenir shops with respectable looking offices buildings and shopping interspersed in between. All of them closed. There were still a handful of women soliciting, most of them very young. She had been warned to be wary of them (another of Karl's rules) as many simply posed as prostitutes but were in actuality thugs preying on tourists to rob. She passed a few clustered here and there. Occasionally one would tease her in Slovak for a trick. At one point a very short and overweight girl with long wavy chestnut hair dressed in a red and green knit scarf and cap jumped in front of her, looked her up and down and made a comment in Slovak that had the rest of the group in stitches. She kept moving fast, keeping her gaze forward and down at her snow covered boots. She told herself to slow down, to not walk so fast after she saw the blurs the boots were leaving in her quick-panicked strides. Too American. Europeans don't hurry. She was calling too much attention to herself. Karl would have a fit if he saw her racing around like this. She put her hands in her pockets and took on the more casual approach of the locals to blend in. She passed a car with its interior lights still on. A man and woman were inside having sex. She kicked off a condom that had latched onto her boot and was flopping in the wind.

Her legs were tired and cramped from all the walking and cold. And at the same time, she could barely feel them. She was tired. She needed a rest. She felt heavy and numb. As her eyes scanned for a bench to plop down on she saw Karl.

He was dressed different. He still wore jeans but they were of a different cut and the shirt he wore beneath his jacket was button-up. His hair was slicked back. And he too had taken on a different energy to his normal gait. He was across the street. He was ambling towards a home at the end of it, casually, as if out for a daily stroll. His hands were submerged in the pockets of his coat. Her heart began racing. *Was Olive near?*

She knew he didn't see her as his back was to her. If there were more people on the street, she might not have recognized him.

She looked at the home he was walking towards. It was plain and flat without any adornments and without trees or landscape. Very few windows. It seemed to be a post war cream colored stucco building surrounded by what looked like an electrical fence that decided who entered and more importantly, who got let out.

The gate of the fence flew open and at first Ivy could not place the man walking out but then realized it looked like the man from the Kvapil bakery.

The man stood at the sidewalk, eyed the street both ways and headed straight across. He then started down the sidewalk straight towards Ivy. Her eyes could now adjust as he was lit more by the street lights and closer. He wore a black leather bomber jacket with metal studs. She could not see his arm or tattoo but was sure it was the same man. Just as he had left the house, Ivy saw Karl make a quick turn to one of the side streets alongside the house.

Ivy's heart pounded and not knowing what else to do she continued her gait in the same direction. It would only be a matter of moments before she and the man would inevitably pass. The moment came and Ivy did not look up.

She was certain that he recognized her as his gait slowed for a second and she could feel him turning around to do a double take. She told herself to be casual and walk, walk, walk away.

She made it to the end of the block where she turned to get out of his line of vision if he were to look back again.

She stopped behind a pale salmon-colored and brown trimmed, baroque style building that housed a real estate agency. It was the last building on the block.

The side street she was now standing on was dreadful and as much as she did not want to continue down Vajnorska, it looked as if it may be the wiser decision, but she wanted to see what was going on first.

She peered around the corner of the building to Vajnorska Street. She folded her hair behind her ears so it wouldn't fly out in front of her; the chilly wind was becoming unkind, stinging her face where her hair left gaps allowing it to nip.

She saw the bakery man exit a building a few minutes later. She wasn't sure what building it was but thought it was a market as it was the only thing she remembered passing that was still open. The man clutched a brown paper bag with a package that was too large for it and it jutted out of the top. The man looked up and down the street carefully before heading back to the house.

Ivy got a look at the package he was carrying. There was a picture on it. It was a baby. The package was diapers.

Frantically she eyed the street up and down for Karl. He was nowhere to be found. The cell phone! She called him.

"Yes." He answered in a low voice full of irritation.

"She's there. There. The home you were just walking towards. The one with the fence!"

Karl was in an alleyway behind the home timing himself to pick up Dalena before any other suitors could. He hoped like hell to avoid being seen by Andel, Arnost's brother, whom he wanted as little contact with as possible.

As Ivy rambled on frantically on the other end, Karl had no choice but to hang up on her. Dalena had left the home and was about to walk past him. His intuition was right on. She was working an earlier shift for the holiday. If he was quick he could get her. Andel had just walked past with a bag of diapers sticking out of the bag.

Karl was so close. So close that he knew any errors from this point on would sabotage the entire effort. He hated it that Ivy had just phoned him. He was inwardly panicking about her presence. Panicking was not something he normally did but this involved an infant and he feared Ivy was losing control. *What was she doing out here? Dammit!* She never listened to a single thing he told her. He wished like hell that he had never let her come along. She wasn't the passive young woman he had met in Misty Falls any longer.

"Hello," Karl said as Dalena strutted past him. He was sure the American voice would be far more enticing than a locals or a British accent. He was also hoping she would speak it or at least understand it. He had weighed this choice heavily, knowing that at the same time an American could raise suspicions in the household of Vojtech. But when Karl had been there the last two nights, no one seemed to care or notice. Probably because most everyone was drugged out or further occupied. Plus Vojtech was very well known for its arrogance as the group had gotten away with far more than it hadn't.

Dalena did a 180. Her hair was a thick and smooth auburn. Her hooded green eyes were dotted with black flecks dancing in her irises, her lips fleshy and soft, protruding cheek bones, milky skin. Her nose was unusual-small but slightly odd shaped with a round bump towards the tip. One of those flaws that couldn't detract from the otherwise overwhelming beauty. She wore a forest green beret, her face was without makeup except for thick black eyeliner on her upper lids. She was bundled up in a wool trench coat and stiletto heeled boots that gave her profession away as no one else in their right mind could walk in this ice without breaking their neck in them. Silently she looked him up and down with her nose and chin in the air. She turned back around and started walking again.

"Wait, wait, please!" Karl called after her.

She kept walking.

He did a slight skip to jump start himself into a run to catch up with her.

"Please go away. I don't want no trouble."

"I won't be any trouble. I promise you. Just talk. Please just talk?"

She kept looking around to see if anyone was watching.

Karl kept in stride alongside her.

Frustrated with his tenacity, she stopped dead in her tracks. "I want you go now. No talk, no nothing" she told him firmly, still looking around as she did so.

Karl, unwilling to cause attention to them, stopped following her when she took up walking again.

He stood there in the snow watching her walk away.

He turned around and began to walk in the direction of the home again.

He was sunk. Why was the girl so adamant about not being with him? Did she know anything about him? Or was she just paranoid of customers who didn't want sex?

Then suddenly she was there by his side walking with him again.

"Please, turn. Get off this street" she begged him.

Karl turned on the next cross street. It was quiet and dark. Only a few twinkling strings of Christmas lights in the small square apartment windows above.

"I don't know you. I know not who you are. But I have feeling you lie. You see the other girls two nights and no sex. I don't trust you-you American right?"

"Yes, I am American. My wife died...."

"Yes, I know. I hear story. Is bullshit."

"No, no it's not bullshit. Why would I come here otherwise? Please, no offense but the only thing your city is famous for in America is a horror film about a hostel where everyone turns into a hamburger," he watched the madness in her eyes set in and then a small corner of her lip turned into an upward pointing arrow when he finished, "and.... its beautiful women." He waved his hand towards her for reference. "Please, I am serious. I am lonely. I want company. I traveled far. I am not here to cause problems. I have just seen you the last two nights but others always beat me." His attraction was real but his story was so full of shit and he prayed he could get her to buy it like the others. She was the ticket to solving this. He knew it.

"Where are you from? Sound like Texas."

He laughed, "Close but no cigar as we say back home. Mississippi."

"Mississippi?" She could barely say it and laughed at herself as she tripped over the word.

"That's right" he smiled at her.

She smiled back.

She turned around again to see if anyone was watching and then remembered she was on a different street.

She stared at him again. Up and down.

She was too smart, Karl thought. He wasn't sure if she'd bought his story or not. His heart was racing in his shivering body. He wondered if he had just botched up everything without Ivy's help. Speaking of Ivy, he hoped like hell she had left the scene and gone back to the hotel. He made a mental note to keep an eye out for her on Vajnorska street once he got back there again.

"So what's it going to be? You want to be with me? The lonely man from M-I-SS-I-SS-I-PP-I?"

She laughed only to regain control of herself quickly.

"Okay" she said. "But I want paid now."

Karl agreed and handed her the money. It was good for at least two hours, he thought. If all went well he might not need that much time.

He had to get in the house again and this time he needed to get a good look at the baby. And he needed to get the baby out of the house discreetly if it was Olive and he was most certain it was. He wasn't sure how he would do it but he trusted that he would know at the time. He learned the hard way not to plan too far in advance in situations with so many variables. Pure instinct at the right time usually worked best.

The girl turned back to walk towards the house. Karl just a few steps behind her.

After a few steps she turned around and seemed hesitant to continue. But she carried on and together they entered through the prickly gate.

CHAPTER NINETEEN

Ivy lost track of Karl after the hang up. In an odd feeling of pure desperation, panic and steely determination she crossed the street back towards the house.

She looked for surveillance cameras but didn't see any. She kept her head low though, just in case.

If someone was to come out of the house and ask her what she was doing, she would have no idea what to tell them.

She walked the sides and back of the house searching for answers. The front of the house was out of her league as a barbed wire fence surrounded it and the front door. At the back of the house, a girl looked down on her from one of the above windows. Ivy was hoping she wasn't waiting for her to save her. They locked eyes for a second but then a man's voice yelled out at her. A hand grabbed her by the shoulder and yanked her away from the window.

Then he appeared. It was the bakery man. He looked at what seemed directly at her. She pressed her body in as tightly as she could into the building and prayed a crazy incoherent prayer, thinking that she was going to see her life flash before her eyes any second. But the man closed the window and nothing else happened.

Ivy knew she was playing with fire being so close to whatever was going on in this house. But she knew Olive was there waiting for her. She knew it like she knew her own name. A part of her wanted to leave before something terrible happened, but the other part of her made her stay as she remembered the most terrible thing would be never seeing her again.

She crept alongside the other side of the house and was edging her way back around again when she heard the code of the gate being punched in and then watched it slowly creak open as Karl and a young girl walked through. Ivy wasn't sure who the girl was. She didn't look like the other girl who watched her from the window. This girl looked alert and attractive. The other girl looked strung out and sloppy.

She thought Karl might have just seen her at the very last second. Something internally seemed to shift in him and she thought it was him seeing her. But she couldn't be sure.

It was freezing. Ivy's pants were wet all the way through from the snow and ice, and a collection had gathered on the outside of her jeans of mud and dead plant debris. Her jaw shook in fear and from the chill. She sat down against the frame of the house feeling frozen, paralyzed. She couldn't feel her legs or feet.

Just wait, she thought. As she did, she became more and more scared and cold with each passing minute.

CHAPTER TWENTY

The young girl led Karl through the parlor. It was decorated with a sticky red tile floor with thin trails of gold paint threading throughout. A cheap attempt at looking opulent. Through a plaster archway to the left was the kitchen. A wobbly table covered with needles, crusty plates and the package of diapers sat on the edge.

The inside of the house was loud in contrast to its quiet exterior with radios blaring and people arguing. Once in a while there was a loud thump as if someone was being thrown across a room. Karl strained for the telltale sounds of an infant but heard nothing.

The young girl made her way up the stairs, leading her American client, who was going by the name of "Ted," to her private room. She was the only girl who had the use of one room solely for herself. The others had to share rooms and take turns with clients.

As they started up the stairwell, Andel stood atop leaning over the railing watching them.

He gave the girl an intimidating look, showing his disgust with her and her new client when she looked up and caught his eyes.

"Who's this?" he asked her in Slovak.

She answered back in Slovak that it was none of his fucking business, that he would be paid so leave her alone.

Andel gave Karl a snarl as they walked past.

Andel laughed inside at her. *The bitch.* She thought she was something special. He was pissed that Arnost had given her so many privileges. *Why? Just because she was born beautiful?* He hated her. Hated the attention she got. He wished Pavol had stuck to his real taste with the trampy whores he usually dragged in. *Where in the hell did she come from anyway? And why did she always get the fucking Americans and Englishmen?* Andel was a true xenophobe. He hated everything and everyone that wasn't from where he was.

He smiled to himself. At least now with Maruska back and Arnost and Pavol gone he could probably dispose of her in due time. In the meantime he needed her help with the infant until that was taken care of. Maruska wasn't around much and he had his bakery front to keep up with. Getting rid of her would also get rid of the foreigners she dragged back to the house as well.

All the other girls had taste; they picked Slovak men as their customers. He knew it was really because none of the others could speak English like her, but he didn't want to think about that. He loved his brother and part of him wanted to kill Maruska, too, but he knew her offer was the best thing-sell the baby to the right buyer and put her back to work in Vojtech. With his brother gone he had too much power with the Russians depending on him and was scared of it. Maruska had the skills and the knowledge and already knew too much anyway. *Women. Always a fucking problem.*

The thought of getting rid of the baby and eventually the girl relaxed him a tiny bit and he went back into his room.

The girl led Karl into a room that was surprisingly pleasant compared to what he had just walked through. There was no proper bed, just a mattress on the floor that was carefully made up and the walls were covered with posters of U2 and Sophia Loren. She unzipped her boots, took them off and sat on the mattress. Quietly, she told Karl as she pulled him down next to her that he had to get undressed with her. She explained that he had been lucky the last couple of nights without being caught but if Andel walked in on them and things didn't look normal it would mean a lot of trouble.

Karl agreed and proceeded to undress himself self consciously layer by layer and then jumped under the tattered comforter before she could get a good look, but something told him she already had and was pleased with what she saw. His skin slightly brushed against hers. The sensation was suddenly warm and tingly.

The tips of her glossy hair lightly dusted his chest and shoulder and her nipples stuck out from the comforter as if they were playing peek-a-boo with him.

She noticed the shift in sexual tension and then pulled the comforter up to cover them.

"So. What you want talk about?" she asked slightly irritated.

"What is your name?"

"Dalena."

"Dalena? That is a very beautiful name."

"What was your wife's name?" she turned to look him square in the eyes.

"Elizabeth."

"Elizabeth what?"

"Elizabeth Edwards."

Silence.

She shifted back down in the comforter and stared at the ceiling.

Karl thought she was trying to picture what an "Elizabeth Edwards" looked like and wondered if she was picturing an image that looked like the Elizabeth Edwards in the American news if she followed it-the one that had been married to the cheating senator.

Quickly she turned over to him again.

"I know not what you want but I know you no tell truth."

Karl waited for her to reveal herself.

"I know suddenly baby here and then you here. The man who want talk only. Is strange, no?"

"What baby?"

She looked deep into his eyes and studied them.

"The girl baby." She sat upright and grabbed a packet of cigarettes from a table next to the mattress. With hard slaps on the bottom of the package, she finally got one to succumb.

She lit it and took a long hard drag and then stared back at the ceiling again, the ashes drifting to the comforter. "I tell you what I want talk about. This fucking hell hole. Three years I be here. Me and maybe four, five other girls. All on heroin. I see this right away. I cooperate and help so they don't inject me with the drugs but what good do? I still here. I escape once they make sure I never forget. And now a baby. What the hell they do with a beautiful innocent baby girl? Inject it with drugs, too? Make it perfect girl who never ever know different?" She buried her head between her knees.

Karl watched her in silence. He wondered if the next time she raised her head if there would be tears.

She lifted her head back up. There were no tears but much anguish behind her dark green eyes.

"So, Mr. America? What you want talk about?"

The music that was blaring from downstairs abruptly stopped. A hard thud of footsteps was making their way up the stair case. The thin door to the bedroom shook with every step.

Dalena snubbed out the cigarette on the linoleum floor and jumped on top of Karl wrapping the comforter around their waists covering their private areas below.

The door to the bedroom swung open all the way and Andel appeared in the frame silently watching, his arms folded.

Dalena turned around to look at him as if to tell him to mind his own business.

He looked at her, sneered and closed the door.

Dalena stayed on top, fearful that Andel would come snooping again. They heard the footsteps go back down the stairs. The music was turned back up.

She bent down and whispered into Karl's ear.

"You come for baby?"

"Yes," Karl said praying this was the right answer.

"Why?" she asked.

"I know the mother," Karl answered realizing he answered too quickly and it didn't sound exactly right.

She sat up away from his face and stared hard into it again trying to make sense of the answer he had just given her. At first Karl thought he really blew it, the answer couldn't have possibly made sense to her under the circumstances, but then she unstraddled herself and got up from out of the makeshift bed. The smooth porcelain skin of her soft and narrow body practically glowed in the dark. She cracked open the bedroom door and peeked through looking both directions. Quickly and quietly she closed it.

"Second room on right. Go now. Hurry. He go with his girl now. Go before he tell you to leave and he bring baby back to my room." She was standing now, her hand motions frantic. "You only opportunity. Go, get baby. Do not come back never!" She screamed in a whisper.

Karl wasn't sure he was hearing right. He was supposed to get the baby out of the second room?

He looked at her quizzically. It was all so fast, he wasn't sure he was hearing right or being set up.

"Now!"she said "Now!"

Karl tripped over his pants as he pulled them on in haste. His sweater was inside out and his undershirt tangled up inside of it making them uncooperative from all the cold and moisture they had collected and so he carried the twisted bundle with him under his arm.

Barefoot, he crept down the hallway to the second room. Unclear if this was a trap, he kept his back pressed against the hallway wall as he lightly pushed the door in. No reaction.

He turned his head in to look. Light bubblegum pink paint covered the chipped walls. Three mattresses sat on the floor. On each one lay a girl who appeared to be peaking in a warm, drowsy, cozy state from a recent heroin injection. He pushed the door open further to reveal the entirety of the small square room. There was a bassinet in the right hand corner. He tiptoed towards it. In it was Olive.

He heard the creaking of a door at the end of the hallway. Someone was coming towards him. Karl realized whomever it was would see him if he didn't move quickly. With nowhere else to hide besides behind the door to the bedroom, he jumped behind it bringing the door flush to his face and pushed his back hard into the wall behind it and stopped breathing out loud.

It was Andel. He stopped and looked into the room from the door frame. Karl could make out his white t-shirt through the crack. The switchblade cross tattoo on his arm appeared in different segments as Andel flipped on the light switch. Apparently satisfied with what he saw, he flipped the lights off and closed the door. Karl heard his heavy footsteps lead towards Dalena's room.

He could hear Andel questioning Dalena about the American. They argued and whatever she said in Slovak had the sound of a desperate plea.

What was going on? Did she tell him where I am? Or who I am? Or did she lie? There was no point in trying to figure it out. If there was a language that had few if any ties to English this was it. It was a waste of time to speculate.

There was a lone window in the bedroom. It was above the bassinet and to the left, a naked rectangular mass of thick warped cloudy glass that hadn't been cleaned or used in decades.

Karl crawled on the ground on his hands and knees through the darkened room towards it. He had to stand on his tip toes to see out of it. It was like looking through the bottom of a soda pop bottle but he could also tell it would be impossible to escape from. The building dropped with a straight edge, was too far up, and had no other protrusions that could help an escapee. He watched for movement. Then he saw her like a thick ground level cloud. Ivy. She was still there.

Her body was barely visible through the murky glass. She had dressed in an off white coat and jeans of the same color that blended in with the snow. If there wasn't moonlight he probably would have never seen her. And if he hadn't seen her earlier and known where to look for movement he might have missed her.

Karl pulled the handle hard at the bottom edge of the window towards him. It was one of those windows that only opened halfway with the bottom portion. The upper portion was separated by pane, which allowed only the bottom glass to move, creating too narrow of an exit even for his lean frame. Years without use and the thick paint that coated it had sealed it almost permanently shut. Out of breath and with some of the girls becoming more alert he knew he didn't have much time. Finally the window gave him some leverage. A harsh cold draft enveloped him. He saw two of the girls stir in their beds. Olive was asleep but stirring too. He could tell it would just be a matter of seconds before she would start crying which was the last thing he needed. Her little body was only dressed in a diaper without even so much as a blanket. Karl looked around the room. The unobstructed moonlight made it much easier to see. He needed something to get Ivy's attention closer to her level. Then he remembered his belt. He unfastened it and draped it down the window sliding across the outside wall. He got on his tip toes again and saw Ivy reacting. He could tell she was scared and he had to let her know it was okay, it was him.

"Ivy. It's me, Karl" he whispered loudly out the window.

She stood up.

She was about to go hysterical he could tell, which would not be good.

"Listen to me" he commanded. He waited a moment for Ivy to settle down so she could take it in. "Olive is okay."

At that moment he heard the footsteps again. This time coming faster down the hall toward him.

Instinctively, Karl grabbed Olive, tied his entangled sweater around her tiny body and as fast as he could, fitted her through the window and pushed her out towards Ivy.

"Catch!" he screamed at her.

His heart raced as he forced himself to peel his eyes open to see if she did catch her child or if this was the end.

Ivy caught her!

"Run!" he demanded. "Run! Get out of here. Hurry!"

The door flew open and Andel came leering towards him with a switchblade.

With all his might Karl yanked the entire window off the frame by its crank handle and slammed the thick bubbled glass plate over Andel's head.

He had to get the hell out of here.

CHAPTER TWENTY-ONE

She had Andel wrapped around her little finger, she thought with a wry grin. The gay little prick that hid behind the real accomplishments of his brother. He was really just a baker she scoffed. A muffin man. Yes, he was a damn good one, as she would even tell everyone, but what a stupid, useless thing to do with one's life, she thought. His pride with baking was to the point of ridiculous, especially now. Why Andel hadn't simply gotten rid of him a long time ago was beyond her comprehension. He simply wasted space. "He isn't a true Vojtech," she mumbled to herself in disgust. He had insisted on his other vocation as it gave some sense of normalcy to the people who inhabited the house at the end of the street. At first he had argued his point with Arnost and now she was the lucky one who got to hear his whimpering whiny excuses about making chocolate and cream puffs all day. But it worked in her favor as he had always depended on Arnost for direction, so he was easy to play and would do as she said. He was like a child when it came to real power. He was the type who lost himself around it, shrinking like a stick of butter melting in its real presence.

She had found a buyer for the baby. A Russian named Viktor. He was the one who had trusted only Arnost in the past and Andel had been the one, of all people, to set up it with Maruska. The timing couldn't have been more perfect. She appeared with a baby just when Viktor's people asked for the youngest girl they had in their stall. Viktor was someone Vojtech had tried hard to please in the past, always falling just a hair short. But this time they were sure they had him. This would be their in with Viktor forever. And life would be good as long as they could keep pleasing him.

Viktor was very much the New Russia; flashy, emotionless, and rude. But he was also a billionaire. He made his fortune in the diamond trade. A total sleaze bag with many an enemy who paid off many of his cohorts in contraband, so Maruska knew how lucky she was to have the cold hard cash. At first he tried to bribe her with trading his SUV for the baby. He bragged of its gold plated bullet proof windows and diamond encrusted dashboard. It was almost tempting and certainly worth over a million dollars but then he revealed its interior was made of whale penis leather. Maruska, even with her questionable morals, had a hard time swallowing that one. So she insisted on the cash and won out. She smirked to herself about the irony of it all. She was now on her way to headquarters. She thought about being set for life but something about a million dollars wasn't quite enough. She wanted power. Real power. And it took money to have it. Not millions in this lifetime. But billions. She had to be equal or greater to the schmucks like Viktor to have any real clout. She wanted him bowing to her, not the other way around. No one would write about a mere millionaires in the history books she laughed to herself. Fucking history books. No, she wouldn't be in them but maybe on the History Channel? The show on cable in the U.S.? They often times featured American gangs. Seemed like every time she had turned it on, it was a story about the Crips or the Bloods or Hells Angels, which she always found amusing with the way the media glorified its most brutal in the United States of America. She laughed again at herself, her sense of self lighter than usual. But this was a start. Time to give Andel his delivery orders. Someone had a good Christmas coming their way if all was done right.

By the time she pulled onto the street of Vojtech, it was already Christmas morning. The snow had delayed her somewhat and so had the anticipation of the money that was to come. She hadn't driven straight back. A little stroll in the old square had beckoned her to see what she might be spending some of her cash on. She hadn't bought any clothes in a while and it was time. She was going to make history, yes, she was, she had made up her mind, and she was going to dress for it too. In time she would have the scar above her left eye fixed and maybe another breast augmentation to even things out a bit more, and the lines under her eyes revamped. The possibilities were endless. In the meantime her hair camouflaged the scar on her forehead. So much time had passed since she had been cut by her mother that the pinkness of it had nearly faded to the same white color of the rest of her. Perhaps in time her teeth could be fixed, too, but she had learned so well how to not show them- to the point that it was the least of her concerns. No, she would live with the teeth. The alternative wasn't in her plans. The thrill of her new life and new look sent an exhilarating shock wave up her spine.

It had been an odd night to go shopping for oneself, Christmas Eve, but it wasn't every night you knew you had a million dollars coming your way either. The town square had been virtually lifeless with only a few stragglers and the boutiques were closed only leaving the window lights on for post holiday shopping. Before the effects of her last line wore down she had driven herself around the city to try to take the edge off. She knew going back to Vojtech and trying to rest was out of the question. She drove around thinking about the disappointing display of mostly teenage Hip Hop clothes she had just witnessed in the store fronts and about the exciting holiday gift exchange that would take place in a matter of hours.

Before getting out of the car, she took out a small package of plastic wrap out of the glove compartment. She unfolded it carefully not to spill any of the contents and poured the powder on her dashboard and then scraped and cut it up the coke and heroin mixture in two thick short lines. Just a little treat for her good work. Just a little something to enhance the feeling of euphoria that was already taking place. *All done,* she thought as she pressed her left nostril shut with her index finger, snorting with extreme back and up through her right one. The stuff was too good to let any go to waste. She fumbled around in the dim light of the glove compartment for another baggie. She caught herself with surprise realizing that she was overdoing it and needed to stay in control. She slammed the glove compartment door back shut. She didn't allow herself to get disappointed though. In time there would be so much to go around she would never have to worry about running out or rationing.

She let herself out of the of her car into the freezing cold. Yes, the shopping had been disappointing but nothing else was ever going to be, everything from now on was going to be wonderful! She felt it. She knew it was cold outside but she felt nothing but a warm glow. She felt relaxed, happy, superbly confident. She had it made from here on out she kept reminding herself. She just had to give the dough boy his orders and make sure all was done right, that was it.

She punched in the code and the gate swung open. The snow had iced over the two low lying front steps and had a man's shoe print in them going in the opposite direction. Hopefully not Andel's. He was such a fool. How many times had she told him not to leave the girls and the customers in the house alone?

Andel didn't check to see who came through the door. She was going to have to get on him about that again too. She wanted to go look at the baby. Not because she cared about her but because she was curious in her new state to see what a million dollars looked like to someone else.

She climbed up the stairs into the main room where most of the girls were asleep and where the baby had been kept in the bassinet in the corner if Dalena was busy, which was typical at this time of night. The baby's crying and constant neediness had worn her thin, so putting her in a room full of drugged out girls was the best solution. The baby wouldn't get on their nerves. They were too high most of the time. The heroin made them mellow and unlikely to become agitated. Dalena did not have a habit like the other girls. There was no need to get her hooked. Her futile attempt to escape after they first captured her taught her to be well behaved. And, it left more to go around for everyone else. Dalena liked the baby and could be trusted with her, unlike the other low lifes when they were busy. Everything was falling together so perfectly. Maruska threw her head back and swallowed the gasoline like taste that dripped from her nose down to her throat.

She opened the door. The first girl she saw was Svelta, which surprised her as she hadn't seen her in years. She had been her first recruit. She was surprised not only to see her but that she was still alive after all this time. Maruska flashed back to the afternoon she picked her up. Svelta looked no older than twelve. A rare beauty even by Slovakian standards. The kidnapping had come almost by accident. Maruska was on her way to pick up a prescription for the girl that Arnost and Andel held captive, the one that Jeff got to spend time with- Zuzana. Maruska had been surprised that they let someone with a condition stay and on top of that give prescription medication to them. It showed the desperate stage the two brothers were in. It was something that she would not tolerate once she got back to headquarters. It was too risky. Just that once she would pick up the asthma medication but it would be the last. The girl was going to have to disappear.

As Maruska strode down the aisle to the pharmacists station, she passed Svelta and her mother looking at a few of the training bras the shop offered. Svelta was sullen, her arms crossed and looking defiant at her mother. Apparently there had been an argument between them and young Svelta was reluctant to have to wear such an ugly thing under her shirts from now on. Maruska did a once over of the girl's chest. Her breasts were just beginning to show. Small firm mounds that would blossom into voluptuous tear drops some day. The young Svelta caught Maruska staring, and Maruska in order to save face, stuck her tongue out at her mom behind her head as she strolled past. The girl almost peed in her pants from the sudden burst of laughter she couldn't contain. Her mother agitated and perplexed with her daughter beyond momentary repair, proceeded with the undergarment to the cash register. At that very moment, Maruska, who anticipated that to happen, turned back around and grabbed the girl by the arm and pulled her out of the store with such force and suddenness the girl didn't have time to register what was happening. Maruska then shoved her into the car and sped off with the child.

Once she got into a remote area, she injected Svelta with the needle. Svelta passed out almost immediately and she made her first money that night from her own girl as she almost effortlessly segued into her new career.

Arnost couldn't have been more pleased. Svelta way surpassed his expectations and Maruska had taken such initiative as well.

Maruska looked over Svelta more closely. She was a hard core junkie now but still beautiful. Maruska knew beauty when she saw it and Svelta, though not the young flower she once was, was still more than most men could hope for in their lifetime; she scoffed to herself as she proudly relived her accomplishment. How beautiful everything was all of a sudden. And what a coincidence and omen to run into Svelta. A reminder that she was the best at anything she set out to do. She looked around the room some more. Most of the girls were in bed except for one girl who sat in a corner of the room staring at the floor, her face ghastly. Maruska couldn't make out what she was staring at. She had to get to the other side of one of the mattresses to see.

It was Andel. Half of his face had been shaved off by a pane of glass. The frame around the glass embraced his neck like a necklace. He lay motionless. She checked his pulse. There was none.

Quickly, she turned towards the bassinet, the suddenness of events quickly sobering her. "What is going on?"she demanded of the girls, but they could not answer her. The baby was missing.

Maruska flashed to a strange sight she had seen earlier in the evening. As she was leaving the town square after her futile shopping expedition, she had seen the strange sight down by the river of a woman running through the snow with a bundle under her arms towards a hotel. It all became clear. Ivy was here.

She dialed the police and reported that her child had been kidnapped by an American named Ivy Weiss. She placed a second call to Juraj. And a third call to Konstantin at the SIS, or Slovak Information Services, who reported directly to the Prime Minister. She had helped Konstantin in the past with an abduction of the former president's son. She had contacted him when she first arrived back home and had explained her situation not realizing she would need to depend on him. She was glad she did. After all, he was indebted to her.

Konstantin spoke English as perfectly as Maruska. "Maruska? How lucky can someone be to hear from you twice in a week? How can I help you, my beauty?"

"Listen to me." She had crawled back into her sedan and was sitting outside the Vojtech Headquarters.

Konstantin recognized her tone and feared for a minute that the police had arrested her and his name had been brought up again. "What's going on Maruska?"

"The baby has been kidnapped. You understand? She took the baby. The fucking American girl. I lost her. I just reported it to the police you understand?"

"I see. I am on it," he replied, relieved. Yes, he would do anything to help her. He had to. He was indebted.

And just like that both parties hung up. No need for pleasantries. The message was loud and clear.

CHAPTER TWENTY-TWO

Her legs were like two huge frost bitten Polish sausages. She could have never guessed she had it in her to run the distance as she had in the elements such as they were. Her fingers were so numb and her hands shook so badly, she could not grasp the key card to let herself inside the hotel room. Time and again it slipped out of her fingers. At last, she was finally able to grasp the key card and slide it through the lock making the tiny circular light turn green and made it to the safely inside.

Through her haste she had not even been able to look at Olive. Now that was her top priority. Thankfully Karl had the tangled up sweater and t-shirt to wrap her in because other than that she was just in a diaper. She looked less robust but Ivy's heart sang that she was with her now and alive.

She wrapped Olive in the comforter on the bed and snuggled in with her without her icy wet clothes touching-keeping the soft warmth of the bed spread in between, only their faces touching.

She snuggled her face into the crevice of Olive's neck to take in the familiar scent that mom's become addicted to and kissed her what must have been a hundred times. She fed her a bottle of water. The room was still freezing cold even with the windows shut. Ivy took off her clothes and ran a warm bath for Olive and her to share together.

Just as the water began running her hotel room phone started ringing.

Was it Karl? She suddenly jolted back to reality that the nightmare wasn't exactly over. She was still in this country and God only knew where Maruska was or what she knew.

Should I answer it? She frantically searched for her cell phone. She couldn't find it.

Her heart began racing as the tension started building back up. She turned the water off and got dressed quickly.

The phone ringing stopped. Then started back up abruptly.

Shit! Who was it? What if it was Karl for some unknown reason.

Cautiously she picked up the phone as though it might explode.

"Ivy?"

It was Karl's voice.

"Yes."

"It's time to listen to me carefully. You lost your cell phone. I have it. Get to the airport in Bratislava immediately. Go home now! There is no time to discuss this. Go now! Do not wait!"

Click.

Her heart switched, beating from fast to medium fast to speed racer fast. Her hands trembled as they held the handset tight against the base. Her mind scurried to collect the data of what she must do first: get Olive clothed, pack, call taxi. No, call taxi first; they weren't quick around Bratislava.

She called the taxi with the front desk's help while attempting to dress Olive with her free hand, which wasn't working. She had a lot to do in a short amount of time including finding her passport, which seemed to have vanished. She finally found it when she flipped over the hotel desk and it fell out of a drawer.

She quietly told herself to get it together as she set the desk back upright. She knew enough by now to keep calm. She reminded herself that keeping calm had gotten her this far which was practically a home run. All she had to do now was get on the plane and go, go, go. Just focus on that. Get the hell out of here. Don't worry about Karl now. *You've got Olive. Just scram.* Her mind raced a million miles a second. She peered through the curtains of her third story room to see if she could spot any taxis already awaiting passengers. Instead, she was greeted by the sight of uniformed police men showing a composite sketch of someone to the concierge who must have been on his way home. The concierge looked up and saw her staring out the window. He pointed to her but she shut the curtains before they could see her.

The phone rang again. Karl? The sinking feeling reappeared. She answered.

"Halo?"

"Yes?"

"This is Leos at front desk. You have taxi?"

"Yes, yes. Ďakujem."

That was too fast. She wasn't quite ready yet. She had to finish dressing Olive.

She slapped on the rest of Olive's clothes as quickly as possible. Olive had fallen back to sleep, her body full of dead weight in one arm and baggage in the other as Ivy went downstairs by the stairwell straight to the taxi. The police were in the elevator going up.

The driver never looked at her or said anything. He just nodded. His shaved head moved slightly in response to her request to go to the airport.

The taxi driver began driving off from the hotel before Ivy had told him where she wanted to go. She wasn't sure what to make of that but decided the people of this country simply did not like English speaking people or maybe it was just her and the new energy the whole situation had given her.

She concentrated on Olive who had opened her eyes. Ivy wished for a sign of recognition from her but did not see one, although her eyes were the same soulful steel gray pools. Ivy fed her a bottle of water and held her tight, keeping her tucked in the blanket that she had wrapped around her.

The driver stared at her through the rear view mirror. Another chiseled cheek bone model type with narrow blue eyes under dark straying eyebrows and inky black eyelashes. She smiled lightly at him in response, but he just stared at her and then looked away.

She returned her attention back to Olive. Olive needed to be seen by a doctor. She was sure Karl had thought about that and had a plan for someone to meet up with them at the airport. She at least hoped so.

When she looked back up, the taxi driver was doing something with his right hand. Ivy couldn't tell what as it was pitch black in the car now but saw a flash. Metal? Something glistened in the dark. A knife? No, he wasn't handling it like a knife but what was it?

Whatever it was disappeared and she convinced herself she was being paranoid.

Out the window she watched as they passed Vajnorska Street in the wrong direction. This wasn't the way to the airport.

"Excuse me," Ivy tapped the driver on his left shoulder. "I need to get to the airport."

She looked expectantly at the rear view mirror for some kind of a response but got nothing.

Maybe he doesn't understand English, thought Ivy. She wracked her brain for some Slovak words.

Finally it came to her.

"Letisko prosim?" Airport please.

She wasn't sure if she was making sense but it was the best she could do. Besides, the front desk had told him the destination, too.

Maybe this is a back way, she wondered as she tried to make sense of their direction.

Or, maybe he is taking them to the Vienna airport!

"Letisko prosim, *Bratislava.*"

Still nothing.

He picked up the radio and called someone.

She tried to make sense of the language but there just weren't any commonalities to English she knew of except for the words mama, hotel and radio, which were almost useless.

He was talking to a woman with a low husky voice. Was she the dispatcher? Surely she must speak English.

Ivy signaled for the driver to give her the radio. "Radio?"

For the first time he understood and handed it to her after chuckling with whomever he was talking to.

"Hello. Do you speak English?"

The driver's eyebrows and eyes were staring at her in the rear view mirror.

There was some crackling static and then, "Hello Ivy. This is Maruska. How do you like my country?"

Ivy not sure how to hang up the radio simply dropped it on the floor. No further words came out from the radio but Ivy could have sworn she heard Maruska laughing besides her feet.

The street lights sashayed a ray of light in the car that washed over the dashboard. The metal she had seen earlier was aluminum foil. The driver placed tin foil over the GPS tracking device so the taxi company would not be able to track his whereabouts.

Clever.

Now it was time for her to be clever in return but she was at a loss.

The driver pulled onto a side street, a dark uninhabited area. A heavy aura of its former Communist self still intact. They were now at the base of the Carpathian mountains. The forest was near but they were in the midst of a handful of warehouses and factories. At the next side street, the driver made a sharp left hand turn that had the car spinning. Ivy held Olive tightly to her chest. She was awake and crying. The sirens had jolted her listless body into hysteria.

Ivy turned her head around. The police were chasing after them. The sirens wailing louder in such close proximity behind them. The louder they became the more peaceful Ivy became that the game was over.

Juraj pulled the taxi over. The police pulled up behind, almost rear ending the taxi, and two officers emerged, one after the other with pointed guns that they directed at her. Through the glass she stared in disbelief thinking the dark was playing tricks on her mind. "Get out of the car." They were talking to her.

Still holding Olive, the police informed her she was under arrest for kidnapping.

What? Her whole world was coming undone. One officer took Olive while Ivy tried to fight back. The officer was too strong and Ivy couldn't compete with his grip that felt as if it was going to tear Olive apart. While Ivy was fighting the man the other one in one swift movement had both her arms pinned in back of her and handcuffed her and twirled her into the back seat by the back of her head that bumped and scraped hard against the jagged metal roof. The officer that handcuffed her got in the car behind the steering wheel. As she looked out the window she saw the taxi driver being handed Olive by the other officer who slapped his hands together and smiled as if he just got rid of an explosive. The taxi driver eagerly took the baby, put her on the front passenger seat of his taxi and then sped off in the opposite direction.

The two police officers were now sitting in the front seat. The driver had never turned the car's ignition off so it was ready for take off. The pressure of the accelerator made Ivy slam her nose hard into the front seat and then her whole body hard against the back seat almost rolling over herself. The two cops laughed at her and made comments in Slovak. She turned her back to one of the passenger doors and slammed her back hard against it until she felt the blood. It was no use. She was trapped.

The policemen, Lubomir, the driver, and Peter, his partner escorted Ivy to the front door of the police station. Once inside, they asked no questions, their mission accomplished as laid out by Konstantin.

The holding cell was small with cold damp concrete floors that reeked of urine. No chair, no bed, just one hundred percent concrete and steel. The tears were burning, the helplessness blazing over her body as she had never felt before. *What was going on?* Maruska must have set her up. It was the only explanation she could think of. She walked to the door where a small window divided by two iron bars let her see the world outside. Lubomir and Peter were nowhere in sight. There was what appeared to be a secretary at one desk; a woman with long black hair with uneven ends and thick cracked pancake makeup covering her face who flirted with the other officers and occasionally typed on a computer and answered the phone. Ivy called for her but no matter how hard she tried, the woman would never make eye contact. There was a man sitting across from her. Apparently on break. He had caught Ivy's eyes at one moment but looked away quickly. He sat on a stone bench eating an apple, talking and flirting with the woman. He seemed to resign himself to the woman's wish of him not looking at the American woman in the holding cell.

"Please please. There's been a misunderstanding. My daughter's been kidnapped. You've got this all wrong. I need help. Please please!" As uniformed officers walked by and out of the building, no one paid mind to her.

Now the only people left in the building besides her were the man and the woman who stopped talking for a moment and just smiled at each other, waiting for the crazy woman to shut up so they could hear each other again.

"Please! I have been set up. That was my baby they took from me!! My baby girl! Please someone please please help. I have proof." Ivy realized she was lying as she looked around. There was no proof. All of her belongings including her purse that had Olive's birth certificate and her name only on it, had been left behind in the taxi.

Ivy thought hard to herself. These people were not going to believe her and even if they did they were not going to help her. Going hysterical was not going to help the situation either. *Where was everyone else who worked here, why had they all left?* She looked out the window and scanned the office. It wasn't an official police station she was sure of it. But surely there had to be more people than this man and this woman? All she needed was just one who would understand. Someone who would help her.

Ivy wondered where she was. The old town square's location was not somewhere she could imagine from the holding cell. All the strange directions the taxi driver had taken along with the police had left her disoriented. She had to think. Think hard. Maybe Karl knew of everything. Maybe he knew she was here. Maybe more importantly he knew where Olive was. Hopefully he had been following them.

Ivy looked back out the jail cell window. The woman looked as if she was ready to call it a night. She was getting up from her desk, straightening out items in her purse while digging for her car keys. She finally pulled them out, setting them on her desk momentarily and then grabbed the fake fur collared jacket hanging on the back or her chair and put it on. The man sat pale and limp in the chair still making idle chit chat with her. He looked up again at Ivy when the woman wasn't looking and raised an eyebrow at her. Ivy wasn't sure what to make of that but it didn't feel good. Was he flirting with her now? Yes, he was. The man was bored out of his mind and the place was going to be left in his hands momentarily. Ivy stepped away from the window and waited for the tell tale signs of the woman leaving. She finally heard a chair's legs screech against the concrete floor, footsteps, what must have been "goodbyes" in Slovak, and the front door open and close. The place became eerily silent. She didn't want to look out the window anymore.

The quiet clanking of keys was heard just before her cell door was opened. It was the man. He was now sharing the small space with her. He looked harmless except for the small dark eyes that were set too close together. What was he doing? He came closer to her forcing her to back up in a corner. He ran his sweaty hands through her hair. The blood curled through Ivy but she knew she had to play along now. She was supposed to be some bad ass crazy kidnapper and she was going to take the role to the hilt. The man pushed his body up against her, pressing into her. She could feel the short and narrow length of his soft erection. Harder and harder he pushed into her thrusting and gyrating painfully pulling her skin upwards. The friction from her clothing started chaffing her. But Ivy leaned back against the wall and let him do his thing. *Let him get good and worked up,* she thought. All the men she had ever known could never have gotten off this way. They needed more; even hands would usually do but never had she seen a man come to fulfillment through this method. She hoped Mr. Snake Eyes wasn't any different. His breath was hot in her ear now as he muzzled his face into her neck. As he moaned, his excitement had been growing but was turning the corner into frustration now. He unzipped his pants and groped around inside of them trying to find it. He lifted his penis through the fly. Ivy looked down at it and turned her back so her hands could touch. A vile liquid rose up inside of her and she had to swallow hard in order not to throw up. He probably wasn't buying it but it didn't matter she thought. Anything to get him to need more of her.

He moaned more and then turned her around. He lifted both hands to run through her hair again and then over her body under her clothes. The cold had made her nipples hard but he thought it was him as he pushed fingers through barricading straps and fabric, laughing and tugging at them. He pressed his mouth to hers, his tongue pushing through her teeth. She resisted, which turned him on further. He stepped back from her and took hold of himself and began sliding his right hand up and down as he stared at her. He pushed her hard down on her knees and gathered her hair in his free hand and forced her head down on him. This was too much. She didn't want to participate in any of this but this was out of the question. But she stayed in character. He pushed his small penis fully and forcefully into her mouth. And Ivy bit right through it.

The man screamed to the likes that Ivy had never heard before not even in the worst horror flicks that Punch would beg her to watch with her. He fell down on the floor hard on his side, legs

curled and gasped for air as he clutched his crotch screaming
and crying. Now she had to find the right key and get out of the
handcuffs. She should have figured out where it was first. But it
was too late now. It was find it, or else. The key ring was clipped on
to the man's pants, which was going to make things difficult since
she was cuffed from behind. She kicked the man hard rolling him
over on his back with her feet and with as much speed as possible
she unclipped the chain. The man was foaming at the mouth calling
her names she had never been called before. His face was pinched
in pain and bright red. He was reaching for his gun. If she didn't
move fast, it was going to be the end.

She took a chance with the key that looked the right size. *No.
Next. Yes, next was probably it.* But the man was sitting upright now.
Getting out of the cuffs was second priority. Getting away from
him was first. Ivy made a run for the front door bumping into
the sharp splintered edge of the secretary's wood table that badly
bruised and cut her thigh. She turned around backwards to open
the front door with her hands that were clasped closely to her back,
the man only seconds away from her face, and flew out of it as soon
as it was open. Luckily it was still dark as she beelined towards a
warehouse across the street. She would hide in its shadows while
trying to free herself.

The night was quiet. It seemed as if there was no one on the
planet but her and this raging horny cop who now had half a penis.
If that wouldn't make a man mad, what would, she wondered. Ivy
trembled in fear as she heard him only feet away from her several
times. If he had had the sense to bring a flashlight she was sure he
would have found her crouched down against the building a long
time ago. Ivy looked up. She was huddled at the foot of a metal
door decorated with black graffiti. His footsteps were less than
twenty feet away, coming closer, closer. She grabbed the handle

of the door and tugged it gently towards her. It opened. She crept inside the small crack she made for herself and gently shut the door behind her. There were voices inside. American voices. Voices that reminded her of Pastor King. She realized what looked like a warehouse on the outside really housed an historic opulent theatre that must have just had a touring gospel concert for Christmas Eve. The musicians were on the stage about fifty rows in front of her, joking around and exchanging high fives complimenting each other on a great gig. Some of them were packing their instruments in cases. They were all American and black with one white woman who appeared to be their manager, telling them the tour bus would be picking them up in thirty minutes to take them back to Prague. The bass player sat on a stool trying to work out the rhythm of a particular song that must have given him some grief in the earlier performance. The drummer tapped along on the rim of his snare with a stick and a beautiful black woman sang out the melody, "Sometimes I feel like a motherless child.... sometimes I feel like a motherless child.... sometimes I feel like a motherless child.... I'm a long way from home. A long long way from home," while her hand fluttered in the air in rhythm with a slow snapping of her fingers. Ivy wondered if she could wait the thirty minutes and hop on the bus with them. Surely they would understand and help her. Or *would they?* No, not with the police station across the street. It would be obvious to them that she was an escapee. She kept her crouch low behind the red velvet seats and quietly opened the door she had entered through. Hovering in the shadows, she watched him as he limped back across the street to the police office. He must have known about the other Americans inside the building.

Time to get out of the cuffs once and for all. It wasn't an easy process and the time it took made Ivy all too aware of the possibilities of what could have happened to Olive yet again. But at last she undid them and slid her sore raw hands out.

She made her way in the opposite direction of the police station and the warehouse, the direction from her best guess that would lead her in closer proximity to civilization. In what felt like at least ten miles, she began to recognize the twinkling of the city square up ahead in the distance. The dome of St. Martin's Cathedral was awash with a pale blue light. The bridges that led there were brightly lit, like someone had decorated them with enormous strings of Christmas lights. The lights reflected on the black water of the Danube. Riverboats lulled, floating heavy guests on Christmas cruises. The disgusting taste of the man and his blood still sat heavy in her mouth and the urge to throw up was halting her progress. She had to get back to the hotel and put it out of her mind. And think clearly. She had to call Karl. Hopefully she could sneak back into the safety of her old hotel room clean up and place the call.

Passing motorists stared as she crossed the city streets making her way to the Novy Most- her bridge to the only life she knew in this strange land. Her hair disheveled, her pants torn and leg bleeding, she wished she could ask for help but her condition was scaring people rather than inspiring them to be merciful holiday participants. At last she made her way to Hotel Pressburg. As unobtrusively as she could, she would make her way in and up to her old room. She still had a key card that she accidentally left in her coat pocket. Hopefully they hadn't changed the code yet. The hotel was about fifty feet away now. A taxi awaited in the half circle driveway for a customer and the lights that lit up the rooms inside gave her renewed hope. As she passed the taxi to make her way through the front sliding glass doors, one hand reached out and grabbed her around the waist and pulled her hard in the opposite direction. Another hand was placed over her mouth. Ivy kicked the legs of the person holding her and screamed, but for as lit up as the hotel appeared, no one was aware of her muffled cries. She was forced backwards and shoved through the small opening into the back seat. She was back with Juraj, the same clear window with the small gap of broken glass separating them. The same taxi. And Olive was still with him riding in the front seat in a bundle of towels.

As he sped out of the hotel driveway, his eyes began searching furiously for a safe place to pull over. Driving was impossible with a baby in the passenger seat. Maruska would probably chop his balls off if anything happened to her. He found a quiet side street that lacked any signs of life, lights or buildings. He got out of the taxi, quickly strode to the passenger side of the car, opened the door, grabbed Olive then pressed a button on a key chain to unlock the back door and handed Olive over to her mother without a word. Seamlessly, he locked the two of them in the back of the car and made his way back to the driver's seat and took off again.

Ivy's tears of pain had turned to tears of joy and confusion. She was holding Olive for what was probably the last time she realized. She held her close, the blood from her thigh soaked up through the towels Olive was in and her wrists burned from where the hand cuffs had sliced into them and her skin, making them pink and raw. Her head pounded and she felt delirious, as if she had downed a thousand bottles of champagne. But Olive was here now. She savored the moment unsure of what was to come; she knew it couldn't be good. She had lucked out too much already. *Eventually luck runs out.*

The driver zoomed across one of the bridges and cruised through blocks and blocks of the city. On and on he drove, the twinkling of city lights far, far behind them now. They were in the country now. Amongst the other wolves.

Suddenly a pale gold, four door sedan swerved into the unmarked intersection they were crossing barely missing the taxi by a thread.

When Ivy's dizziness ended and the cars came to screeching halts, she heard the other car's driver's door slam shut.

It was Maruska who was striding towards Ivy's door. She heard the pops of the locks open thanks to the driver.

Ivy tried in vain to lock the door to keep her out but there were no buttons or ways to control the locks. The driver had full control, again.

Ivy rolled over to the other door and gripped the handle to push it open but it was sealed shut.

She sat still and stared out the front window. All the silence that surrounded her was created by her instinct to survive. She shut the world out and it came to her. *Do what you just did; just comply.* There was no one here to hear her scream. There was no way out. *Befriend the enemy when all else fails. Befriend to win them over and when they least expect it blindside them.* There was nothing left but to try.

Maruska opened the rear passenger door and motioned for Ivy and Olive to get out with the pointing of her K-100 power pistol.

Ivy obliged and took in her surroundings, off in the distance a few towering street lights dangled from long skinny poles and lit the snow banked roads. There was no life in sight. Black smoke trailed out of one of the distant chimneys into the nearby woods. The sight reminded Ivy of a particularly grim fairy tale that scared the daylights out of her when she was a child. Maruska was now the real life child devouring witch.

Maruska, in her throaty voice ordered Ivy to give her Olive. She then pressed the nozzle of her gun in Ivy's back and began leading her into the woods.

Olive was screaming now. But it didn't matter as no one would ever be able to hear her this far out.

These people aren't stupid, thought Ivy as every idea she had to outsmart them, she had to reject as they were at least one step, if not more, ahead with their plan.

She prayed a silent prayer this time not to God and not to Santa Claus but to Jesus. It was Christmas. There was no Santa Claus in Slovakia. Jesus was their gift deliverer. "Please make sure Olive lives through whatever is about to happen. Please. I know I will die but please please please don't let anything happen to my baby."

If Karl was still alive and going to find her, he could tell her how much she loved her and how hard she had tried. And if that was to fail, if the Father, Son and Holy Ghost would please make it known in Olive's heart and soul. Tears streamed down her face as the notion of her mistake of bringing a baby into the world with a father like Jeff wormed its way through her bloodstream. But she caught herself. It was too late to let any more of these types of thoughts take over.

Where was the driver? She had completely lost track of him. She turned around to look back and could make out the subtle glow of the taxi's paint under the moonlight. She also got a quick glance of Maruska's irritation from a baby screaming in her ear.

"Maruska. Please. Olive is severely dehydrated and will not survive without water. This will all be a waste for you if she does not. Please, can we get to the taxi and get her a bottle?"asked Ivy as she eyed the scene of the driver and taxi. The driver was standing, leaning his back on the car and smoking a cigarette.

In response, Maruska pushed the gun hard into Ivy's back almost tripping her forward.

"Please Maruska. I know you will kill me. But please while my baby is here and alive, you must realize you will only get the best deal for a healthy baby. No one wants a sick child."

"Shut up. I go get bottle after I am done with you."

"Please Maruska. She is not doing well." Ivy wasn't sure she would buy it. But it was a good lie if it could be called that as there was truth to it. Her mind was too worn out to come up with anything more complicated.

Reluctantly Maruska edged the gun nozzle so that it pointed left, tipping only part of the cylinder into Ivy's back swinging her around.

"Okay. We go get bottle. This is it."

They trudged through the snow and branches they had only just moments before crushed on their way back to the taxi. The driver dropped his cigarette butt on the snow, reached in his coat pocket and pulled out the almost empty pack. He tapped the bottom of it with his other hand. A reluctant cig scooted out. He threw the empty pack that drifted slowly to the snow covered ground. He lit it up the last one and continued to lean against the car.

Maruska opened the back door for Ivy and allowed her to crawl into the back seat. She fumbled around for Olive's bottle. Her hands were so frozen that she could barely recognize the texture of its smooth plastic roundness. In a moment of panic, realizing if she didn't produce a bottle things were going to look fishy for her, she looked out the windows. Maruska and the taxi driver were silent. They were waiting for her to be done but were eying the surroundings more than watching her. She saw the driver's identification badge on the front passenger seat. His name was Juraj. And now, if she could do what she really came back to the taxi to do.

In one swift move, she swiped the tin foil off the GPS system. Suddenly Maruska and Juraj started screaming at her to get out of the car and Juraj reached into the back seat, grabbing her by the collar of her coat, and threw her out.

As she fell hard down on the snow, she sat waiting for them to readjust the GPS system again, but astonishingly, they did not. They must have just seen a flash of her arm and panicked, reasoned Ivy. She couldn't believe her luck. *Perfect.* She just needed one more thing; for them to turn the car back on before she entered the woods again.

"Maruska, here is the bottle but she also needs warmth. Please turn the car on with the heat and leave her here. There is no sense in your taking her into the woods with me. Please?"

She didn't answer but pulled Ivy up by her hair with her free hand, the one not carrying the baby and the gun in. Once she had Ivy standing, she shifted the weight of Olive into her gun free hand and nudged the barrel hard into Ivy's left shoulder blade. Then she told the driver something in Slovak. He got in the car and turned the engine on. Maruska then gave him the baby and ordered him to put her in the car and leave the heat on.

∽✵∾

CHAPTER TWENTY-THREE

Maruska led Ivy back into the woods. It was bitter cold. The moon was the only source of light, but it only shone in quick flashes as it was obscured by the dead branches reaching overhead as if in worship. The sharp edge of the K-100's barrel pressed hard into Ivy's back threatening her to fall forward if she lost her grip on the crippling ice and uneven mounds of snow and debris below her feet. The words spoken to her were Slovakian. Ivy could not understand a single word. *Probably cussing*, Ivy surmised which wasn't fair as she wanted to cuss too but wasn't willing to take any chances of paying unfairly for any more sins. "Holy crap," she muttered to herself as her right ankle twisted inward causing a shooting pain to bolt up her leg. She was directed by the gun to spin around. It was like a stick of dynamite going off. The trigger was pulled again and again. At first she stared in disbelief and then Ivy went flying backward like a comet before landing in the soft snow hard on her back. The pain was unbearable like a mad renegade jack hammer going crazy inside her chest. And then every feeling, every last memory and every lingering haunting question faded to black.

CHAPTER TWENTY-FOUR

Karl had barely made it back to the hotel. Andel's knife tip had caught him at one point and sliced his face in a crescent shape from just above his left eye outward, tracing the outline of the inside of his ear to the corner of his mouth. The amount of blood pouring out would flood his eyes from time to time, making it impossible to navigate. But he made it, and now had managed to get back in the hotel without causing too great a stir for a bare-chested bloody tourist. The desk clerk eyed him curiously as he walked past. "Fucking English drunks won't stop at nothing for a girl," he explained taking on the role of a rough redneck who had just gotten back from a beer brawl. It was a pretty easy role as the truth wasn't that far fetched. The desk clerk grinned and nodded and gave him a proud look, hoping he beat the shit out of whoever it was.

Karl had to get bandaged up to stop the hemorrhaging. That was his first priority he thought as he made his way up the stairwell to his room. Now was not the time to get stuck in the elevator with strangers. And right along side of stopping the hemorrhaging was making sure Ivy and Olive had left the country.

He lay down on the heavy earth-colored bed spread with his head elevated, propped up against the tufted leather headboard. With his left hand he put pressure to his face with a gauze and with his right he called the airport.

The woman who answered had an odd way of saying no to the same question she just said yes to a second earlier. He slammed down the phone in frustration.

He got up, put on a new under-shirt and sweater and took the stairwell up to the next floor to Ivy's room. The door was precariously open, just touching the lock. He pushed it in revealing a room once inhabited by someone in pure haste but without any evidence of that person's belongings.

There was no way to get in touch with her now. He still had her cell phone that he found in the snow just outside the Vojtech quarters. He held it in his hand and cartwheeled it over and over in the palm of his hand with his thumb while he thought about his next move.

He jumped up from the bed. He needed to go to the front desk and make sure a taxi had picked her up. He checked with the clerk, the now overly eager to please youngster. He confirmed that he had seen a woman with a baby take a taxi and that he had been the one that called it in and had notified her it was waiting for her. He also told Karl of the police coming to investigate her room after she had left.

Karl thought about that. It had taken him by surprise. Something was seriously wrong. No police, no legitimate police should be questioning Ivy without his knowing about it through Tibor, the chief of the Bratislava department. He still had one major concern at this point- Maruska. Where had she been and how much longer would it take her to find Andel? He knew it wouldn't be long if she hadn't already. And now he listened to the clerk tell the story of how the concierge had been the one to lead the police up to the room while he stayed downstairs and helped customers. He was sure Maruska had found Andel and the bogus police were her doing.

He walked out the glass sliding doors into the misty chill. There weren't any civilians milling around at this time, which gave him no other witnesses.

He thought carefully about his next step. He had Olive's health in mind and placed a call to the FBI to have someone look into her well being at the Bratislava airport and at JFK. Without any better options he decided to go to the airport and get eyewitnesses or some other proof that Ivy and Olive were on board a plane to the states. Hell, he might even join them if they were still there. They could use his protection if Maruksa was on their trail. The basic task had been done, which was reuniting Olive with her mom and if they hadn't gotten on a plane already and could still manage without Maruska's interference, he could leave the rest to the FBI from there on.

He walked to the front desk and ordered a taxi. The clerk apologetically told him it would be at least twenty minutes. Karl tried to push for it getting to the hotel more quickly but the clerk just shrugged and made a remark about it being a holiday. He thought about hot wiring a car in one of the nearby parking lots, but that was risky, especially in a foreign country and he didn't even want to think about driving here in this kind of weather.

Karl's head was still throbbing from Andel's cut. He took a seat in the lobby. It felt good to sit down but the exhaustion was catching up to him. He didn't realize how much until he sat down. He got back up again. As he held onto the chair's arm for support, he looked up and caught the clerk staring at him as if he had finally witnessed a real life super hero. From the looks of it, Karl was sure the kid had been bullied plenty in his life and had had fantasies of some crazy jerk that his new persona took on standing up for him. The clerk, embarrassed, pretended he was thinking about something else; skewed his glance just to the left of Karl in a more thoughtful pose, and then bowed his head back down to the paperwork in front of him.

Thirty-five minutes later a taxi arrived. The driver was apparently annoyed and bitter that someone had called him to actually work and belched and grunted and shifted his suspenders hanging on by a thread to his large pale green waisted pants while Karl told him impatiently to take him to the Bratislava airport. The long wait had made him furious. The driver grunted some more, fumbled around with the meter and slowly took off. When the street lights hit the rear view mirror just right, Karl could see the pastry crumbs like dandruff stuck into his handlebar mustache.

What should have been a twenty-five minute ride at the most was soon turning into thirty when the driver's radio went off. At first both Karl and the driver ignored the dialog until they heard the dispatcher mention the words Hotel Pressburg.

There seemed to be panic or confusion in his voice. The language was such an obstacle in this country. It really had never been worth learning up to this point along with most other languages. Karl told himself this would be the last of any international cases outside of Australia, England or Canada that he would ever take on. He pressed his throbbing head in closer to the driver and the radio trying to make sense out of it.

The driver certainly looked like a country man who spoke little or no English so he would probably be no help interpreting but you never knew until you asked. "Excuse me, what are they saying about the hotel?"

The driver coughed so loud and hard it seemed as if the car was going to roll forward over itself.

It is no use, Karl thought. He would have to make sense on his own. It was probably nothing but the dispatcher making sure he had been picked up by "Mr. Enthusiastic." No, but the tone of the voice was all wrong. There was some note of desperation or concern to it.

Mr. Enthusiastic had responded by reacting negatively or unknowingly to the dispatchers pleas while staring at Karl through the rear view mirror as if Karl had something to do with it or was his alibi. *But what was it?*

Then the voices reappeared. This time they spoke in half-English and half-Slovak. When the dispatcher talked in Slovak, the other voice would answer in Slovak. If the dispatcher asked something in English the other would respond in English. It was the dispatcher giving another taxi driver the third degree for turning off his GPS system. The driver was arguing back calling him a "fucking spy" and at the same time protesting his accusation of him turning it off, insisting it must have been a technical glitch.

"Where the hell are you Juraj? What the hell are you doing in the middle of the fucking forest?" the dispatcher asked.

"I need time out. Just a smoke. Fresh air," the driver responded in his most convincing tone.

More arguing in Slovak.

Then the icebreaker. The dispatcher asked if he had picked up the client at the Hotel Pressburg.

Juraj said he had. He had picked her up and taken her to the airport.

More arguing in Slovak then both voices were replaced in sound bites with static until they completely disappeared.

Now Mr. Enthusiastic laughed, his big belly like sloshing waves rolling up and down. He craned his squatty neck back at Karl for approval and grunted something that seemed to require an agreeable response; *it's always so much fun watching one of our coworkers get in trouble on Christmas.*

Karl was not amused. The name Juraj had conjured up something for him. It was a name that had come up in research the night at Ivy's home back in Misty Falls. His heart banged hard. Maruska had two other siblings. One was a twin sister that records showed had died at birth and the other was an older brother named Juraj.

Shit. How was he supposed to convey to this nimwit that he needed to go somewhere else now? He was sure that Ivy and Olive were with Juraj. He didn't believe the part about taking them to the airport. And why would he turn the GPS back on if he was still in hiding in the forest? And where exactly in the forest was he? This was a scenario Karl had become all too familiar with in his line of work: once you think you're heading for a touch down, you get blindsided.

Karl signaled for the driver to pull over.

The driver's brows furrowed in confusion in the rear view mirror.

Karl grunted at him in the caveman like language he seemed to understand the best and gestured again, this time more forcefully.

The driver complied, the car slid uncontrollably at first on a sheet of ice along the roadside.

When the taxi finally spun into a stop, Karl got out, shut the door and walked over to the driver's side with his thirty-eight pulled out and ordered the driver to get out of the car.

The driver seemed to be suddenly compliant, amused and scared simultaneously; he got out of the car with surprisingly great ease.

Karl jumped in the driver's seat and stepped on the gas silently cursing to himself of his inability to escape driving in this country. He eyed Mr. Enthusiastic in the rear view mirror watching in bewilderment as he was abandoned on the empty street. Karl wasn't sure where he was going but at least he had a car now and its intricate tracking device.

As soon as Mr. Enthusiastic was out of sight, Karl turned onto the next available street and then pulled over.

He looked out the frosty windows. He was parked in a residential area lined with thick cobblestone roads and clumps of housing stacked on small winding hills giving view mostly of tiled roof tops. No street lights in sight. His view was simply from whatever little moonlight was unobstructed from the falling sleet and snow. He stared at the tracking device for a second and then impulsively swept the car around and drove back the way he came.

The headlights shone on Mr. Enthusiastic who was sitting down on the curb of the road that served as a barrier from the thick snow-covered field on the other side. His thick legs stuck out as if waiting to get run over. He looked so comfortable Karl almost felt guilty for a second for having to make him move again.

Karl eased the taxi alongside of him. The driver, who's real name was Vinca, jumped up as fast as his cumbersome body would allow and tried to run away. But it was like running through water in the soft snow and within three steps Karl had a hold of him.

The man must weigh four hundred pounds, thought Karl as he wrestled him back in the taxi's driver seat, the gun helping to get his point across.

Karl had the keys with him. He got into the passenger side, the gun pointed at Vinca's temple. He told Vinca to call the dispatcher more with the gun than with words.

Vinca had always been suspicious of Americans and their over the top ways, but this was absolute confirmation. He had no idea what the crazy American wanted. He had never completed school and wasn't even proficient in his own language so there was no way he knew what this man was saying. Most Slovaks even with Vinca's limited education could speak at least a little English. But Vinca made it a point to never learn a word. He favored the Arabs if you got right down to it, and besides, it was the Americans who helped end the Second World War, ruining a perfect world. That's what his dad taught him when he was a little boy and his dad was always right as he taught Vinca by taking him into the barn bending him over with both their pants gathered around their ankles. Afterwards he would get some chocolates for being a good boy.

The American looked like someone he had seen on TV on an American Western. Vinca had to admit that he did enjoy those and thought one particular funny talking legendary cowboy named John something was particularly handsome. Kind of looked like his dad. This American staring at him was different though; younger, thin and more modern. For a brief moment Vinca flashed a scene through his mind where he and this crazy American man both got down and dirty in the snow, their sweaty bodies writhing, heating each other and then celebrating post coital by spoon feeding each other sweet custard.

Karl grabbed the radio with his left hand and spoke into it calling the dispatcher while keeping a steady aim at Vinca's fat head. He was certain Juraj had most likely turned his radio off after the dispatcher had found him hiding in the forest.

The line was full of static for a few seconds before his voice broke in. Karl couldn't understand what he said so he took charge. "Listen and listen carefully. There is a baby involved. If you help me out everyone stays alive. If you don't, you may be blamed. So here's the story. You tell me where the taxi is, the first one to go to Hotel Pressburg."

"Who are you?" the dispatcher asked in earnest.

"Never mind who I am. Just tell me where the taxi is."

Mr. Enthusiastic suddenly blurted something in Slovak with a squealing neurotic tone.

The dispatcher continued, "I do not know where it is. I have been trying to find it."

"You said it was in the middle of the fucking forest only a few minutes ago. So where exactly are we talking about?"

"I don't know. That was then but the idiot has turned his GPS back off again."

Karl tinkered with the system mounted to the dashboard in front of him. It spoke Italian, Hungarian, Swedish, and a multitude of other European languages. Finally Karl discovered that it spoke English. "So then, Mr. Dispatcher, you tell me what you know."

Again, Vinca interrupted with his own pleading in Slovak. Karl gave him a little tap on his thick skull to shut up.

"The last I knew they were near mountains in forest. About 30 kilometers maybe more. East."

"Can you be more specific? There isn't a lot of time!" Karl stared at the clock on the dashboard as the minutes ticked on.

"You give me Vinca. Let me speak Vinca. I tell him, okay? No know English good enough. I sorry."

Karl held the radio towards Vinca and he and the dispatcher proceeded to share the information. Karl noticed the strong emphasis on the first syllable of the words like a classical musical piece starting out with a charge before withdrawing into its softer side. Vinca ended the conversation with a grunt.

The dispatcher told Karl he had given the driver the location as best as he could but by now the taxi could be anywhere in any direction as their conversation was broadcast to all who had their radios turned on so he should not be blamed if something went wrong because he did the best he could and then he disappeared into the static abyss.

"Go!" Karl screamed at the driver. With a look of shock the driver took the keys from Karl and began driving. Karl studied the GPS system now in English in front of him making sure the driver was heading in the right direction and not pulling any fast moves. Almost twenty-five minutes later they were at the base of the mountains at the edge of the forest.

They got to an area of the forest too thick to drive any further. The snow had piled up in thick banks as if protecting the wilderness from mankind, and the trees had grown closer together at this point. It was hard to tell where the actual road had ended. It might not have been a bad idea to leave Mr. Enthusiastic out of things at this point, but if he did and he were to make contact with the enemy first, there'd be no telling what he'd do, so Karl led him out of the car by gunpoint.

"Where?" Karl demanded eying the wilderness laid out before them. Vinca shrugged his shoulders and snorted, looking at him as if he was some former dictator reincarnated.

Karl would have liked nothing more than to get rid of Vinca right then and there. His slovenly ways and exasperating attitude would have made even the most patient grade school teacher turn psycho in a matter of minutes.

The density of the coniferous trees blocked any moonlight. Karl went back to the taxi to search for a flashlight and found one under the passenger's seat up front. It was still sticky from whatever Vinca had last eaten while using it. He grabbed it while never losing aim of Vinca's beach ball head that made him now look like some perverted snow man. Karl placed the taxi radio in his jacket pocket and aimed the flashlight with his free hand.

"Go!" Karl wasn't thrilled with the time delay. At this point it had been close to two hours since Ivy had been picked up by the taxi.

They trudged through the snow, Vinca leading the way.

About five minutes later the radio went off again. "Vinca! Vinca!"

"Yes" Karl answered. It was the dispatcher.

"I have the taxi back now."

Damn it! Karl's head was spinning. *How could this be so?* "Let me talk to the driver."

"Oh, he no here. Go home family for Holiday."

"Bullshit. You fuck with me one more time and I will blow the head off fatso here, you hear me? This is about a baby, not you, or fatso or any of your other sick drivers. You got it? I am warning you."

Then Karl heard a sound coming from about twenty feet away. Whimpers from some type of life.

He pushed the gun hard into Vinca's back, edging him towards it.

Thick tree branches had fallen from the weight of the snow and were now buried underneath making the icy slush cripplingly uneven. Both men's ankles took turns twisting at various steps. Remaining skinny branches on trees pointed outwards threatening poked eyeballs as they pushed their way through.

There was a clearing up ahead in the distance like a shallow snow bowl and something was moving inside of it. The forest was known for having more bears, lynx, and other predatory wildlife than any other forest in Europe so Karl proceeded cautiously.

At first he could only make a small part out. It looked like a small animal. It was barely moving and making strange cries. When he got closer he saw that it was Ivy's head. The rest of her had been covered in snow.

She was clearly in pain but she was alive, hanging by a thread. Karl brushed the snow away to see if he could get an idea of what was going on. Through her parka were burnt tattered holes. She had been shot through the chest.

It was almost unbelievable that she was still holding on to life. "Olive. She has Olive.."

"Okay Ivy, take it easy. We're going to find her. Don't worry."

Vinca had been waiting for a moment like this. The crazy American was busy attending to another American lying in the middle of the snow. He couldn't make sense of what was going on and he wasn't interested in trying. He just wanted to get home to the comfort of kolaches and some hot cocoa. It was Christmas and he always celebrated by himself in his tiny apartment by masturbating with his favorite porn collection while simultaneously gorging. He needed to get back to his routine and away from this nonsense. His fat legs tackled each other as he ran out of sight. Karl caught a glimpse of him through the corner of his eyes running to his demise towards the middle of nowhere. Unfortunately for Vinca, Karl had more pressing issues.

Karl tried the radio but it wasn't making contact with anyone. He had to get in closer range. That meant carrying Ivy with him. He bent down with his quivering knees and scooped both palms up underneath her. If he could just get back to the taxi and make his way to a hospital before it was too late he might at least have a chance of saving her.

As he backtracked through the woods he gently told Ivy to hang on. He talked about anything and everything he could think of to keep her alert.

He looked down at her face and scanned the rest of her body. He had to get her to the hospital quickly. The bullets probably punctured her lungs if not her heart, judging by the entry locations.

The cab was still where he left it. He searched for the keys and placed Ivy in the passenger's seat. He walked over to the driver's side and let himself in. He slammed the door shut, turned on the ignition and began to drive off when the radio started making noise again and then it went completely dead.

From whatever memory he had of getting to this location in the forest, Karl tried to recall it backwards. He had seen the major hospital in Bratislava days earlier and had made a mental note about its location in case something like this were to happen. The snow had covered the road and made it unclear where it led and where intersections took place. A lot of the streets at this point were unmarked this close to the wilderness. He remembered the GPS System, and normally would have laughed at himself for forgetting except for the dying passenger next to him. He turned it on and eventually it started a map read out and found his way back to Bratislava.

Luckily it was not a busy morning for emergencies. The parking lot near the emergency entrance was virtually empty. There was only four patients in the waiting room, the only other ones that clearly needed help were a young couple with motorcycle helmets resting on their laps. Their clothes were ripped and had blood stains. It was hard to tell if anyone else was in need of help or simply waiting for someone else less fortunate. The hospital was impressively clean, probably due to the lack of business lately, and the nurses all spoke English fluently. They reacted with professional urgency and rushed Ivy in for immediate emergency surgery.

As much as it killed him to have to leave her now, he had no choice. Once the stretcher went rolling into the operating room, Karl whispered in her ear and squeezed her hand. He then turned on his heel and beelined it back out the thin automatic sliding glass doors. The car was still in the semi-circle, meant for emergencies only, where he left it. He jumped back into it and had the GPS system guide him to the dispatch location.

It was just a hunch but that was all he had to go by at this point. He raced the taxi through the snow and ice. The sun was starting to make its appearance, melting the road's coating. The light was good but the sheets of breaking ice it created were not so good for Karl's driving. He thought about what he whispered in Ivy's ear. It was time once and for all to nail these scum of the earth.

Nine minutes later he was there. The building was a dismal gray brown structure devoid of character. It was located in the middle of two parking lots. One small and for taxis and the other larger for general parking. Karl parked at the far end of the taxi parking lot and ran to the front door of the building. He stepped onto a patch of ice on his way that slid him to the front door as if he was riding a skateboard. With all his might he controlled his body to not hurdle into the door, which resulted in him falling hard on his right side. If he didn't know better he would have thought he had broken ribs but he knew it was the air knocked out of him, which sometimes felt just as bad or worse. He pushed himself up with his hands and got his bearing again. He turned the handle of the door. It wouldn't budge.

Karl skipped around to the nearest side of the building, which was to the right. There was a window placed absurdly high for a one-story building. He scanned the parking lots for makeshift ladders and returned minutes later pushing the taxi in neutral towards it so as not to make noise. Once he had it angled close enough, he climbed on top of the roof but still had to stand on tip toes to peer through the window.

At first there appeared to be nothing going on. The building was a rectangular mass inside without any walls or barricades, giving him full view of its contents. The linoleum floor was stained from various food sources and spilled coffee and buckling in various portions as if mini volcanoes had erupted underneath. A gray haze of cigarette smoke muted the room. It was the type of place that once you had been inside you could never get rid of the stench it left on you unless you took a long hot shower with harsh detergent soap, and even then you would still smell it in your hair as it burned your eyes. The only other doors led to restrooms. One for each sex, both painted army green. There were a couple of desks with dirty ashtrays, computers, and vending machines and a makeshift kitchen with a pot of thick black coffee in it. The coffee maker was turned on as indicated by a small circular red light. He guessed the dispatcher, and whom ever else had been left working, accidentally left it on in their haste to get home to their families for the holiday. Karl leaned back to see if there were any other windows he had missed earlier. There weren't.

He stared in a few minutes longer. The woman's restroom door swung open and an anorexic thin, tall, white blond woman appeared carrying a baby. She seemed high strung, pacing around nervously for a few minutes until the men's bathroom door swung open. The man that appeared looked familiar but Karl couldn't place him. He was short with an average build and had dark brown hair that was cut in a choppy bowl cut. Karl amused himself momentarily by thinking he looked like a grown up version of Damien from the

Omen. He wore a golden shiny sable fur coat that probably made him look bigger than he was. He reached out his hands to take the baby from the woman. A flash of an enormous sapphire and emerald ring on his right index finger gleamed in the subtle rays of morning sunlight beginning to appear through the windows. Karl was able to place him now. He was a Russian named Viktor. He had seen a bulletin on-line about him back home. He couldn't remember the details exactly but knew he was a dangerous mother fucker who gave South Africa a run for their money in the diamond trade. He also gave quite a few others a run for the money if they got in his way, but he would often settle on a tortured death.

So, this was the buyer Maruska had found. Karl had to give her credit as Viktor would have the type of money she was after. He also gave her credit for the obvious way she must have seduced him to come by himself. He watched through the window, backing off enough so his breath would stop forming fog rings.

Viktor held the baby against the bright green silk lining of his fur coat, cradle style. He cooed, smiled and tickled her. Then he held her upright, an arms distance away from him and checked her out from head to toe. He turned her around and did the same.

Maruska watched with a plastered closed half smile on her face as if she was pretending to be at ease with him. She sat down at one of the plastic desks but had jumped back up once Viktor had completed his inspection. She reached out her hands to take Olive back but Viktor pretended not to notice.

Loosing patience, she pointed to the duffel bag that sat at Viktor's feet, the bottom of his fur coat partially covering it. Her lips were moving, speaking to him about it.

She got no response. Just more cooing at Olive.

Viktor placed Olive on one of the desks and was proceeding to undress her by unbuttoning her sweater. Maruska was becoming more and more agitated, her hands reaching in across his, silently telling him her end of the bargain had already been signed, sealed and delivered.

Viktor was not moved and puffed up like a peacock, his fur coat spreading, his body appeared a foot wider and taller. He took out his Makarov from deep within the silky bowels of his coat's pocket and pointed it at her face.

Maruska backed off, literally.

Karl's heart was racing now. What was he planning to do with Olive? Was this merely another inspection or did he have other ideas in mind? He didn't want to find out.

Suddenly footsteps and the sound of tin rolling on pavement appeared from out of nowhere to the back of Karl. It was a man whose gaze was shifted downward as he casually kicked an orange, brown and white can of Kofola through the parking lot towards the building. Kofola was the Slovak's soda beverage of choice containing more caffeine and less sugar than it's American rivals, Pepsi and Coke-a-Cola. The man didn't seem to notice Karl or the odd parking job so Karl quietly jumped off the car landing in the space between it and the building. The footsteps became more audible as pebbles of ice crunched underneath them. Below the car, Karl saw them walk past and towards the front door of the building. Karl carefully made his way back on top of the taxi as the young man entered the building with a key. The disturbance had sent Viktor into a frenzy, his eyes and veins bulging as if they were going to explode. The gun was now pointed to the door. Maruska was trying to tell him something as if to pacify him, but it was too late. The gun fire went off and Juraj lay face down in a pool of blood.

The front door was left partially open now and Maruska's screaming could be heard clearly. Viktor had just assassinated her brother and she was not happy about it. Olive was screaming now too.

Viktor yelled something in Russian to Maruska that sounded like a warning, grabbed the duffel bag with the gun still pointed between her eyes and was making his way out the building careful not to trip over Juraj or to get any blood on his fur. As he was walking backwards out the front door something grabbed his right arm with such force and surprise, it sent his gun careening into the open air like a golf ball. It crashed back down on the hard linoleum and then slid and twirled until it came to a complete halt just short of Maruska's boots. All the while, another arm had wrapped itself in a strangle hold around his neck.

Karl pointed his thirty-eight at Maruska and then at Viktor back and forth. Viktor slammed his body back into Karl's and managed to pull the arm off from around his neck while contorting it into circus like positions. Karl pulled the trigger with his other hand while he still had his gun and Viktor went down. The look in Viktor's eyes was that of disbelief. Immortals weren't supposed to die.

Maruska had managed to grab the Makarov in the meantime and had taken a stand next to Olive only a couple of feet away from Karl. She and Karl were going to play cowboy.

The money was his only leverage. Karl bent down and unraveled the bag from Victor's dead body. Maruska settled the gun on a deadly spot on Karl's head but then she got a crazy look in her eye, smiled a smile that flashed her rotting baby-like teeth and pointed the gun at Olive who was laying on a desk courtesy of Viktor, instead.

"Now Maruska, you don't want to do that."

"Like hell I don't," she answered.

"Look Maruska. You can still get the money. It's right here. Just put the gun down and we'll do a little tit for tat." She didn't budge.

"How much is it Maruska? A million? A million and a half?"

No answer.

"Two million? Come on Maruska, this is your big chance."

"You give me the money first" she said.

Karl let out a small chuckle. "No, I don't play like that. I get a baby in good condition-let's say before she falls off that table there for example, and you get your money. Wasn't that the deal?"

"It was the deal with him, not you." Her gun pointed to Viktor on the word "him" and Karl flew into her. She fell hard to the ground but the gun was still in her hands. She wrestled with him, trying desperately to aim the gun back at him but Karl had her arm in a deadlock pinned to the ground. She broke the grip for a second and a shot rang out. Olive screamed a blood curdling scream. Karl turned around. She had fallen off the table but thank God had not been shot. He turned back to face Maruska. He was on top of her now. Her breasts still hard from the saline pouches sewn in below her skin and for one imaginary moment he fantasized about puncturing them with two blasts. As much as Ivy would like that, he decided not to. It would be best to get her taken alive and as a lead to the Slovak government as a hopeful informant. *Damn!* Now she was on top of him. The gun pointed into the cut on his face. She had wedged some of the skin apart again with the nozzle and was tracing the cut back up and down with it.

With one hard thrust, as if they were making love and he was giving her the "big surprise" of his manliness deep inside her, he thrust hard and her body flew off in a backwards somersault. Now the money bag was within reach of her. Karl sprang up to his feet and sprinted the three strides towards her and as she pulled her trigger, he shot her first.

CHAPTER TWENTY-FIVE

K arl raced back to the hospital. He made a makeshift bed for Olive on the floor board of the taxi out of a thick wad of his coat and the money bag. The Slovakian police had been informed as well as Interpol and were on their way to clean up the remaining investigation in conjunction with the FBI.

"Hold on little tiger," Karl purred to Olive. Tears were forming in his eyes. The outcome still unclear at this point. *How would the story turn out?* He rhapsodized, replaying it in its entirety in his head. He prayed for the first time in years.

As efficiently as before, the nurses took Olive into the pediatric ward for immediate attention.

They were adamant about Karl being seen as well, but he had something else he needed to do first.

He walked down the slick hallways to the shiny chrome elevator. He punched the button with the upwards arrow to take him to the third floor to intensive care. He introduced himself at the patient service's desk as many nurses and doctors gathered around. *Oh no*, he thought. Then they all broke into smiles. A doctor and a nurse respectively led him to Ivy's room. "She be okay," the doctor said as he entered the room and smiled at his patient. He gave the nurse some instructions in Slovak and left his dosing patient with the other two. Karl sat down next to Ivy while the nurse continued with procedures and protocol. Ivy looked better than before. Some flushed pink in small patches had returned to her cheeks. Her hair was damp and softly splayed across her forehead. He gently brushed it back. "Olive?" she said as she opened her eyes and registered him.

"She's all yours" Karl replied.

A painful looking but endearing smile spread across Ivy's face and two teardrops,one from each eye slid down her face. "Tell me" she whispered with all her might.

"First lets talk about you. Moms come first you know?"

Ivy let out a small groan anxious to hear about Olive rather than herself.

Karl continued, "You'll be out soon my partner in crime. You need to rest Ivy. Olive's okay and she's going to be fine. I just came in to check on you. I have to go now. Meet the police and FBI at the crime scenes. Be back soon. We'll have plenty to talk about then."

Ivy tried her best to get him to stay and talk by trying to not let go of his hand. But Karl won out from her weak grip. He explained to her again that he just wanted to set her mind at ease about Olive. Everything else could be saved for later. She needed to rest. It was of utmost importance.

Karl returned to the hospital the next morning. The previous day had been exhaustive with meetings, phone calls, and keeping meticulous records for himself while it was all still fresh. He had gotten a good nights sleep back at the hotel before returning to the hospital the following morning.

Ivy was sitting up in her bed much to his amazement. She still looked out of it but was far more alert than she had been the previous evening. He continued to make appearances at the hospital. On the fifth day she was coherent and could talk with more ease.

"What happened to me?" she asked as she reached out for his hand.

He held her hand in his and thought about how to tell the story. "You got shot Ivy. You're really lucky to be alive but I assume I am not the first to tell you that." Ivy didn't respond so he wondered if he was the first filling her in. Then he chuckled to himself. The accents of the nurses and doctors probably made it especially hard for her to understand in her current state.

"Just a sprained ankle." He joked with her to lighten the mood.

Ivy looked at him not sure how to react.

"Two bullets trooper. The most damaging bullet passed first through your left lung and then through your right one, paying a little visit to your heart in between." He motioned with his hands like a little boy the directions the bullet took. "Then it lodged itself in between your two ribs. You're lucky to have survived it. Very lucky Ivy."

Another cheat at death, thought Ivy. She hoped it was her last.

Like an enthusiastic child sharing a special adventure with his mom, he sat at Ivy's bedside replaying all the gory details of what had happened.

"Well, where to start partner?" He waited for Ivy to see the humor in the statement which she finally did. "I see, now don't blame it on the pain meds now."

"No, I am normally slow I guess. Remember how long it took for your rules to steep in with me?" The long question had Ivy winded but they both wound up laughing at it.

"You'll be happy to know that Maruska is dead. I had the opportunity to shoot each breast and knew you'd be happy with that, but in the end she got hit in her heart. If she had one that is. Just thought she should know what it felt like."

Ivy was silent. It wasn't exactly something that made her happy. Someone dying due to their involvement with her, but she realized it was probably the best answer.

"Don't feel bad Ivy. Olive was the youngest but she by far wasn't the first. We have reports going back that Maruska probably trafficked at least eight girls. Probably much more." Karl could tell Ivy was going to ask if they had made it out alive too but wanted to change the subject fast before she could. The others weren't so lucky. "The men in Austin she killed at the hotel were her former boss and his sidekick. We suspect they came to get her to come back to work for them. Looks like things didn't turn out the way they wanted though. She went back to Slovakia anyway but with her former boss's brother, the bakery man you'd encountered. Twice."

Ivy nodded along now. It was all slowly coming together.

"Yep, Maruska came home with intentions of being the leader of Vojtech by making a devil's bargain to sell Olive to a crazy son of a bitch Russian named Viktor Krukov. If you ever watched "America's Most Wanted" you surely saw his ugly mug. Rap sheet all over the world. He's gone too Ivy, as well as the taxi driver that picked you up from the hotel. He walked in on the middle of the exchange of Olive between Maruska and Viktor. Not a wise decision. You see, none of these sorries sons of bitches are anyone you'd want your worst enemy to marry Ivy."

Ivy didn't react. She simply sat back taking it all in with her eyes closed.

"It's you, me and Olive, Ivy. We're the only survivors."

Ivy flashed back to the dirty cop and the other two fake cops that arrested her for kidnapping. She wondered what happened to them. Did Karl even know about them? She asked Karl about it.

Karl stood up off the bed. These were three people at least he wasn't aware of but he knew she had been taken by phoney cops. He couldn't believe she remembered it and got descriptions of all three men and the heavily made up receptionist who worked across the street from a warehouse that housed a beautiful theater holding a Gospel concert. Karl excused himself to put in a call to the FBI. He knew with Ivy's rich description it wouldn't be long before they were wrangled in for arrests as well. Hopefully. If they still had their phoney store front. Anything could have happened by now.

Karl returned to Ivy's room. He wanted to change the subject and not go back to the three or more who might have gotten away. It was important to keep her spirits up. "Hey." He lightly tapped her knee to make her aware of his presence again as he sat next to her holding her hands again. "Most important thing of all of this is that Olive is going to be okay."

"Are you sure Karl? Please don't lie to me to make me feel good."

"No, Ivy, I ain't lying. Wouldn't lie about something like that. She's a miracle baby all the way around Ivy. Really and truly, she's gonna be just fine. She did suffer, I ain't gonna lie to you. Harsh environment. Dehydration. But she's kicking butt."

Ivy chuckled. That was her Ollie.

"Okay, so that's basically the scoop here in this wonderful city of Bratislava."

Ivy and him both laughed.

"Seriously Ivy, what happened here could have happened anywhere. Child trafficking is big even in the United States. But you should see the city in different circumstances once you are up to it. It really is quite peaceful and beautiful."

Ivy thought about it. *Maybe.* It could be cathartic. She had blamed so much on the country and the city. But Karl was right. These things took place all over the world all the time. She thought she'd remembered hearing that the state of Maine was high in child trafficking incidents. Whatever the case, it may be a while she thought, before she came back as a tourist.

"So, let's talk about back home in the States and what's going on." He took a moment to gather his thoughts and choice of words. "Well, Jeff got three years of prison time for child endangerment. He's got plans for drug rehab at a center outside of San Antonio upon release. Seems to be serious about kicking his ways this time according to his parole officer. But don't take him back whatever you do." Right as he said it, he wished he hadn't. Ivy didn't laugh. He continued quickly.

"Yeah well, without Maruska what else is there for him to do anyway?" They both thought for a moment. Ivy knew they were both thinking about Jeff but wondered what specifically Karl was thinking about him. She herself wondered what her life would be like with him once the three years had passed. Hopefully enough had happened that he wouldn't have any visitation rights. Karl must have been reading her mind because right then he said, "Don't worry. Not going to happen."

Ivy looked up at him wondering if he was really answering the question.

"I'll be your number one witness Ivy if it came down to that and no judge is going to want him near a child after this. If he stays clean for a certain number of years it will be supervised only. And as my gift to you, I will volunteer to do the supervising," he said as he brushed his jacket back revealing the thirty eight. Karl was serious. He wasn't out to kill, but there was no way he would ever allow Jeff to be with Olive if he could help it. Ivy knew his loyalty was real and could count on him if that day ever came.

"Be right back," he said as he hopped off the bed.

Moments later he returned carrying Olive. He handed her to her mom. He watched as she held her, her eyes closed, her mouth semi-smiling. The sight reminded him of the very true stories about mother's picking up cars that had fallen on their babies. Ivy couldn't have had much strength in her arms but it wasn't stopping her. He apologized to her for keeping her so distant throughout the whole ordeal and without need, reiterated the importance of it to have gotten the job done. He told Ivy it was thanks to her that Olive was okay. He joked with her calling her an "escapist" a "modern Houdini" and that maybe she could try out for the San Antonio Spurs once she got home since she could catch so well. The snort chortle that was Ivy's laughter burst forth, exasperating her pain.

They talked some more and he even teased, prodding her to join him in private investigating. They both chuckled at that one remembering how Ivy couldn't obey any orders. All of her life she had been a follower, but she had heard the mind worked differently under severe pressure and now she was a believer.

"And there was another young lady who we owe a whole lot of gratitude to," Karl added, feeling a little foolish as maybe he was overwhelming Ivy with too much at once.

Ivy's face was expressive with puzzlement as she stroked Olive's face.

"Her name is Dalena." Karl watched Ivy's reaction, which was primarily focused on cradling and caressing Olive with her eyes closed, smiling. Karl spoke quickly hoping the subject would be dismissed as quickly as it was brought up. "Well, um, really, she was the ticket to solving this. Without her help and willingness to risk everything, I would have never been able to get to Olive without being caught first."

Ivy could hear the nostalgia and longing in his voice. He fancied Dalena. It was obvious. You didn't have to be a wedding officiant to know when love bit. And she couldn't ever remember him talking so much or being so animated in their short time together. He had a new life to him.

Ivy, too weak to speak clearly anymore, the morphine kicking in, made a motion with her hand. Karl looked at her confused. She did it again. One hand stretched out flat, fingers close together swerving in the air like an airplane. "Shoo now. Go find her." She finally found enough strength to say something clearly.

Karl thought about it and wondered where she was right now. Anything could be possible. Hopefully she made a run for freedom but the chances of someone like that going back to a normal life were slim. She probably had no one and had taken up with another prostitution ring.

"Ivy, you are a hopeless romantic. I don't think so. She's probably long gone. But just thought I'd tell you about her. But thanks for the encouragement anyway, sport. Listen, let me take Olive, give her a kiss if you can. I'll take her back to the nursery. You need to get some rest. It's very important." But she was already asleep.

Karl reached back down to take Olive back to the nursery before leaving the hospital. He thought again about Ivy telling him to go find Dalena as he walked down the corridor on his way out and laughed amusedly to himself. He wished it was that easy and couldn't even imagine where he'd start looking for her in this strange city after all she had just risked. Besides, it was time to go home. Another unique case was waiting for him. Maybe he could find her from there. There would still be more time that he would have to be involved with this case, even if he was overseas. These cases didn't just disappear overnight especially dealing with international crimes. If it was meant to be, she'd resurface. No sense in hanging around here any longer.

The next morning he went to visit Ivy and Olive. It was also time to say goodbye. Ivy was in good hands now. No more bad guys or girls for that matter to put her or her daughter at risk. And just in case, she had been assigned all privileges of having a private stay under a false name in the hospital. Olive's name was falsified as well to Alanna, a nice Slovakian sounding baby girl's name and stoic security guards stood erectly with their backs to her room and the nursery with weapons clearly visible, giving the hospital an intense new energy that excited the staff, although they weren't quite sure what to make of it. Ivy was sad to see him go, but Olive was okay and back with her, the funds had dried up, the case was solved and he was due back home to work on a local apparent hit and run investigation. Karl had shared the story with her of the quarterback for Nelson High in Austin, Tim MacNamara, who had been struck and left for dead walking home from school after practice a few days ago. The route he had taken was a shortcut through a soccer field that an eyewitness could account for. The cops theory back home was that he had actually been killed there, at the soccer field, but then the suspect or suspects placed his body on a dirt country road later that night with no street lights, setting up the perfect scene for it to look like a hit and run that took place there. If it weren't for Tim's missing right hand, it would look like a typical hit and run, but the police were suspicious of the case becoming a first or second degree murder over involuntary manslaughter because of this one missing detail. The hand could not be found.

Most kids didn't walk home through the soccer field like Tim. But there was plenty going on there that evening including the rival high school's football practice, which the witness said Tim had been studying as he walked past. He said that Tim thought it was funny that their practice field would get rained out forcing them to give up their secrets right in front of him and because he wasn't in his usual football garb no one seemed to pay him any mind or recognize him. He said he walked the rest of the way home alone because Tim wanted to take his time loitering, checking things out while he had the golden opportunity-the two teams would be playing each other in a week's time. Lots of the students and jocks parked their cars at the field. It was theory back home that someone eventually recognized Tim.

Tim's mother had called Karl the night he was found dead. She was besides herself. Her son was a good boy, well mannered, good grades, excellent grades- an honor roll student and besides which, everyone loved him.

Obviously, not everyone, thought Karl. And sometimes it didn't take much to end up in a position like Tim's: stare too long at someone else's girlfriend, or maybe the girlfriend spoke of you a little too fondly, or maybe being the star athlete made others assume you were a dick and deserved to die. The night that Tim's mother had called was the same day Ivy's doctor had told him Ivy and Olive were on their way to recuperating just fine. With all the other help in place, Karl felt the urge to return home and help others who now needed him. It wasn't easy saying goodbye. It wasn't unusual for him to find himself more emotionally involved in most cases than he planned on. But usually he could contain it.

But Ivy and Olive were different. Olive and Ivy felt like family now and he promised they would see each other back home.

It would be another month before Ivy was released from the hospital and finally allowed to fly back home. Slovakian hospitals granted their patients much longer humane stays than American hospitals that acted like fast food chains, trying to get you in and out for as much money as possible as fast as possible. And for this Ivy was thankful. She wanted to be good and ready before returning home and being Olive's sole care giver. Punch flew to Slovakia the day Karl left to stay the four weeks before Ivy was allowed home.

Punch appeared at Ivy's bedside describing a city that Ivy had never been able to see, one that Punch described as being "rad." She'd delight in sharing with Ivy her adventures of the day and for Ivy it was a warm replacement for the cold thoughts she harbored against the city. Slowly but surely she found Punch's stories defrosting those layers of her heart bit by bit, piece by piece.

CHAPTER TWENTY-SIX

One day after Punch took herself to the Blue Church for mass, she brought back a white chocolate penis and encouraged Ivy to bite down on it hard. It goes without saying that the part of Ivy biting the man's penis in half was her favorite part of it all. She was so proud of Ivy. For herself she bought a dark chocolate vagina and licked it until it melted all over her mouth and hands much to Ivy's dismay. "Seriously, Ivy, you should reconsider," Punch said as she licked the remaining streaks of chocolate off her long fingers. "It tastes much better."

Ivy knew she was full of shit for the most part but was trying none-the-less to convert her-yet again. She didn't feel the need to even respond to that one. She thought back to the boyfriends she had in her life from the first one, Bob, to the last one-Jeff. Even as terrible as it all turned out, she still couldn't feel any desire for a woman. Maybe to be alone yes, but no urge to do a complete about face. Once she had even heard that many lesbians have sex with their straight male friends because they needed the real deal every once in a while, so what was the point? She wondered if Punch had ever been tempted.

She finally couldn't keep quiet any longer on the subject. "Punch, it'd be as hard to turn me into a lesbian as it would be to make you straight. Did you ever consider that?"

"Hmm," she responded as her mouth paused on her middle finger and rested on it in a pseudo bite at the top knuckle. She removed it slowly, twisting, as if she was teasing a horny john desperate for a blow job. Ivy turned away and rolled her eyes.

"Guess not. Oh well, you can't blame me for trying. Especially now that I've seen all your goods through that designer garb that is your uniform around here," she scrunched her paper napkin in a wad and dipped it into a glass of water and cleaned up her chocolate streaks vigorously.

"Thanks for the compliment. If I ever change my ways, you'll be first to know."

"Yeah, well, I ain't holdin' my breath," replied Punch as she aimed for the waste basket. She made the shot.

"You know Punch, I've been thinking. We're pretty odd birds. You know, for what we do and all and the fact that we're darn good at it. I can't write and you can't speak properly but we do well. It's been on my mind a lot. Hard to explain. But I just don't feel so bad about writing terribly anymore the more I listen to you speak."

Punch got up, removed the wad from the trash can and threw it at Ivy.

"Ugghhh. See, not only can't you talk properly. You simply have no class."

At that they both started laughing. Ivy was startled at what she just said. She wondered if the medications she was on were making her tongue loose. She looked up at Punch who was staring down at her adoringly.

"Punch, can I ask you something?" Punch didn't answer but Ivy knew the timing was right.

"Do you remember when you told me that all the signs were there for Olive coming home? When I called you from the hotel? I am just curious if you don't mind sharing what you were referring to?"

Punch took in a deep breath and held it for a moment. "Karl was in Oregon trying to track down Misty and passed a restaurant not only with the name Olivia in it but it was really called Olivia *Union* Station. That was it."

Ivy thought about the name. Yes, it was a coincidence. "What else?"

"That's the best answer you're going to get. But since I know you won't stop probing I will just say it was simply because the first song on the radio I heard the morning you went to Slovakia was that song about the chicken and egg dish on that menu he saw."

Ivy had no idea what in the world she was talking about and made a face. "What?"

"What's his face. You know. Used to be in the trio. Big guy. Famous. Oh, Lord. You know the song that the guy wrote called "Mother and Child Reunion.""

"Oh, the Paul Simon song?"

"Yeppers. Geez. My brain is fried. Yeah, he wrote it after he saw a chicken and egg dish on a menu in New York called Mother and Child Reunion."

"Punch, you are crazy."

"Not kidding Ivy." She looked up at Punch who was as serious as could be. She wasn't going to ask her about any more signs. That was all she could take for the day. The menu item made her flash back to Kirk again and the remembrance of her throwing out her *365 Ways to Cook a Chicken Cookbook,* before he would stumble upon it.

Back home, Karl was feeling the drain of the two cases intermingling. Mostly Ivy and Olive's case was done on his end but it didn't mean his phone didn't almost ring daily regarding it one way or the other; either reporters, the FBI, Interpol, or someone from the police department in Bratislava who was either being nosy or had legitimate business. Sometimes it was hard to tell. Karl hadn't worked any other international cases and he was pretty sure he'd say no if ever asked again. But, he knew better than to be so sure. It wasn't all hell. The girl, Dalena, was haunting him. It didn't seem right to just leave without knowing if she was okay, but that wasn't his job. Hell, if he worried about every nice person he came across working a case, or every pretty girl for that matter, he wouldn't get anything solved. But she was different. Yes, she was too young for him. Yes, she had a terrible past, and God only knew what else hid behind those beautiful eyes and beautiful... Karl felt himself longing for her. *Was Dalena even her real name?* He owed her more than just disappearing-it was true, she was key to solving the case and getting Olive home safe. How could he have just left the country without at least trying? He wanted to kick himself. She may not care, but he did.

As luck would have it, Tibor, the chief of Police in Bratislava called him the next morning. They had hit if off well while Karl was in Slovakia and parted with Karl giving him an open invitation to come visit the States anytime. Tibor was thrilled with the hospitality and couldn't wait to take him up on it, but it would have to wait. The kids were back in school and mischief was all around the city at this moment in time, but in the meantime there was always the phone.

"Hello," Karl answered seeing the foreign number but not sure who in Slovakia it was.

"Hello there! This is Tibor from Bratislava!"

Karl had to restrain himself from laughing. Tibor's nature was unlike any he had ever seen before in his field in the States. He was always enthusiastic.

"Hey there Tibor. What a pleasant surprise. How you doing man?"

"Just fine, fine. Am I disturbing you?"

"No, I've got a few minutes. Tell me what's happening in Bratislava."

"Oh, you know, the freezing cold, the bad attitudes everywhere. Nothing new!"

"Well, I guess that's the way it is. You sound good, like you're holding up real well."

"Yes, thank you. I again thank you for all your help to puts these sons of bitches where they belong. You know, Karl, I tell you honest. Vojtech no more. But no mean much. Someone new come take place eventually but we enjoy while it lasts," he chuckled during the "while it lasts" part.

"No problem Tibor. Happy to be of temporary service."

"Yes, thank you. I go see Ivy yesterday in hospital. She told me she go home soon. I forgot to ask her about crazy son bitch boyfriend back in the states. You know what happened to him?"

"Sure do. Three years prison for child endangerment. Hopefully that will be enough time to clean him up. May take a little while." They both agreed on that one and ribbed each other with a few more put downs and jokes on Jeff's behalf. "Well, great. I'm glad you went to see Ivy. How's she doing? How'd she look? Did you get to visit the baby too?"

"Yes, yes, everyone look wonderful. Very happy. Beautiful baby. Maybe we keep in Slovakia?"

The joke was in bad taste but Karl chuckled anyway to play nice. Hell, since Tibor was in such a great mood he figured he'd hit him up for a favor that may equally be in bad taste.

"Tibor, let me ask you something. Your team ever come across a girl that was held by Vojtech named Dalena?"

Karl could hear Tibor go silent on the other end while he thought about it. "I do not know the name. You have last name?"

"No, wish I did."

"Ahhh, I see. You like Miss Dalena. Slovakian women always get the Americans in trouble."

Karl couldn't help but agree as he thought of Ivy.

"Let me see what I can find. And I call you back."

"Sounds good, partner."

"Yes, sounds good, partner. I call you back."

Karl hung up feeling embarrassed. He could imagine Tibor making announcements to the whole department that he was on a hunt for a Dalena for the American detective and them all rolling their eyes as yet another foreigner fell head over heals for one of their women.

Karl went back to work on the MacNamara case. It was turning out that his mother was wrong. Not everyone loved her son. Especially a particular cheerleader from his opposing high school. Her name was Sam, short for Samantha, and rumor had it she was overly protective of her boyfriend, the quarter back at her school and she took sports way too seriously. Karl was going to pay her a visit.

Karl got back home late that night after working the field on the MacNamara case. Sam was useless or a great liar. Probably both. She had a perfect alibi for the night, cheerleading practice, of course. She said she left immediately afterwards and had witnesses to prove it. But Karl was still suspicious of her and was certain she had cajoled some jock, maybe even her own boyfriend, to get rid of the star from across the tracks. *Hell,* he thought, *she probably came along for the ride.* Sam was striking with the tan legs and toned hamstrings that cheerleaders get and the long golden hair that fell in layers past her shoulders. Her makeup by itself was pretty-iridescent purple eyeshadow accentuated her hazel eyes while sparkling pale pink powder dusted her cheeks and enhanced her Scandinavian heritage. A bright burst of transparent cherry flavored lip gloss shined her lips. But she had a cold and hard arrogance, a truly narcissistic persona that showed no remorse for what happened to Tim or empathy for his grieving mom and dad. The detail of the missing hand was something police were keeping mum. Karl knew next time he saw her, they would have a little discussion about that detail.

The phone rang. It was Tibor.

Karl picked up the phone as he walked over to his computer to continue working while talking.

"Tibor?"

"You are one lucky son of a bitch! I believe I found you woman."

"You're kidding. That was fast. So, tell me, anything ugly besides the obvious?"

"No, what we going to get on her here, you know? Prostitution legal. Solves many problems. When the States going to catch on?"

"Well luckily you're a happily married man and still will be by the time you come out to visit, cuz I guarantee you partner, it ain't ever going to change out here."

Tibor became serious and quiet for a moment. Karl wondered if he was having marital problems and wanted to have an anonymous rendezvous with an American woman. Was that the real reason why he sounded so anxious to come to Texas? Karl knew it wasn't, but it was fun to pretend.

"Hey Tibor, don't let that get you down too far. You can always go to Las Vegas and find something legal to do there. But don't tell your wife I had anything to do with it. Don't even tell her I mentioned it." Karl could picture his wife, a huge German woman, coming after him with a rolling pin. Tibor didn't respond right away.

"No, no, I no think about that. I happy. My wife good woman. Two greats kids you know. Boy and girl. Why complain? I have everything man needs," Tibor explained to Karl without need. One of these days he'd get him to understand the benefits of having more of a sense of humor especially in their line of work. "No, I quiet because I was looking at the papers of the Dalena. There is nothing. Not even last name. Sorry. I thought maybe we hit jackpot but no. She just in home one night during drug raid. That's all. But she clean. No arrest for her, unfortunately for you."

Karl could feel his heart almost land in his boots in one big thump. "Tibor, thanks for trying. It was a silly idea. Forgive me for wasting your time. When you going to come visit?"

"No problem. I come visit soon, take the family to Schlitterbaun." Again, Karl had to contain a chuckle. Schlitterbaun was a children's water park in New Braunfels that housed the world's first surfing machine. "We keep in touch, no? Take care Karl. We talk soon again."

"Thanks Tibor. Take care. Say hello to Fredda."

Karl hung up again feeling out of sorts. It was that same feeling he got whenever he worked at the Austin Police Department; helpless and out of control. He knew if he didn't take action on it right away, the feeling would spiral into a fierce depression.

Dependence was not his specialty. It was time to take the matter into his own determined hands. In the meantime, he'd give Sam some time to get nervous about his interview with her while taking a small trip back to Slovakia.

Punch had rented a small apartment in the town square for her stay. The flat was located in the spacious attic of a sixteenth century medieval home. It had a large terrace that offered stunning views of the red roofs of the Old Town houses and the St. Martin Cathedral and the Bratislava Castle for a price you couldn't find anywhere back in the States. Punch was ecstatic. She loved being there as well as the excitement of being in a new and exotic location. Having Olive at her side to take care of was the icing on the cake. And knowing Ivy was going to live through it was even better. The cherry on top, she thought.

Ivy's mother had loaned the money to help but Ivy had been careful not to say it was for Punch exactly. It was for help with the "care of Olive" until she could get back home and get back to work. She knew most kids never repaid their parents but she was going to. She was sure her mother would get all sorts of weird ideas about the money going to her overtly lesbian friend, especially after she had just cause to turn away from men, so everyone was in cahoots to keep mum about it.

Punch had set up a corner in the room for Olive whom she was in full charge of these days until her mom was released from the hospital. She was excited to get the call from Karl, it would be fun to have someone else from back home to hang out with. She told him the quarters were tight but he was welcome to stay and of course Ivy would be thrilled. She just wondered why he was coming back. And when she hung up with him she became worried that he wasn't telling her everything.

Karl arrived three days later but wasn't around much. *What the hell is he doing,* she wondered. She asked Ivy about it but Ivy didn't have any idea. She told Punch to let him do his thing. Maybe one more detail needed to be wrapped up for the case.

Punch awoke one morning the next week to Olive crying and a note on the refrigerator. It read: Thanks Punch for the hospitality. Had to get back home for the other case. See you back in the States. Karl."

Well at least she didn't have to think about it anymore, especially after their conversation over wine on the terrace the night before. He had told her everything including the part about the cheerleader back home who turned herself into the police with a plastic ziplock baggy in her purse of Tim McNamara's decaying hand. She had placed it on the receptionists desk at the police department as casually and cool as could be without saying a word. Apparently the reason for cutting off the hand was in case he did live. It was insurance he would never be able to throw or hold a football again. It was to serve as a threatening message.

The receptionist, a recent college graduate, who rarely if ever saw the dark side of the place she worked, promptly passed out and Sam stood by doing nothing but rolling her eyes at the weakling lying on the floor next to her starched white socks and Gucci tennis shoes.

Punch had become addicted to Karl's gruesome stories and they had hit it off very well during his short stay in which she made him promise her that he would fill her in back home from time to time on the other cool stuff he saw in relation to his job. Karl had laughed and said he would share what he could.

Punch decided to go to the hospital and check on Ivy, bringing her lunch of a particularly delicious pagace; biscuits stuffed with cracklings, potato and cheese she had found at a café tucked in a remote alley and a bowl of stone fruit for dessert. She begged the hospital staff to let her the hell out of there.

CHAPTER TWENTY-SEVEN

Six days later, Ivy was wheeled off the plane in Austin. Holding Olive was a moment she would never forget. The gust of warm, humid air was like medicine for her soul as her chair rolled out of the plane onto the ramp towards the gate. She took in a deep breath. It suddenly felt as if she was arriving in a foreign country yet again. And what adventures and trials and triumphs were awaiting her now? She hoped none for a while. The Bratislava staff and hospital had been overwhelmingly concerned with her well-being and it had felt like she was leaving a family. They begged her to come back and give their city a second chance. She believed in second chances and promised she would.

Her last night in the hospital they decked themselves out in their most formal wear and held a party for her completely staffed with waiters carrying trays of champagne and caviar and a DJ. It was a spectacle. The female nurses were gorgeous out of their uniforms and the men were just as handsome. The hospitality was too much and on occasion Ivy broke down in tears, so overwhelmed by their kindness.

The wheelchair was now inside the airport just entering the gate. Punch had been steering her fast down the narrow blue corridor and the speed almost made Ivy lose her grip on Olive a couple of times. When she looked up from Olive she saw them. There standing in a group waiting for her. First she saw her mom. Then Iris and Karl. Then a handful of couples she had married and the staff from Chapel Desiderio and LuAnne. And lastly, Kirk. *Kirk?* What was he doing here? She craned her neck back to look at Punch, who was steering her towards the group.

"Well I fucked it up for you once, thought I could at least try to do something right to make it up to you."

"Punch, but *Kirk?*"

"Yeah Ivy. He's the best one you ever had. He misses you. I think he's the one. And, he really is a good writer."

Ivy looked up at Punch readying herself for a wink or some other sign that the last remark was a joke.

Punch looked down at her. "What?"

Ivy gave her a look.

"I am serious Ives. He's got a new book out. Wrote it while you were away. Says you and your story were great inspiration for the title."

Ivy recognized the tone of Punch's voice. She was edging her on, baiting her to ask what the title of the book is.

"Okay, Punch I give up. What's the title?"

"Great Tits, Loons and Cuckoos."

They both broke into laughter. Kirk caught her eyes and she suddenly felt guilty for giggling at the title. Hopefully he was far away enough for him not to hear her and Punch talk about him. God she hoped so.

Then Ivy's mom and Iris strolled up next to her. Iris gave her a big kiss on the cheek, holding back the tears that were about to burst out of her eyes. In order to save face, she gently took Olive, her niece, whom she had never been able to meet before this moment in her arms and walked away from the small crowd to meet her for the first time.

Ivy's mom, bent down to kiss her too and then said, "This is the best you've ever looked. You finally lost all that baby fat."

Ivy dismissed the comment and her and Iris's eyes locked when she handed Olive back knowing without speaking what their mom had just said. They gave smiles and raised eyebrows to each other.

LuAnne peered over Ivy's shoulder at Olive and said, "I reckon you must be the little one who's been riding the gravy train with biscuit wheels." She pat Ivy on the shoulder.

Ivy looked again at the small crowd gathered around her. The couples held bouquets of flowers and well-wishing cards that they handed to her. Small dolls and stuffed animals for Olive. The staff from Chapel Desiderio whistled and cheered led by Justin who was dreamier than ever but her eyes searched specifically for Kirk. She had lost track of him and was afraid his shyness had taken over and he had left the scene.

Ivy was a little stunned with the initiative that Punch had taken. But then a wide smile spread across her face. Yes, Kirk wherever he was, was a symbol of what is important in love-it being unconditional. The antithesis of Jeff. *But where was he?* Ivy felt a wave roll inside of her washing depression from her head to her toes. She scanned for him again. Found him. There he was! But wait something was amiss. She watched him walking away from the crowd with another woman. *He had shown up with another woman?* Punch had been crazy to trust that he was interested in her after all this. As payback he had brought another woman to be seen with. And just like that she saw the top of a mound of black curly hair break through the group and come running towards her. The man wore jeans and an untucked tropical shirt with bright colored macaws printed all over it and handed Olive a stuffed parakeet. It was Kirk! And his glasses were falling down his nose. The man she had seen with the woman she had mistaken for him. Kirk was far more handsome than the other man. He then proceeded over to Ivy and stood next to her. Everyone clapped, much to Ivy's surprise. She looked up at him. He looked different, better, not so unsure of himself. Or maybe he was still the same and she had changed. In either case she suddenly had a secret desire for him to give her a second chance. And just at that moment he bent down, shoved his glasses back up his nose and kissed her. Not a passionate kiss of entangled tongues, but a respectable kiss in front of her family and friends. They all gathered around Ivy, most seeing Olive for the first time, and became quite a rowdy bunch causing many stares from the rest of the travelers as they made their way out of the airport to make their way to Sueno's Tex Mex for a celebration. Ivy and Olive rode with Karl in his new Ford 150 to catch up.

"Good to see you again Karl. Not to sound like a broken record, but thank you." Ivy was turned with most of her weight on her left side so she could look at him and sneak peaks at Olive who rode behind her in a car seat.

"The feeling is mutual. Glad you are here Super Mama." He gave Ivy two gentle taps on her left knee.

Ivy smiled. She liked the new identity. She looked back at Olive and winked. Olive laughed.

Twenty minutes later they pulled into Sueno's. There was a special table reserved for them in the sun room overlooking the lush gardens and trickling water fountains outside its windows.

Karl found a parking spot and turned the engine off. After taking his seatbelt off, he turned to face her and grabbed her hands. "Ivy, I guess now's a good a time as any to tell you this." They both looked at the clock on the dashboard. They were still 15 minutes early for their own party. "Remember me telling you about Dalena? The young woman in Slovakia we are indebted to for helping find and save Olive?"

Ivy said yes, although she wasn't sure where the conversation was going.

"Well, I did some research on her. And this may seem hard to believe, but…" His eyes searched Ivy's for a reading to see if he could predict the reaction that might follow. "She's Olive's sister."

"What?" Ivy couldn't help the laughter at the absurdness. Olive was laughing too in the backseat. "You're kidding me right?" She thought about it. Was he messing with her just to be funny? No, the look on his face was incredulous that she wasn't believing him. "She's Punch's niece and Olive's sister? Oh, I don't know. That is crazy."

"I'm not foolin'." He looked at her with dead seriousness. "That's why I went back to Slovakia. To find out for sure."

"Oh no." She suddenly thought about Punch waiting inside. "Whatever you do don't tell Punch this news. She'll go hysterical and we can't have that with my mom in there too. It would be too much for her to handle after everything."

Karl grinned a sly grin and informed her that he had told Punch the news in Slovakia over a carefully planned dinner of wine and cabbage soup which they both smirked at for being Punch's favorite thing to eat there. She had brought back a stew and soup recipe book and was already begging Ivy to start making things from it once she was settled in. "When she was at the right stage between warm and buzzed I broke the news. You told me yourself one time Ivy, that Punch, when you get right down to it has a big heart."

Ivy smiled, relieved that she didn't have to break the sudden news to Punch that her niece, the former prostitute, was dating Karl and she was Olive's sister. Ivy had to take a moment and think if she was leaving anything else out. It was so absurd. That one twist really changed everyone's relationships around. Oh yes, she was also Dalena's aunt.

"And would you do us the honors?" He reached to the back of the truck in the seat behind him and pulled out a large manila envelope that was resting on the seat next to Olive. He handed the envelope to Ivy who then slid the contents out: a marriage license. He became silent.

"My, a lot happens when you're in a coma." She gazed at the license in almost disbelief. So much was happening at once. She smoothed the document in her lap, looked out the window at the rest of the bunch entering the restaurant. Iris and Kirk were the last to enter, following her mother. "Are you sure Karl? I mean here in the United States we call it a shotgun wedding remember?"

"I've never been so sure of anything in my life."

Ivy looked back down at the license. It was a lot to take in all of a sudden. She looked back around at Olive who was smiling and kicking her legs. "I'd be honored to pronounce you as family."

"Okay, so it's done," Karl said as he opened the door to the truck and skipped over to the other side to get Olive out of her car seat and into her stroller and to assist Ivy into her temporary wheel chair.

As he was getting Olive out of the car seat he asked her if she wanted to be a flower girl.

"Wower," said Olive much to Karl and Ivy's surprise.

"Yes indeed. Excuse me for calling you a flower girl Miss Olly. You are a Wower girl if I ever saw one."

Olive stared at Karl with bewilderment then broke out in an infectious giggle.

Kirk had seem them park and came forward to help steer Ivy into the restaurant. The four of them strolled through the gardens leading to the enormous round topped mesquite front doors of the restaurant.

The whole sun room had been cordoned off for the event. Everyone was already there including Dalena, whom Ivy recognized immediately as the young girl Karl had walked through the home of Vojtech with. She was quietly sitting in the background taking in her new surroundings with a pleased look on her face. She had clean long auburn hair that was slightly past her shoulders and hooded green eyes. Ivy could see the resemblance to Punch but couldn't entirely place why, except for maybe in the facial structure. *This girl is also Olive's sister?* she thought. The thought set her back a moment. *Olive's sister? Her niece and Punch's niece?* Yes, it was true. This girl was a part of them all now. Karl wouldn't be mistaken about such a huge concept to grasp. How strange that all this commotion would come to this, and how beautiful. *Yes, God does work in mysterious ways,* she thought as she stared at her new family. She was wheeled into her designated seated place at the head of a long rectangular table. The table had a bright striped Mexican table cloth full of large pitchers of margaritas sitting atop. Punch had already helped herself to a glass, toasting the virtues of tequila and Tex Mex to the small crowd as they settled in.

The staff of the restaurant was attentive and jolly obviously aware of what the celebration was about as they kept eying Ivy and Olive curiously, hoping they would be able to report something funny or strange about them to their own friends and family afterwards. Pink balloons were tied to a high chair and goody bags full of crayons and coloring books and tiny stuffed animals sat on the table in front of it, all for Olive.

Punch made a second toast once everyone was seated, "To the day's events." Everyone toasted the unlikely and fortunate outcomes of having Olive home alive as well as Ivy. Their enemies were behind them now and the other happy ending to the story was that of Karl and Dalena's love, which would be consummated in a marriage performed by Ivy after everyone had sufficient amounts to drink.

The afternoon drifted lazily by and it finally came time. Ivy didn't have a ceremony prepared so married Karl and Dalena off the top of her head, the words flowing easily for the first time ever. Kirk sat at the table and watched her with his mouth slightly agape at the new woman who stood before him. He and Punch exchanged glances to each other regarding her, the unspoken sentiment of how proud they were of the new woman they saw standing before them.

Dalena and Karl intently gazed at each other and only looked at Ivy once waiting anxiously for her to give the okay for the ring exchange. At that moment Ivy for the first time saw the apprehension of what they were doing in both of their eyes. The flicker of panic was undeniable.

She contemplated asking them if they wished to continue. This was a first and she wasn't quite sure how to handle it this far into a ceremony. She slowed her speech so the pronouncement wouldn't come so soon in case they wanted to stop. She would let them make the decision if they wanted to. Maybe they had realized by the words she was speaking that they had jumped in too quickly. Little did she know that behind her back walking past the glass doors that sectioned off the room they were standing in, Dalena and Karl saw what must have been the ghost of Maruska walk past. The white hair and skin and the posture were unmistakable. *She was here. But how?*

Karl recognized the shift in Ivy and in order not to upset her returned his gaze back to Dalena. She too had seen what he had, he saw it in her eyes. But how could it be? He had shot her stone cold dead. There was no explanation unless she was still alive. Then he remembered the twin sister.

The pronouncement came and Karl and Dalena were instructed to kiss. The license was signed by Ivy and loud applauding and shouts of congratulations were made. Everyone gathered around Ivy after they congratulated Karl and Dalena.

Karl excused himself to use the restroom. Dalena stayed behind, still a little shy, *a little unsure of herself in her new surroundings,* Ivy thought as she watched her not so new relative. She hoped that by the end of the day they would be friends. Ivy watched as Dalena took a seat at one of the back tables, holding onto the license anxiously awaiting the return of Karl.

Karl searched the restaurant up and down. Out the back door and outside the front. All over the massive grounds of Sueno's. *Where was she?* It wasn't his imagination. Dalena had seen her too. But where did she go? He looked out the window of the front door and saw the white hair of the woman drive past out of the parking lot in a gold four-door Crown Victoria. He raced out the door and jumped into his pickup truck.

He followed the one and only lone road out that led out of the restaurant. In this direction it would take him to a well-traveled country road. He sped out 20 miles over the speed limit. He had seen the car turn right so he followed the lead. Down the hilly road he sped trying desperately to catch up. *Where the hell was she going?* Up ahead in the distance he saw a small glowing circle that almost looked like the sun setting but he knew it was the last trace of the golden glow of the car before it was completely out of sight. He pressed harder on the accelerator. He couldn't catch up. The circle was gone. And then he realized he'd been tricked. He wasn't following Maruska or her twin sister. It was not either one of them that was in the car. He made a sharp left, then made a u-turn, causing his truck to squeal and do donuts before he had complete control of it again. He went back to the restaurant. But it was too late. His wife was gone.

THE END

www.ingramcontent.com/pod-product-compliance
Lightning Source LLC
Chambersburg PA
CBHW021502240626
47154CB00002B/473